MW01491460

Down and Dirty
Interlude
Intermission
Four Play
Game On
Swingtime
Party of Three
All Jacked Up
Top or Bottom
Rodeo Heat
Night Heat
Cupid's Shaft
Trouble in Cowboy Boots

Strike Force
Unconditional Surrender
Lock and Load

The Sentinels
The Edge of Morning
Night Moves
Dark Stranger
Animal Instinct
Mated
Silent Hunters

Cat's Eyes
Pretty Kitty
On the Prowl

Corporate Heat
Where Danger Hides

Erector Set
Erected
Hammered

Anthologies
Night of the Senses: Carnal Caresses
Christmas Goes Camo: Melting the Ice
Treble: Trouble at the Treble T
Subspace: Head Games
Bound to the Billionaire: Made for Him

Strike Force

LOCK AND LOAD

DESIREE HOLT

Lock and Load
ISBN # 978-1-78686-353-9
©Copyright Desiree Holt 2018
Cover Art by Posh Gosh ©Copyright April 2018
Interior text design by Claire Siemaszkiewicz
Totally Bound Publishing

LOCK AND LOAD

Dedication

A lot of people helped me make this book happen. Margie Hager, my ever-faithful beta reader and all-around wonderful person. My son, Steven, just for being such a great guy and for watching out for me. Joseph Patrick Trainor, my wonderful cop friend and former Air Force Raven who answers my endless questions. And my wonderful editor, Rebecca Fairfax, who makes my stories sing. Thank you all. My success is due to you.

Chapter One

Come on, asshole, where are you? Show me your face so I can blow it the fuck away.

Beau Williams flexed the fingers of one hand, relieving the strain of holding them in one position for so long. They had been there for what seemed like hours, he and the other members of Delta Force Team Charlie, waiting for their high-value target to appear.

'Take him out then get the hell out.' That had been the order from their commanding office and it worked for Beau. If the murderous jerkoff would just get the fuck out of the tent where he was holed up.

He was disciplined enough to ignore the hard ground beneath him, the mountainous terrain and the unrelenting heat. When he'd been picked to join Charlie, one of the first things his teammates had told him was that Afghanistan was no picnic — it was considered one of the most forbidding battlegrounds in the history of war. It hadn't taken him long to agree with that assessment. Bitter cold in the winter, hotter than an oven in the summer, there were few roads, water was scarce and only the hardiest of the hardy could survive the brutal environment.

They hit the nail on the head with that one.

But he and his teammates, led by Slade Donovan, were just such men, trained in every skill imaginable to fight in the war on terror. They were part of a unit in the legendary Delta Force—or 1st Special Forces Operational Detachment—which operated as part of JSOC—Joint Special Operations Command—in the ongoing conflict with radical extremists around the world.

At the moment, the team was in the middle of yet another hair-raising mission in the Hindu Kush, an unforgiving mountain range that ran from Central Afghanistan to Pakistan. Almost a thousand miles long and two hundred miles wide, it ran northeast to southwest, most of it through Afghanistan, and divided the Amu Darya River Valley and the Indus River Valley. It stretched from the Pamir Plateau, near Gilgit, to Iran and had over two dozen summits of more than twenty-three thousand feet in height. Below the snowy peaks, the mountains of Hindu Kush appeared bare, stony and poor in vegetation. For centuries it had been referred to as the graveyard of foreign armies.

Beau could agree with that. This wasn't the first time Delta Force Team Charlie had been on a mission in this soulless place, and he was pretty damn sure it wouldn't be their last. They'd plotted and planned with as much care as they could, absorbing all the intel they'd received, but as many times as they'd been here, they knew planning could only take them so far.

Finding cover was difficult as always, but their recon man had spotted them a perfect place to sequester themselves until the target was visible. Good thing, since they'd been waiting two days and two nights. The one good thing about the endless wait, roasting by day and freezing by night, was the wind that had plagued them without end for most of that time had died down at last.

As the team's sniper, Beau hated the wind. An errant one played hell with the accuracy of a sniper rifle, screwing with the trajectory. He'd been serving as a sniper for ten years and had learned how to compensate for nature, how to correct for almost anything up to gale force winds. But he liked it better when the air was still and his spotter could give him exact trajectory and coordinates. He'd still rather not have to worry about it. And up here in the Hindu Kush, the winds were very unpredictable.

Stretched out full length beside him was Trey McIntyre, the man who had been his spotter from the time he joined the team. By now, the two of them were so much in sync they almost had telepathic communication. Trey was motionless, staring through his field glasses at the small settlement below. It was little more than a collection of tents, with camels and donkeys staked out under a canvas ceiling. Their target was a tribal leader who had proven connections with a radical Muslim group and who made money stealing guns from the American military and selling them to other tribes.

Word had reached them that the man they were after would be visiting this outpost and would be more exposed than at any other time. This would be the optimum time to take him out before he could do any more damage. With their commander, they'd plotted the mission with great care, trying to cover every angle.

But damn it all, the fucker they were after was still holed up in one of the tents that made up the camp and hadn't shown his face. Their four-man team had been dropped into place more than a mile away from where they now waited, the place where the helo would pick them up when their mission was completed. Getting more than one team in there — even a full team of their own — would be impractical. The more people who were dropped into a hot spot, the greater the chance of discovery. Lean and mean, as Slade always said.

The two days they'd been there felt like two weeks as they waited for their target to show himself, and subsisting on energy bars and bottled water which they used sparingly. It wasn't as if they could run into the local Walmart to replenish their supplies. They had taken turns standing watch then taking light naps, something they'd been well trained to do, watching for signals of the arrival of their target. But the monotony of the activity below them hadn't changed. The men in the camp rose at dawn, gathered in the central area of the yard for prayers, prepared their breakfast over a central campfire and ate as if they had nothing else to do. Which, Beau thought, seemed to be pretty much what their activity was for the rest of the day. At sundown, they prayed again, ate dinner and retired to their tents.

They had a three-day window, but that time was about to run out. The Apache gunship that had dropped them off wouldn't hang around beyond the target date. Too dangerous. Even now, they all hoped the pilot had managed to find a place out of sight, maybe in one of the many desolate canyons.

Beau was happy they had found this little niche to conceal themselves. Slade and their recon expert, Marc Blanchard, were stationed behind them, scoping out the area and covering their backs.

Looking at Beau Williams when he was not in mission mode, most people would have dismissed him as a surfer dude, and often did. But he was one of the most well-trained snipers in Delta Force, one hundred percent focused on every mission and with a growing kill book. The carefree surfer look he wore like a suit of clothes camouflaged a man who was very controlled and lacking any deep emotion.

Now, however, stretched out on the rocky ground, his ears tuned to every sound, he looked every bit the top-level sniper—cold and efficient. He cradled his very effective .50 caliber Heckler & Koch SG1 almost as if he was holding a baby. The lightweight, super-efficient semi-automatic sniper rifle had lethal accuracy and a large magazine capacity. Its soundless bolt-closing device made it ideal when absolute silence was required, as it was with almost all of their missions.

As the hours crawled by, Beau's training took over, keeping him and the rest of the team alert and ready. Every two hours, they changed watch shifts, although for Beau even Afghanistan and their mission couldn't drive away thoughts of the leggy blonde he'd met in Texas who had pushed all his buttons.

Hanging out at Slade's ranch during downtime had given them all a chance to work the kinks out of their bodies and enjoy some relaxation.

"Don't forget the party tomorrow night," Slade had reminded them, as they'd all gone off to shower. "Barbecue tonight, party tomorrow night."

"Yeah, yeah, yeah." Beau had paid lip service to the invitation but parties weren't his thing. A cold beer and a hot body took care of all the relaxation he needed.

But twenty-four hours later, as he'd stood next to a hot, sassy blonde, he'd had to rethink that. She had a body that wouldn't quit and gorgeous sun-streaked hair he wanted to run his fingers through, and he'd wondered how fast he could get her out of there and into bed.

Megan Welles had been a treat and a half. Sexy, smart, with a sassy tongue and a body that had made his cock stand up and beg and beg and beg.

"Lucky asshole," Beau had told their team leader when Megan went off to the powder room. "You hit the jackpot tonight."

Slade had laughed. "But I had to wait five years for it to happen. I'll never be that stupid again."

But Beau had thought it stupid the man had carried a torch for five years to begin with. To his way of thinking, no woman was worth that. Not to him for sure. Love 'em and leave 'em was his motto.

But then Megan was beside him again, and something inside him had made him wonder if he wasn't about to change his mind.

Remembering it now, Beau had to acknowledge that party had been a petri dish for the entire team. Mouthwatering, feisty Megan Welles, a sports reporter for an online magazine, had pushed every one of his buttons. The sizzle that had sparked between them had lit up the room and they'd spent that first night together enjoying some of the most erotic sex he'd ever had. By the time morning had arrived, he'd been shocked at the connection he'd felt to her.

Megan had given him a week to remember, one of the best in his life. He'd soon discovered she also had a strong side to her personality, which had added more spice to the sex they enjoyed. He'd spent every minute of his leave with her when she was available, hating it when they'd had to return for their next assignment.

Beau had never been one to get himself tangled up with a woman for more than a few nights. Neither his family experience nor his career as a sniper had made him open to people. Most women didn't like the prospect of a long-term relationship with someone whose emotions were so closed off. The few people he connected with were the members of Team Charlie and that was the way he liked it. He did his best to ignore Slade's remarks about all of them getting older and needing something solid in their lives. His something solid was his sniper rifle.

But ever since he'd left Texas, he'd woken up more than once with his hand wrapped around his dick, sweating from dreams about the things he and Megan had done together. He'd just been damn lucky nobody had been watching at the time.

In his mind, there had been no mistaking the link between the two of them, one that was both emotional and physical. He'd never had that before. Never wanted it. He'd always believed that relationships were destructive. He'd never had one that wasn't. Until Megan.

Maybe he was deluding himself, but he wanted the chance to find out if that connection was real or imagined. If she felt it, too. If, as unexpected as it was, he'd found someone he could think about for more than just the moment, shocking as it was to him.

And if he could trust the situation. Where his social life was concerned, Beau was a loner. Things just worked out better that way for him. He didn't trust the commitment level of women. That was just part of who he was The Army was his mistress, his lover, his commitment.

Not to mention the fact that he never knew when he'd be home or how long he'd deploy for. He was more than aware, however, that a career like his didn't quite help the situation. He'd seen too many relationships fail due to the stress of constant separation and the inability to settle into a normal pattern during downtime.

What do I bring to it, anyway? Sixteen ways to kill someone? He wasn't sure women found that romantic.

But you've seen others succeed, too. Like Slade and Kari. And if Slade is willing to take a chance, maybe it can work.

And maybe not.

Despite the fact that Megan had agreed to spend time with him when he had leave again, there was always the chance she'd meet someone else while he was off playing soldier. God, he hoped not. *Because Megan…well, Megan is different. Isn't she?* When his cock had been buried deep inside her, he'd felt something he'd never felt with any other woman.

He kept in touch with her via text and email, a strange aberration for him since he almost never connected with women after the fact. He was once and done. But the moment they landed in San Antonio again, he was heading for her townhouse. For the first time in maybe ever, he wanted to see where a relationship could go.

He shifted, trying to get comfortable in his position. This was no time or place to be thinking about down and dirty sex. He needed to use his big head, not his little one. He had serious work to do here.

"Tangos at three o'clock."

Trey's whisper was so soft that if not for his acute sense of hearing, Beau might have missed it. It jarred him out of his thoughts. He blinked to clear his vision and sighted through the scope, a dual-illumination system that had an automatic adjustment, and an aiming-point brightness for existing lighting conditions. Yup, there they were, sharp and clear — two Jeeps lumbering like slow-moving animals across the rocky ground into the camp. The guards stationed at either end of the camp went on full alert, rifles at the ready, scanning the surrounding area for any sign of movement as the Jeeps moved into the center of the encampment.

But Delta Team Charlie was like a wraith, a phantom that faded into the background, so silent they couldn't even hear their own breathing. They all waited, patient, Beau more than any of them, for the men to exit the vehicles. The target was easy to spot, the one that every single man bowed to and who was distinguished from the others by his colorful clothing. His *chapan*, a robe of vivid purple and green reflecting the moonlight, was worn over a *peren*, the typical baggy cotton trousers, and a *tunbun*, a cotton tunic. The headdress he wore designated him as a person of some note.

The Taliban leader stood erect as he accepted each man's homage and allowed himself to be embraced for a brief moment by what appeared to be the two primary guards. The greetings out of the way, the group began to move in slow motion toward the largest tent set just to the side of the central yard. It had flaps enclosing it all the way around. As they walked, the men were talking, gesticulating. Beau was sure none of them expected enemy invasion in the unforgiving landscape.

In a moment, they would separate, just an infinitesimal amount, and he would have his shot.

Wait for it. Wait for it.

Next to him Trey began whispering the wind velocity, the range to target measured with his spotter's scope, the angle of descent. A spotter was trained to memorize formulas for range, wind, elevation, temperature and target movement and be able to make calculations with or without a calculator. And Trey was one of the best. Beau trusted him without reservation.

Wait for it.

Beau held himself still as he tracked the tribal leader with his rifle, aiming at the dead center of his forehead. The moment would present itself. He just had to be patient. He drew in a deep breath then let it out in a slow stream, his finger ready on the trigger, Trey continuing to feed him information.

There!

The target separated himself just a little from the other men while one of them lifted a tent flap for him to enter. For a moment he turned a little in Beau's direction.

Now!

He squeezed the trigger, just the right pressure. And the .50 caliber bullet streaked through the night air to pierce the forehead of his target. There was no sound except a slight puff from the suppressed instrument. He knew Trey was tracking the round by the slight vapor trail it left, already recalculating in his head in case by some wild-assed chance Beau had missed. But as always, Beau was right on target. They watched the man jerk then crumple to the ground.

Even as the men in the encampment shouted, bending over their fallen leader, scanning the surrounding countryside, aiming their rifles and firing burst after burst toward shadows, Delta Team Charlie was already up and on its way. It took Beau eight seconds to break down his rifle and stuff it into his backpack. Slade, already speaking into his radio, led the way as they moved like ghosts to the exfiltration site.

They waited, crouched in the sparse scrub surrounding the landing zone, Glocks in their hands just in case, until they heard the distinctive *whump!* of the rotors. Then the big Apache helo pulled up over a tall outcropping and hovered over the landing zone, low enough for them to get on board. Even from the distance of the camp, the shouting voices of men carried on the now still night air. Beau knew before long they would be combing the rocky landscape looking for the intruders. And the sound of the helo was impossible to disguise. They needed to get the fuck out of there *now*.

Hands reached out from the bird to help pull the team members into the cabin and they were lifting off even as the last two men were still scrambling to get inside. A fast exit was always best in situations like this. No telling how soon the men from the outpost would be up there looking for them.

Beau leaned back against the cabin wall, legs outstretched, and closed his eyes. One more for his kill book. One more bad guy eliminated. One day closer to a week of leave and time with Megan.

He looked over at Slade, who grinned through the black grease on his face. He nodded and gave Beau a thumbs-up then did the same to Trey. Using his sat radio, he reported in on the success of a mission then he, too, let himself relax. The noise of the rotors and the open doors prevented any real conversation so they all just bumped fists and settled back until they landed at the base. As they headed toward their barracks, Slade answered a call on his cell phone. When he finished, he looked over his shoulder at his men.

"It's a fluke, but we've got transport day after tomorrow, a military flight to Fort Sam. You guys all ready to rock and roll? And Teo will pick us up and take us to the ranch, just like the last time."

Fort Sam was Fort Sam Houston, one of five military installations in and around San Antonio. Not as comfortable as a commercial flight, but a hell of a lot cheaper. There was a chorus of yesses and hoorahs as they walked across the tarmac. Slade's ranch was just south of San Antonio, a small spread by Texas standards but it was well run and appeared to be profitable. A good place for them to unwind. Beau in particular thought it was great, since if not for that last visit he'd never have met Megan.

Trey cleared his throat. "So the big day's all set, Mister Getting Married?"

Slade laughed. "Kari's got everything set for two days after we land in Texas. That way she and I can have some time together before we're wheels up again. Bring your uniforms."

Trey frowned. "You guys are going the whole big, fancy route for the wedding?"

Slade shook his head. "No. Kari wants to keep it small. Neither of us has parents still living, sad to say, so it's just going to be our closest friends. Maybe some of the people she works with. That's it." He looked from one member of his team to another. "But that doesn't mean I don't want this to be very special for her. She's gone all out on her dress and I want to make this a day she'll remember forever. She's an exceptional lady."

"You can count on us," Marc assured him.

Beau glanced over at him, surprised he'd even commented. Marc still carried the baggage of a disastrous marriage and the results had turned him into a silent, gray presence with an invisible wall around him. Beau and Trey had wondered if they'd have to pound him to get him to the wedding. *Good for him for stepping up.*

"And you know," Slade added, "while I'm honeymooning with my bride, you guys can hang out at the ranch if you want to. Teo will have everything at your disposal. But..." He looked from one to the other.

"Am I right in assuming you'll be hooking up with the women you met?"

"Does the sun come up in the morning?" Trey joked.

"Not even a question," Beau added.

Marc said nothing, although they all knew he'd met someone, but everyone was afraid of jinxing things if they opened their mouths.

"You know Kari sent each of them invitations," Slade said.

Except Marc, Beau thought, since no one knew who the hell the woman was and Marc was not sharing.

"That's very nice of her," Trey said.

"She enjoyed meeting them the weekend we were all together at the ranch," Slade told them. "She's happy they said they'd be there."

"Great." Beau winked. "As long as it's not catching."

"You never know. I sure didn't expect it." He checked his watch. "Okay. I'll go make my report and afterward we'll have a couple of days to debrief. Then we're outta here."

Beau knew the first thing he'd be doing as soon as he showered off the dirt was texting Megan. Already his cock was swelling in anticipation.

* * * *

Megan sat back in her desk chair in her home office, picked up her coffee mug and punched up the latest edition of *Sportsweek*, the hot online sports magazine for which she was a reporter at the low end of the totem pole. The first thing she saw almost made her spew her mouthful of coffee.

Star Quarterback Candidate for MVP
By Linda Alfonso

Online publications didn't have the fold that print editions did, but the article was placed above where it would have been, right next to the headline story.

Damn!

Shitballs and crackers!

She'd been working her ass off at this magazine for three years and she still couldn't get asshole editor Gus Kendrick to give her a decent assignment. The cream went to Linda, who had been there for six years, since the magazine had started. Next in line was Rose McMillan, who specialized in personality profiles and had in fact won awards for some of her articles.

Then there was her, Megan Welles, still clawing her way up the ladder, fighting the two female reporters and twenty-three male writers whose asses Kendrick kissed on a regular basis. She supposed she could have gone to another publication. She'd sure thought about it at least a hundred times. But *Sportsweek* was hot, and if she made her bones here, she could write her ticket in sports reporting anywhere. If she could just get Kendrick to see her talent. Or at least not see her as a woman.

Shit!

The problem with an online publication was there wasn't a lot of face to face. Kendrick ran the office with a limited staff, with most of the writers scattered over far and wide. He held meetings once a week and, for those in the area, attendance was mandatory. Others Skyped in. It was hard to argue with someone who could, with a punch of a finger, cut the connection and leave her hanging.

She sat there, staring at the screen of her computer, her mind running in twenty different directions. She needed a hook, something that would interest hardnosed Kendrick enough that he'd sign off on it. But it couldn't be anything so interesting he'd yank it and give it to someone else. She didn't know which would be worse, handing it to one of the other female writers or giving it to one of the guys. Either way sucked.

I should sic Beau on him.

She grinned at the thought of her Delta Force…what? Boyfriend? Lover?…going after Kendrick. The image brought a wider smile to her face, even if she knew it was impossible.

Sipping on her coffee, she closed the document and started surfing the Web to see what was out there that might catch her eye. One headline made her sit up and take notice.

He's Still Got It at 36
Hawks' Senior Citizen has Fifth Straight 35 Point Game

Megan scrolled through the story on Manny Rushmore, who'd scored thirty-five points for the San Antonio Predators for the fifth game in a row. In fact, he was consistent in scoring more than any player on the team. The pundits were calling him the Senior Citizen Wonder.

There has to be something here. How is Rushmore doing it? What's his routine? What does he eat? How does he exercise? Is he taking special vitamins? She'd love to do a profile on him. He was a very popular player and she knew a profile would draw a ton of readers. She just had to approach Kendrick the right way. Make her proposal interesting but not so he'd take it and give it to one of the guys.

As she sat there, holding her coffee that had cooled to beyond drinkable, an email notification popped up from one of her sources. She read the message, shocked at what it contained. She blinked twice, to make sure what she saw was correct.

Hey Megan,
Tony Gagliardi died last night. They're saying heart attack, but his wife insisted he didn't have any heart problems. Poor guy was just getting ready to announce his retirement, too.

Megan stared at the message. Tony G was one of her all-time favorite players, a high scorer, a team leader and very involved in the community. Just last week one of the channels had done a retrospective of his career, showing some of his highest scoring games.

She typed back —

What happened? Where was he?

At a friend's. Report says he was very thirsty, drank down two bottles of water real fast then clutched his chest and collapsed. No history of heart problems.

How devastating. When is the funeral? Send me details.

When the answer came back, she entered the information in her Notes on her cell phone. *Tomorrow.* The funeral was tomorrow. She'd attend, no question about it, but the news bothered her. This was the third high-profile athlete to suffer the same fate in as many months. The first one, a sudden heart attack, she'd seen as an anomaly. The second one not so much. *But now, with Tony G's death, could there be a pattern?* She pulled up her Notes section on her tablet and read what she'd jotted down. Yes, this was number three.

Her reporter's nose was twitching like a rabbit's. This couldn't all be just coincidence. Three deaths, all players about the same age, all turning in superlative performances, more spectacular when their ages were considered. She scanned her notes yet again, looking for something she might have jotted down that would jog something in her memory. She was pretty damn sure it could not be performance-enhancing drugs, at least those on the known list. They would show up in routine urine tests. Besides, none of the players who had died had ever been associated with PEDs. In fact, they were squeaky clean.

But Megan had learned long ago that things were seldom as they seemed.

Her instincts, which had never failed her yet, were telling her there was something big here, but she'd have to watch her every step. She would need to dig into the story. Do some research. Low profile interview some of the players, if that could be arranged. See if she had the threads of a story to follow.

She'd have to do it all on her own time. If she went to Kendrick with it, he'd either toss it or give it to one of his favorites, and she wasn't going to let that happen. The problem would come if it turned out she had something, a major story, that Kendrick might want her to hand over to someone else. If that happened, she was out of there.

Research first, then write, then sell it.

No sooner had she thought Kendrick's name than the Facetime icon blinked on her computer and her phone rang.

"Hey, Megan, are you all set for today's interview?" Kendrick's voice boomed across the connection.

Megan forced herself to tamp down the urge to cover her ears.

"Holy crap, Gus. I'm sitting right here. You don't have to shout. I can hear you."

Kendrick, a thirty-five-year veteran of sports reporting, just laughed. "Just making sure you're not napping in your chair. So about that interview you got coming up. Don't make me regret giving it to you."

Ah, yes, the constant nudging and warnings. He wanted to be sure she knew he'd thrown her a bone after all her bitching.

"All set up for this afternoon," she assured him. "Don't you worry. I'm meeting him at his agent's office. I scheduled a photographer so we can get a picture of him doing the ceremonial signing of the contract."

"I need the story by noon tomorrow," he reminded her.

"No problem." She grinned at him. "In fact, I'm getting my notes together as soon as a certain editor lets me get off the phone."

"Okay, okay."

The Austin NBA team had drafted one of the hottest point guards to come out of college basketball in a long time and that was all anyone was talking about. A lot of people were waiting to read an in-depth interview with the man. There were other more senior reporters on the staff who were griping because Megan had gotten the assignment. But Megan knew Kendrick was testing her and she wasn't about to screw up. Not when she had an idea for a series to sell him.

Since the day Kendrick had hired her, she'd been fighting to earn and cement her position on his staff. The other reporters, some of them asshole would-be jocks, weren't above making crude and rude comments every time she got a tasty project. She'd thought by now there'd be some enlightenment in the media world regarding female sports reporters. But this publication seemed to have its permanent share of Neanderthals. It seemed she fought every day for respect and recognition. Sometimes wearing her strength like a shield got tiring.

Kendrick had sent her on the local college tour when he'd first hired her, throwing everything on that beat at her to see what she was made of. Megan had gritted her teeth and slogged through it, doing her best to earn his respect and that of the editor-in-chief.

She had cut her teeth on four lesser publications before getting to the big time and even at that she'd almost had to start at the bottom again. Whoever said there was equality in reporting today didn't pay attention to what was going on in the world of sports reporting. If not for the publisher's push to hire more females and his fascination with the work Megan had done to get here, she might still be wandering in the virtual doldrums, trying to find a place for herself.

If she was right about the story she was following, though — and the news about Tony G just reinforced what she was beginning to suspect — it could be the making of her career. If this series came together and had her byline, every guy on the staff would have his dick in a knot because of it.

Tough shit.

The coffee in her mug was cold and bitter, so she headed for the kitchen to get fresh. Back at her desk, she sipped the hot drink and took a moment to rub her temples. Then, exhaling a deep breath, she pulled her thoughts together. Today she'd get a killer interview after finagling for a week to set it up, wading through everyone's politics. Kendrick would have to give her good placement for it. Damn it, he'd just have to.

Her concentration was interrupted by a *ding* signaling a text message on her phone. She touched the screen to bring it to life and her pulse leaped when she saw Beau William's name. His Delta Force team had been gone for two months and although he was able to text, email and Skype between missions, it wasn't the same as having him here.

Watch yourself, girl. He might not be not the settling down type.

Hey! We're heading back to civilization.

Awesome!

We're back in Texas in forty-eight. You gonna be around?

Damn straight! Her heart did a funny little skip.

I will.

Will he come straight to my place? Will he hang out with the men first? Should I ask him? She didn't want to seem too clingy. That wasn't her and she sensed that wasn't Beau's cup of tea, either. She smiled at his next text.

Pick me up at the ranch?

Her pulse did a happy dance.

Let me know when.

I'll text you. Everything okay with work?

He knew what a jerk Kendrick was.

The usual. You know.

There was a long moment of silence.

Want me to take him apart for you?

Megan laughed.

Don't tempt me.

Okay. I'll text you when we're close to the ranch. See you soon.

Soon.

Then he was gone.

She sat there staring at the phone, memories of their week together looping through her brain like a video. When they'd met, he'd made it plain right away entanglements were not on the to-do list of all the guys on the team. But now Slade Donovan was getting ready to marry Kari Malone. If the team leader could settle down, maybe the others could, too?

Getting ahead of yourself much?

Of course, she wasn't sure she was marriage material, either. She'd learned the hard way that she and long-term relationships didn't work. Either she picked the wrong men or she wasn't meant to couple up. The last one had exploded more than a year ago and she'd made a solemn vow to quit putting herself through that emotional wringer. So she was done. Ended. Finito.

No forever for her.

Then she'd met Beau and a nugget of hope had begun to grow inside her.

They'd had no more than a week together, during which the sex had been hot and plentiful, then he'd been gone. In that ten-day period, she'd felt something bubbling beneath the surface. Something that had been more than the sex. *A connection. Whatever.* It both frightened and tempted her. She'd known it would be weeks before she saw him again. *So, take it for what it is, right?* A hit or miss friends with benefits.

But there's something about Beau...

Quit dreaming, she told herself, *and focus on what works here. Great fun and hot sex.*

She did want to run her idea about the athletes past him. Beau was smart and had an analytical brain. He told her it was necessary for snipers, who had to calculate so many variables before they took their shot. He'd tell her if she had something to follow or not.

Buoyed by her texts from him, she looked up the number of Manny Rushmore's agent. Maybe she was pushing her luck, not getting Kendrick's okay first, but she didn't want him jerking it out from under her. Besides, how often would someone turn up almost on her doorstep that she could question? She had to strike while the iron was hot. Fifteen minutes later, she had a meeting set up with the man himself in a couple of days.

"Lunch?" she'd asked.

"Lunch is good," he'd said. "Like friends. Better than offices, which I think are too stuffy."

So did she, so they were on the same page there. She just wondered if he'd be so quick to accept if he knew the real reason for the interview, and the series she hoped it would give birth to.

So, the meeting. Would Beau be interested in going with her? Then there was Kari and Slade's upcoming wedding. So much to cram in and so few days to do it. Would they be able to pick up where they'd left off? The pulse deep inside her throbbed with anticipation and her nipples beaded into hard tips. She couldn't wait for the next forty-eight hours to pass.

Swallowing a sigh, she gathered her tablet and her handheld recorder, slid the strap of her purse over her shoulder and headed out on her current assignment.

Chapter Two

It was late afternoon by the time Teobaldo Rivera, Slade's longtime ranch manager and friend, picked them all up at Fort Sam and ferried them to the ranch in the helicopter. Slade bumped fists with everyone and left them to Teo's tender care. He was already on his cell with Kari as he headed toward his bedroom. Trey McIntyre had his own cell out, no doubt calling the hot lady lawyer he'd met last time they'd been here at the party given by friends of Slade. Beau chuckled at the thought that both Slade and Trey had taken attorneys to bed. Of course, with Slade it had gone way beyond that. In two days he and Kari Malone would be married and Slade was like a kid waiting for Christmas.

Marc Blanchard was a silent presence, saying very little either on the trip back from overseas or on the way to Slade's ranch. He had showered in less than ten minutes then asked Teo for the keys to one of the ranch trucks and headed into town. The others were all too well aware of Marc's disastrous marriage and even more devastating divorce. If at last he was finding his way out of the dark, they were all for it. And no one was going to upset the apple cart by asking too many questions.

Beau thought about showering and changing at Slade's while he waited for Megan to pick him up, but decided against it. What he wanted most was to shower at her place, with her. The images of their bodies slick with water, the two of them gliding their hands over each other, Megan facing the wall while he slid into her from behind were so vivid and appealing he had to send a message to his eager cock. He hoped she wouldn't think he was too grubby when she saw him.

Although he often dreamed about women, most times those dreams were one hundred percent sexual in nature. He figured it was because he wanted sex, and plenty of it, and he was always up front about it. He just didn't see himself committing to a woman. He belonged to Delta. He was the team's sniper. That was his focus. All of it. Some people might call him a plain old horn dog, since the parts of him that ever got involved with a woman was his sexy smile and his cock.

But Megan pushed buttons he didn't even know he had. She was smart and feisty and funny. He found himself relaxing with her, something he never did with women. If he thought about it, most of the time he played a part, the surfer dude they thought he looked like, carefree, fixated on hot sex and as much of it as he could get. He kept the real Beau Williams under the same tight control he used when in sniper mode.

But somehow Megan got past all that and into the core of who he was and, in a way, it frightened him. He wasn't sure he wanted anyone to see that far into him.

But Megan was something special, no doubt about it. He had a history that had made him isolate himself on an emotional level up until now. He got the sense from Megan that she was in the same place. Maybe one of these nights they could open those steel doors and look into each other's souls.

The thought of it frightened the hell out of him. He just hoped he didn't fuck this up.

The honking of a horn interrupted his mental wanderings and he looked up to see the woman herself pulling into the parking area. When she climbed out of the car, he took a moment to appreciate the sight of her. Her skin glowed with a light tan and her honey-blonde hair was pulled back in its usual ponytail, emphasizing the smoky gray of her eyes. The pink T-shirt and skinny jeans she wore hugged the curves his hands had memorized every night they'd been together. His cock stood to attention and saluted at the sight of her, and he had to use all his brain power to control it.

"Welcome home, soldier. Glad you're here." Her lips curved into a smile.

He could tell she wasn't sure just how enthusiastic to be, despite the intense week they'd spent together and the many texts and emails they'd exchanged since then.

Beau opened his arms.

"Come here and let me wrap my arms around you."

She walked into his embrace and he hugged her close, loving the soft feel of her breasts against his chest. The enticing scent she wore teased at his nostrils. This was the first time in, well, maybe ever, that he'd felt excited about a woman in more than a physical way. Almost all the time, his habit when he was on leave was to hit the bars running, searching for new faces and hot bodies.

Anything where he could shut off his brain and have mindless sex and a few laughs.

This was different and all of a sudden it scared the shit out of him. *What if I fuck it up? Make a huge mistake?* But then her arms were around his neck and she was kissing him with such enthusiasm he forgot to be worried. Her mouth was so sweet and her lips so soft and velvety. He thrust his tongue into her heat, coaxing hers to slide with him, to dance with him. He closed his eyes and just lost himself in her, the erotic flavor of her erasing the aura of death and destruction he'd lived with for the past several weeks.

When a wolf whistle from the porch pierced his brain, he looked up and saw Slade watching them with a big grin on his face.

"Y'all want to borrow a room before you take off?"

Megan broke the kiss and Beau loosened his grip on her just a little bit.

"Thanks, we're good," he hollered. Then he looked down at Megan. "Sorry. Didn't mean to embarrass you."

"It's okay." She waved to Slade, who nodded to her.

"Don't forget Sunday," he called out. "Five sharp."

"We'll be there," she assured him and glanced at Beau. "First of our team to get married."

"Yup." He didn't say anything else. What could he say? That he never intended to get married? Not a great way to start a couple of weeks with a woman who had him all twisted up inside.

"You ready to get out of here?" Megan asked.

"You bet."

She scanned him from head to toe. "Let's get you to my place and into a shower."

He put his mouth close to her ear. "I will if you get in there with me."

She laughed as they walked to her car, a teasing sound. Again his cock demanded attention and his balls ached. *Good Christ*. His body seemed to be on fast forward with Megan Welles and he didn't know quite what to make of it. He just hoped he could behave himself until they got to her place.

All the way into San Antonio, Beau couldn't stop himself from touching her. He brushed the softness of her cheek, stroked the silken tail of honey-streaked blonde hair, squeezed her thigh through the fabric of her jeans.

"You keep doing that," she joked, "and we might end up on the side of the road."

He leaned over the console and put his mouth close to her ear. "I'll do my best to behave myself," he breathed, "but it's damn hard." He gave a rough laugh. "*I'm* damn hard. But I'll do my best to behave because I have plans for that shower."

Take it one day at a time, buddy. And don't fuck it up.

Megan was having her own troubles with control, riding in the car with Beau. One look at him after all these weeks and every part of her body pulsed with joy. Except now that he was here at last an unfamiliar feeling of shyness crept up on her. They had been so relaxed and free with each other the last time. He'd spent every minute of his leave with her from the moment they'd met at the Huttons' party. But she had the sense Beau didn't do repeats with the women he met and she sure hadn't had any kind of continuous relationship since, well, forever.

Would he have a sudden awakening and think he'd made a mistake? Decide he didn't want to hook up with her again? Maybe give her the wrong idea? Or come to the conclusion she wasn't what he thought she'd be after all? And what if she was disappointed in *him*? Discovered he was an asshole like too many of the men she met these days?

Drive yourself crazy much, Megan?

As all the conflicting thoughts banged into one another, Beau reached over and rested his hand on her thigh, giving it a gentle squeeze. A wave of heat flashed through, nudging her pulse to overdrive, most of all the one between her thighs. Her foot slipped a little on the accelerator before she pulled herself together.

Goodbye thoughts, hello hormones.

"I missed you like hell." His voice was deep and rough, the sound of it scraping along her skin.

She gave a short laugh. "I'll bet you tell that to all the women. I'll bet you were too busy over there in the jungle or the sandbox or wherever it is you went on this mission." She knew he could never discuss the details with her and she was fine with that. Proud, in fact, that he was in Special Forces and committed to fighting for his country.

He squeezed her thigh again, sliding his hand over the curve of her leg. Her muscles tightened beneath his palm and he squeezed again. She wanted to tell him to slip his fingers just a little farther, press a little harder, to still the pulsing in her needy sex. Or maybe she could pull off the road someplace and jump on him for a quickie.

Crap, Megan! You're thinking like some sex-starved maniac.

Which she guessed she was where he was concerned.

"You'd better keep your hands to yourself," she warned, "unless you don't mind if we crash on the way home."

His rough-edged laugh lit a blaze in her body.

"You glad I'm home, sugar?"

"Damn straight." Okay, maybe she shouldn't tell him how much she'd missed him, but what the hell? He was the first man she'd ever felt this way about. If it crashed and burned, she at least wanted the best ride she could get.

"Good." He lifted his hand to stroke her cheek with the backs of his fingers. "But I'll bet not half as glad as I am."

His touch sent shivers racing up her spine. She never remembered being this aroused by mere contact or so filled with rampant desire for a man in her life. But there was a special something about Beau Williams that affected every part of her body. She just hoped she wasn't biting off more than she could chew here.

"So catch me up on what's new with you." He dropped his hand back to her thigh. "What's going on at *Sportsweek*?"

"Funny you should ask." She glanced over at him. "I think I stumbled on something that has the potential to be a blockbuster story. I want to tell you about it first, though, so you could poke holes in it or tell me I was imagining things."

"That right? I'm not an editor, Megan. I can't tell you if Kendrick would jump on it or not."

"First of all, you are so much smarter than he is it isn't funny. Second, you have the ability to get through bullshit. If I am making something out of nothing, I want you to tell me."

He laughed. "I love it when you stroke my ego." He lowered his voice. "Along with other parts of my body."

"We'll get to those parts soon enough."

Yes, indeed. We'll do just that. She maneuvered past a car moving too slow in the wrong lane on the Interstate. No time to waste today. She wanted to get Beau to her place *now!* She tried to focus on telling him her idea.

"I ran across a couple of interesting items," she began, "just in the process of digging for story ideas. One was about a basketball player getting up there in years who had an unbelievable scoring night, one of many in recent games. The other one was about a player almost the same age, also coming off a super best season, who died of a sudden heart attack. Then I got an email that Tony Gagliardi had dropped dead of an apparent heart attack, with no warning at all. Just like the others. Three similar players with the same cause of death seemed a little weird. Oh, and they both had established new, incredible scoring records this season."

"And you're seeing a pattern," he guessed.

"I know two events don't always mean that, but I've just got this itch, Beau. There's been no hint of performance enhancing drugs for either of them, but something has to be going on. I'm already trying to dig into Tony's death and his recent playing history." She sighed. "Beau, that funeral was so sad. His wife was devastated. She could not stop crying. And his children. God. It all broke my heart."

He reached his hand over and squeezed her thigh. A potent combination of caring and desire ignited every nerve in her body, burning hotter when he moved his thumb back and forth in a slow, sweeping movement.

"So you're asking me if I think you should do some research. Right?"

"Yes." She nodded. "You always get straight to the heart of the matter. If this is nothing, I want to know now, before I invest any more time in it."

"You think there's something odd about it?" he asked.

"Do you?" His opinion would give her a hint if she was chasing shadows or not.,

He paused but just for a moment. "I do."

"I could be chasing a wild hare here, but damn, Beau. I think this story, if it's real, could pull me out of the underbrush where Kendrick keeps sticking me. I'm tired of Linda Alfonso getting her pick of stories, or the other top-drawer ones going to the guys." She tightened her fingers on the steering wheel. "And sick and tired of Kendrick telling me I'll get there soon enough. I'm not eighteen years old, for crap's sake."

"He plays favorites." It wasn't a question.

"Well, yeah. And okay, so she's good. But so am I. I just need the one breakout story. Or series." She blew out a breath. "Manny Rushmore is in town for two weeks. He's gotten a lot of coverage of late on his unbelievable scoring runs. On my own, I went ahead and scheduled an interview with him."

"No kidding?" He sat up straighter in his seat. "I don't have time to follow sports as much as I'd like, but he's one of my favorite players."

"Well, one of your favorite players had an unbelievable scoring night, and it was one of several in the last couple of weeks. Call me suspicious, but I can't shake the feeling he's getting some chemical help."

"I'd hate it if that were true. Did you talk to him about it?"

"I arranged to meet him for lunch. He thinks it's for a profile piece. I'm not saying a word to Kendrick or anyone about it until I get the whole story together. If indeed there is one," she added and slid a glance at Beau. "Maybe you'd like to come along with me. It's the day after tomorrow."

"You bet." He squeezed her thigh again. "I can meet a real sports hero and get to watch my girl at work at the same time."

His girl? Okay, but she wasn't counting her chickens. She knew they had something strong and intense going, but she still had no idea where it would end up. And she knew they both needed to be extra sure before they made any commitment.

For some reason the traffic was heavier than usual and the drive to her townhouse seemed to take forever. Or maybe it was just that she was so anxious. But then, at last, they were there. She parked in the garage in the back of the townhouse and they entered through the side door. She spared a moment to give thanks she'd taken the time to clean the place that morning.

As soon as they were inside, Beau dropped his duffel and pulled her against him. She didn't care how dirty or sweaty his body was. She just wanted to be close to him like this.

He grabbed her hand and pulled her around to face him, burying his fingers in her hair so he could hold her head in place. His mouth was hot and demanding on hers, his lips scorching as they moved over her mouth. She opened at once to his tongue, sliding her own over it and scraping it with her teeth. The kiss was deep and sizzled her clear to her toes. She pressed her body against his, feeling the hard plane of his chest and the even harder length and thickness of his cock.

Beau slid his free hand down her back to her ass, cupping one cheek and squeezing it, all the while continuing to plunder her mouth. When they ran out of breath, he lifted her head, his eyes glazed with heat and need and want.

"Shower," he gasped. "You. Me. Naked. Now."

Stopping to pull something from his duffel, he grasped her hand and almost dragged her from the hall into her bedroom. He took a scant few minutes to take off his own clothes before stripping Megan of hers then tugged her into the bathroom. Before she could blink, they were standing under the warm stream of water and Beau was stroking thick, sudsy lather over every inch of her body.

His hands were warm, his fingers strong as they massaged and caressed, his touch erotic and teasing. The pinch of a nipple between his thumb and forefinger, the light squeeze of a breast, the glide of his hand down the valley between her breasts to her navel and at last the quick stroke of his fingers through her slit. Nipping the lobe of her ear, that soft place that was a hot spot for her body, his breath a hot breeze over her skin. And all the while, he murmured in her ear, telling her every erotic thing he wanted to do to her.

She clung to his shoulders, holding to him as she shook with need. When she tried to squeeze her thighs together to trap his hand and keep it locked to her sex, he eased it away, extending his fingers to spread her legs. She hitched her hips forward, a silent movement urging him to slide those same fingers inside her, but he gave her a low, rough laugh.

"Not until I'm ready, sugar."

She slid a hand between them and wrapped her fingers around his swollen cock, giving it a gentle squeeze.

"Feels like you're ready to me right now."

He sucked in a breath. "Don't do that, babe, or it will be over before we've even begun."

"See?" She gave a soft, almost hysterical laugh. "That's what I mean."

"And what *I* mean is, I haven't finished having my fun yet. I've been dreaming about this since we were deployed." He stroked the flesh of her sex, rubbing his finger over the tip of her clit with slow, rhythmic strokes. "I couldn't get the feel and taste of you out of my head and I haven't anywhere near had my fill yet."

"You're driving me crazy, though." She tried her best to ride his hand, but it seemed he was just as determined to be in control.

"That's the idea."

He turned her to face the wall of the shower and began the slow process of sliding the lather over the skin of her back. His strong fingers kneaded her muscles as he worked the body wash into her shoulders, along her spine and down past her waist. When he reached the curve of her ass, he eased his soapy fingers into the hot crevice, teasing the sensitive flesh and sending jolts of electricity through her body. She tried to push back against him, to clench around his fingers, but his low chuckle vibrated through her.

He shifted her body again so she faced him and the heat in his eyes almost melted her bones. He cupped her chin, tilted her face toward him and took her mouth again in a ravenous kiss. He tasted like seven kinds of sin, every one of them wicked and wild and so addictive she wondered what she'd done before he came along. He licked every inch of her mouth, sweeping his tongue along the sensitive flesh and coaxing her own tongue to do a sensual dance with his.

More body wash. More lather.

Cupping her breasts in his soapy palms, he brushed his thumbs back and forth across her nipples, which were already hard and aching, ramping up the thrum of the pulse beating low and deep in her core. She tried to squeeze her thighs together, but Beau insinuated one leg between hers to keep her from doing that.

She cried out with need when he slid two fingers inside her, rubbing the sensitive inner flesh and curling them to stroke that very hot spot that made her lose her mind. She moaned, digging her fingers into his shoulders as he drove in and out of her hungry sex, his thumb teasing her clit with each smooth movement.

She rode his hand, pushing harder, trying to pull him deeper, lifting one leg to wrap around his waist, opening wider for his explorations. Neither of them seemed to care about the water streaming down on them, and all she could think about was the response he was coaxing from her body, driving her wild.

Banding one arm around her to stabilize her, he took her mouth in another of those drugging, ravaging kisses, his tongue mimicking the movement of his fingers as they continued to thrust in and out of her hot sex. She teetered on the edge of release, reaching for it, every part of her begging for it. Then Beau added a third finger, slid them in deep and the orgasm exploded like a burst of fireworks. Her body shook. Her inner walls clutched at his fingers and spasmed over and over again. And all the time his clever, wicked mouth never left hers.

At last, spent, as he eased his fingers from her body, she slid her leg back down and wound her arms around his neck. He lifted his mouth from hers, trailing his lips across her collarbone then lowering his head to reach the upper swell of her breasts. He held her tight to his body, stroking her back and tracing the swell of her ass. The hard, thick length of his cock pressed against her was a reminder to both of them that Beau was still riding the hard edge of need.

"My turn," she whispered.

"It better be a short turn," he murmured, "because I've been ready to pull the trigger since I laid eyes on you. Maybe even before."

"We'll see," she teased.

Working up her own generous portion of suds, she smoothed her hands across his chest, brushing the tips of her fingers over his nipples and drawing a harsh intake of breath from him. Coasting her slick fingers down over his abs, she paused a moment to swirl a fingertip in the indentation of his navel before sliding through thick dark-blond curls then wrapping her fingers around his shaft.

Dropping to her knees, she slipped one hand between his muscular thighs to cup his balls while the other began a slow, tortuous up and down movement on his cock. Beau sucked in a breath and leaned over her to brace his hands on the shower wall. His body shuddered as she pumped from root to tip and back again in a slow and steady pace, sliding her thumb across the swollen purple head.

She set up a rhythm, slow then fast then slow again, squeezing his balls with her other hand in a rhythmic cadence. Even with the water pounding down on him, the heat of his shaft almost scorched her palm. She stroked and gripped, mesmerized by the pulse of blood in the heavy vein wrapped around the hot thickness, and the sensation of steel beneath the soft skin.

She almost slipped on the tile when Beau grabbed her elbows and dragged her up to her feet.

"What—" Her brain was clouded in erotic fog. "What's the matter?" Her lips curved in a shaky smile. "I wasn't finished yet."

"Maybe not, but I was close. When I come, I want to be inside you and I don't mean your mouth."

He slid the shower door open and reached out to the vanity. When he pulled his hand in, he was holding a condom, no doubt what he'd yanked from the duffel on the way to the bedroom. Megan couldn't help but notice his hands were shaking as he ripped open the foil and rolled the latex onto his cock.

"Put your arms around my neck," he rasped, "and hold on tight."

When she did, he leaned against the wall then lifted her and lowered her with a careful movement onto his cock. The moment she wrapped her legs around his hips, he started to move, slowly at first, rocking into her so his thick shaft filled every inch of her. In, out, scraping her sensitive walls, igniting the nerves that had not even settled from her earlier orgasm.

She dug her heels into the small of his back, pulling herself into him even tighter. He moved faster, then faster still, and everything faded away except the two of them, his cock inside her and the incredible rhythm he'd set. She closed her eyes as sensations escalated and he moved faster, faster. All the while he murmured again in her ear, all the erotic things he planned to do with her. To her.

"Now," he murmured in a hoarse, gravel-sounding voice.

He drove into her one more time, hard, bit down on the lobe of her ear and it was as if someone had pulled a trigger. Her entire body shuddered as he pulsed inside her, the walls of her sex gripping him tight, milking him. She held on tight as the orgasm shook them, and nothing existed except her, this man and this amazing, incredible release.

At length, the spasm receded. Still shaky, she eased her legs down so she could stand, but she still clung to him to steady herself. The water had turned cold, but it seemed neither of them were aware of it. Beau pulled off the condom, moved them in a quick dance under the spray to rinse off and lifted her out onto the bath mat.

She was too spent to say a word, just stood there while he dried her off, then himself. Then he lifted her and carried her into the bedroom, depositing her on the bed He bent and kissed her lips, running the tip of his tongue along the seam, before he smiled.

"I think we should order in tonight."

She laughed, giddy in the aftermath of the stupendous sex. "Pizza?"

"Pizza sounds good. Then you can tell me all about this big interview you have coming up."

Chapter Three

Megan had arranged to meet Manny Rushmore at
Gilmore's, a quiet, well-known restaurant in the
downtown area of San Antonio, for a late lunch, when
the crowd would have thinned out and there was less
chance of being mobbed. Anywhere on the Riverwalk
would have been too noisy and crazy and she didn't see
any sense in driving way out of town to someplace
when this was so convenient. Besides, she loved the
ambience of Gilmore's — the dark paneled walls, brass
rails above the wainscoting, the thick carpet that
absorbed sound. Also, the lunch crowd would be
cleared out by the time they met, so the atmosphere
would be even more relaxed. Plus, in her research,
she'd learned it was a common go-to place for him.

He was already there when she and Beau arrived,
sitting at a booth in a far corner of the dining room.
When he stood to shake hands, he towered over them,
even Beau, who was six foot three. His shirt and slacks
were expensive and tailored for his tall, lean figure, but

it was his smile that got to her. It was warm and genuine and easy. She liked him right away.

"Thanks for doing this," she told him as they seated themselves.

"No problem." He grinned. "It's always good to see you." He looked at Beau. "I'm a big fan of hers."

Beau chuckled. "Me, too."

Her eyes widened. "Of mine?"

"Uh-huh." Manny nodded. "Love your articles."

She laughed. "I should get a testimonial from you for my editor."

"Thanks for letting me tag along," Beau said to Manny. "I'm a fan of yours, so this is a real pleasure for me."

"Anything for Megan. Are you two" — he waved a finger back and forth between them — "together? A couple?"

Megan searched her brain for an answer. "We're — "

"Together," Beau finished, and slid an arm around her, giving her a hint of a squeeze.

Something did a little somersault in her stomach.

"That's great, man." Manny smiled at him. "Megan's a terrific gal and a reporter all the athletes respect."

"You make me blush, Manny," she kidded. "But thanks."

"Good choice of place," he commented, looking around. "I come here a lot."

"So I discovered. I thought you'd be a lot more relaxed here."

He chuckled. "You planning to give me the third degree?"

"Maybe just first or second," she teased.

Beau pressed his thigh against hers — just a light touch as if signaling that he was here for her. Her heart did a funny little tap dance. In all her relationships, such as they'd been, none of the men had ever been concerned about her and made her feel special the way Beau did. She hoped that if this ended, she didn't fall down a black hole.

Lunch and interview, kid. Romance later.

The atmosphere was very relaxed. They made small talk over the meal, the men joking, Beau asking Manny basketball questions, Manny impressed that Beau was a seasoned warrior and quizzing him about the Army. Beau answered what questions he could, deflecting with skill those he couldn't without offending the basketball player. Megan was pleased to see the easy camaraderie between the two men. It helped set the stage for the hard questions she was going to ask.

"Okay," she said, once they had finished eating and were sitting over coffee. "Now comes the fun part, Manny. All my questions."

He chuckled. "Hell. I'm used to questions by now. Fire away."

"Just so you know, I'm doing my interviews and research for a series, so this might not hit the public for a while. Does that work for you?"

He nodded. "I trust you and respect you, Megan. I know you wouldn't be picking my brain if you didn't have something good in mind."

She was flattered that he had such respect for her and felt a little guilty for keeping her real agenda hidden. But when she did write the articles, she'd make sure to do him proud.

"Well, my focus is stars having spectacular seasons in the so-called golden years of their careers. You just had a night that knocked everyone's socks off, and I want to know what makes you tick."

He laughed. "If you figure that out, don't tell my wife, okay? I like to keep her guessing."

She pulled her tablet out of her purse and clicked it to life. "I've got all the usual stuff already. You know, your playing history, your stats, some of your most outstanding games. All that stuff. But the first thing I want to talk about today is this record you've got going. Five straight games of thirty-five points or more. That's unheard of."

Manny laughed. "Yeah, I'm kind of amazed about it myself."

"I don't mean this in a disparaging way at all," she began. "I just want to put that out there. But I don't know of another player in your age bracket who is doing so well. Over the top, even. What's your secret?"

If Megan hadn't been watching him as closely as she was, she might have missed the sudden tightening of his mouth, or paid much attention to the fact he lifted his water glass and took a long slow drink before answering.

"My secret, huh?" He winked. "But if I tell you, it won't be a secret, right? Then all the rest of the seniors would be after it and I wouldn't be unique."

Her own smile felt a little forced. "But I think your fans would be very interested to know how you do that. I mean, it's obvious you're in great shape. All anyone has to do is look at you to see it. What's your exercise regimen? What kind of foods do you eat? Stuff like that."

Again, if she hadn't been so focused on the man, she'd have missed the tiny relaxing of his posture. *Because I stayed away from the subject of PEDs?*

"For one thing," he said, "I work out all year long, with extra emphasis during the off season when it's easy to get fat and sloppy. I have a gym in my house, and off season I work out with a personal trainer three times a week."

"That's some dedication," she commented.

"Darlin', as the body gets older, it needs more attention. Stay healthy, keep in shape, those are the key things."

"So can you share with everyone the details of what your workout regimen is? I know everyone would be interested. After all..."

Beside her, although his posture was relaxed, his appearance easy-going, she sensed that Beau was alert for what Manny was saying as she was. She knew he was listening with as much intensity as she did while the athlete talked about the schedule his trainer had put him on and how he adjusted off season.

"Diet is almost all just plain healthy foods," he said when she asked about it again. "Lean meat, poultry, steamed and fresh veggies."

She walked him through it a step at a time, taking notes on her tablet.

"What about vitamin supplements?" she asked. "Don't you have to be selective about those?"

Again, that slight tightening of the mouth as he nodded.

"Yes. And each person has to take what works for his body."

Megan wet her lips and took her time to frame her next question. She couldn't afford to give Manny the slightest hint of what she was chasing. If he was doing all this without the aid of illegal performance enhancing drugs, then she needed to know that. It was a story in itself. But if he was taking something he shouldn't even be thinking of, then she wanted to dig into it. She wanted to know if the three deaths she'd read about were an isolated incident or if a pattern was developing. And if Manny was at risk. But she would have to ease into it.

"I think a lot of players, with emphasis on the older ones, will pay a lot of attention to what you have to say. At an age when most players are looking to ease back, you and some others have hit a new plateau."

Again, the easy-going smile. "Maybe we just take better care of ourselves than some of the others."

"Maybe. Anyway, all this will be a big help for my articles." She paused, framing her next statement. "I know you must have heard the sad news about Tony Gagliardi."

Manny's face sobered in an instant. "That was a killer, if you'll pardon the pun. Just as he was ready to make the formal announcement of his retirement. It shocked a lot of people."

"No kidding." She frowned. "Do you happen to know if he had heart problems before this?"

And yet again she saw the slight tightening of the muscles around his mouth.

"Not that I know of, but I understand something can come on like that without any warning. I've even heard of people having fatal heart attacks less than a week after seeing their doctor."

"Doesn't say much for their doctor," Beau commented.

"Well, as I said, it happens. Tony will be missed by everyone. His wife is devastated."

"So I understand," Megan agreed. "I should drop her a note of condolence."

"I think she'd like it," Manny told her.

Megan touched on how Manny felt being a senior citizen player and beating the stats of the younger guys. How he felt about his growing record. All the usual stuff.

"I think that's it," she said at last, closing her tablet. "Thanks so much for doing this, Manny. I think the article will be great."

"Do you have what you need, Megan?" He glanced at his watch. "I've got an appointment coming up."

Meaning, I'm done talking, she thought.

"Sure. If I need anything more I can give you a call, right?"

He nodded. "For sure. In fact, if you want to come watch one of my workouts, just give me a ring and I'll tell you when and where."

"No kidding? That would be great. Thanks."

"And one more thing. I'm having a birthday party next week." He chuckled. "Turning thirty-six. I'd love it if the two of you would be able to come." He winked. "Maybe get a picture or two for your stories."

"That's very nice of you. Are you sure it's okay?"

"It's my party, isn't it? I guess I can add to the guest list. I'll just let my lady know to take care of it. We always have security at something like this to keep out the gate crashers." He pulled out a business card and wrote on the back of it. "My address and the time. See you then."

"Thank you very much." She tucked the card in her purse.

"Beau? Thanks for coming along today."

"It's an honor to meet you." Beau shook hands with him.

"No, as a matter of fact, the honor is mine. Thank you for your service. See you next week, kids."

"What did you think?" Beau asked, while Megan took care of the bill. "I mean, it was great meeting him. Thanks for letting me come along. He's a great guy, but there's something there he didn't want to talk about."

"I agree. I'm sure he thinks by appearing to be so open with me I won't look under the covers."

"You're right. Doing what our team does, you develop a keen sense of what people are up to and who might be lying to you. It can save your life. And while I don't think Manny Rushmore out and out lied, he sure left out a lot."

He had his hand at her waist as he guided her from the restaurant. The heat of it surged through her and a tiny pulse vibrated through her body.

"I just wish I didn't agree with you. There's something very wrong and I'm going to find out what it is."

"Just be very careful," he insisted. "You could be swimming in hazardous waters. Illegal drugs of any kind put you with some dangerous people."

They were at the car now and she turned to him, putting her hands on his shoulders.

"I promise to be very, very careful. Okay?"

"I'll take you at your word. I wish I had the time off to go with you on all your interviews and help you do your research."

Her eyebrows arched. "No kidding? Because if you're serious, we can work on it together until your leave time is up. I mean, if you want to. If you're not just saying that."

"I never just say anything, so count on it."

And despite the fact they were standing in an open parking lot, he pulled her against his body and took her mouth in a searing kiss. They were both breathless when at last he lifted his head.

"I think we'd better go somewhere a little more private," she said when she could catch her breath.

"You took the words right out of my mouth." He brushed his lips over hers one last time before getting into the car. "I sure hope the traffic is light so we can make it to your place in record time."

"Getting a little urgent, are we?" she teased.

"No shit. So how about a change of subject?"

"Okay. Here's a question for you." She glanced sideways at him. "You don't think I came on too heavy to Manny, do you?"

He shook his head. "Not at all. If anything, I think you underplayed it."

"Good. I don't want to put anyone on guard until I know for a fact what I'm looking into."

"You're golden." He settled back in his seat. "It was very nice of Manny to invite us to his party," he told her. "Does that happen often?"

"Getting invited to events like that?" She shrugged one shoulder. "Not so much. We're supposed to make sure Gus knows if we are, but ten to one he'd send someone in my place if I do."

"Are you kidding me? Even though the invite was issued to a specific person?"

"I know, I know." She sighed. "Rude, right? But he seems to get away with it. I'd say it's because *Sportsweek* is such a high profile online publication and everyone wants ink in it."

"Don't tell him about this," he warned. "After all, Manny invited us."

"He'll find out later," she warned.

"So tell him I was the one invited and you went with me as my plus one." He stroked the lobe of her ear with the tips of his fingers. "And I'm looking forward to it."

"What do you think about Manny's behavior today?" she asked Beau. "Is he taking some fancy new supplement and doing his best to deflect questions about it?"

Beau was quiet for a moment before he answered.

"I'd say there is at least a fifty-fifty chance of it. In my line of work, you have to be very good at reading people, because your life can depend on it. I read something hidden with Manny and it could be PEDs."

"I had planned to bring up some of the other players his age, but even though he tried to conceal it, mentioning Tony Gagliardi's death made him uneasy. I wonder if there was an autopsy?"

Beau shrugged. "I believe unless there's a suspicion of foul play, no autopsy is required. I think the immediate family would have to request it."

"I don't think anyone did, in Tony's case." She chewed on her bottom lip a moment. "I think I'll ask Kari to check into it."

Beau chuckled. "As long as you don't need your answer right away. Remember, she took two weeks off work, this week to get ready for the wedding and next week so she and Slade can enjoy their honeymoon."

"Oh. Yes. Right, right, right. No problem. I'll make a note to myself and ask her when she gets back." She pulled off the Interstate to the area where her townhouse was located. "Meanwhile, I'm going to do some intense research on other players Manny's age and see what's up with them."

"Anything I can help you with?"

Megan thought for a moment. *Two heads are better than one. No lie there.*

"Yes. I've got both my computer and a tablet. I can give you the search parameters and you can use the tablet to see what you can find." She slid a quick glance at him. "That is, if you're sure you want to."

"Oh, I'm sure. I like doing stuff like that." He reached over and squeezed her thigh, his warm fingers almost scorching her through her slacks. "But I expect to be rewarded in an appropriate manner."

That same heat flashed through her body, ratcheting up her pulse until she had to squeeze her thighs together to control the throbbing between her legs.

"I, um, think I can come up with something."

"I'm counting on it." His voice was pitched low in that husky, erotic way that made her want to rip off her clothes and his as well.

"I'm hoping this story will at last get me some space on page one." She tried to keep the bitterness and resentment out of her voice. She'd thought for sure she'd had it with her last one.

"What gets you that kind of placement?"

"Either grow a pair or change my name to Linda Alfonso." They were at her garage now and she pulled in and shut off the engine. Then she turned to face Beau. "I'm sorry if I sound like a bitch, but Gus Kendrick has a good-old-boy mentality and Linda Alfonso must be banging him on a regular basis, because her stories are not that good."

"Is that so?" Beau drawled.

Megan leaned back in her seat and laughed. "I know. I sound like the bitch of the world and sometimes I feel like it. But damn it, Beau, I've worked my ass off for the last few years for this magazine and I can't catch a break."

"I'm sure this is a stupid comment," he told her as he climbed out of her vehicle. "But why not just go somewhere else?"

"Because *Sportsweek* is considered the top of the mountain in online sports publications. Gus Kendrick always delivers, which is no doubt why the publisher puts up with his irritating, antiquated attitude."

She unlocked the door to the townhouse and they walked in to the cool air. She dropped her keys on the little table in the hallway, followed by herself on the couch in the living room. Leaning back, she closed her eyes to pull herself together. Then she opened them to look at Beau, who was standing in front of her.

"Come here." He reached out his hands to her and pulled her up from the couch. Then he cradled her face in his hands. "I read some of your stuff, Megan. Read it online during downtime. You have a real talent for telling the story without a lot of bullshit. You aren't a wannabe jock trying to prove something or a female who thinks being a sportswriter is cool. And that stuff comes across in their writing. You have a knack for making the news interesting and capturing people's attention. Don't ever doubt yourself."

She stared at him. "Why, Beau, I think that's the longest speech I've ever heard you make."

He grinned at her. "And the last one you'll ever hear. I'm more a man of action."

That grin just did it for her, liquefying her limbs and pumping up her heart rate.

"I wish we weren't meeting everyone for dinner tonight…" She licked her lips as she stared up at him.

"Don't do that, sugar," Beau cautioned, "or they'll be having dinner without us, I promise you. And no showering together, either."

She would have tried to change his mind, except they'd be the topic of conversation. In addition, he and the others had promised to be all in for Kari and Slade this weekend. Swallowing her regret, she stepped out of his arms.

"You're so bad for me," she teased. "In a very good way."

"Just keep that in mind until later." He started toward the bedroom then turned back and pulled her in for a kiss that scorched her inside and out. "Later," he promised.

* * * *

Manny Rushmore pulled into his garage and sat for a moment after turning off the car's engine. He'd been thinking about his lunch today and Megan Welles' questions all the way home from the restaurant. He'd told her he had an appointment to get to, but the truth was, he didn't want to discuss the vitamins any more. Didn't want to say something that would trip some kind of switch in her mind. He was sure that the vitamins had played no part in Tony's death, but if someone started digging up dirt, the supply would no doubt be cut off. And Manny wanted that supply, at least for one more year.

He liked the reporter. He'd read several of her pieces and the consensus among the players was she knew her stuff and didn't write bullshit. He was aware of the competition for top spots at *Sportsweek*, but as far as he was concerned, Megan could kick some of the guys who worked there to the curb.

But that was part of the problem. She was smart, she was sharp and she could zero in on information better than a bloodhound. Which was why he was more than a little concerned about the questions she'd asked today. He hoped with intense fervor that the special vitamins Tony had been taking had had nothing to do with his heart attack. In particular because he, Manny, was taking the same ones. And they had done wonders for him.

He leaned back in the car seat for a moment, counting back to when Tony had first told him he was taking them. The man had gone through a tough stretch with fatigue and the general signs of aging, which were accelerated when a guy played a physical sport. Yes, those pills, along with the special water, had been miracle workers.

"Not on the market yet," he'd told Manny, since they were good friends. "I think I'm kind of like a case study, something to disprove that you age out of a sport when so many players do. But you ought to be able to get in on it. They assured me it's one hundred percent safe and I believe them because of the people who told me."

When Tony had told him who supplied them, Manny had to agree. He'd been assured that they did nothing but good to the body, that there was no danger in taking them. And truth to tell, there hadn't been. Not until recent days, when he'd begun noticing a few signs that gave him pause. Symptoms such as shortness of breath, increased fatigue after a game and an incredible thirst that nothing seemed to quench. But when he'd mentioned them, he'd been told they were just minor side effects and would disappear once his body became more adjusted to the so-called vitamins.

Okay, so maybe he was sticking his head in the sand, but he needed the extra boost. He couldn't afford to take PEDs that would show up in testing, and he'd been assured there was nothing harmful in these capsules. And there was no doubt his game had improved along with his endurance.

Maybe Tony just had a bad reaction.

Yeah, everyone had a different reaction to pills. That had to be it. Or he had a condition that he'd managed to keep hidden. One that wouldn't show up in normal physicals.

Stop brooding over it.

Brooding did him no good. Besides, except for those couple of little things, he felt fine. Better than fine. Better than he had in a long time. And his game was on target. No doubt about it. He was turning into the senior citizen *wunderkind* of professional basketball.

Okay, then, he needed to get his ass out of this car and get inside before Julia came looking for him. Her car was already in the garage so he knew she was already home. Before her usual time, too. Good. She always grounded him, always kept his head on straight. If he continued to have misgivings about the vitamins, she'd be the first one he'd talk to about it. She would tell him what to do.

She was standing in the kitchen when he came in, in her workout shorts and tank, drinking a glass of water.

"Oh, good." She grinned at him. "I hate exercising by myself. Go get changed."

He placed a finger beneath her chin to tip up her face and planted a hard kiss on her sweet lips. She opened her eyes wider, startled, but then she gave him her mouth and slid her tongue over his. Manny had to force himself to back away or they'd both be naked in ten minutes.

"Wow!" She licked her lips. "Whatever brought that on, bring it back."

He laughed. "After we work out."

She cupped his face in her palms. "I think I'd rather have this kind of workout."

"How about both?" He brushed his mouth over hers again. Then he reached around and gave her a light tap on her very nice ass.

"Wow again." She grinned. "What's with all that?"

He shrugged. "Just letting you know how much I appreciate you, and what you've brought into my life."

"You can tell me any time you want." She picked up her glass and drained the rest of the water. "How was your lunch?"

"Great. I'll tell you, Gus Kendrick is stupid if he doesn't know what a gem he has in Megan Welles."

Julia nodded. "I agree. I love her articles. And she always gets it right, unlike a lot of writers who want to manipulate the truth for their own ends."

"She had a very interesting guy with her today."

"Oh?" Julia lifted an eyebrow. "A sports fan?"

"Better yet. A Manny Rushmore fan, and a Delta Force to boot."

Julia grinned. "So did you fanboy all over him?"

"Just a little. But I did invite them to my birthday party. I hope that was okay."

"It's your birthday. You can invite anyone you want. But it was nice of you to do this. I'd like to get to know her better, anyway." She winked. "And her Delta Force hunk."

"I'm the only hunk you need to be concerned about. And now I'm going to change so we can start on part one of our workout."

As he took the stairs two at a time, he thought about how good his life was. He'd be pissed beyond anything if something was wrong with the vitamins and that screwed it all up.

Chapter Four

Slade married! Beau gave a mental headshake. *What a concept.* It wasn't until the team had begun taking their downtime at the ranch that any of them could even see their leader in a permanent relationship, planning for the future. Operating in the dangerous situations they did, they were often just happy to get to the end of a week.

Not that Beau was complaining. He was dedicated one hundred percent to being a part of Delta Force and Team Charlie. But he'd begun to realize that the things that made him a good sniper also closed him off from personal relationships. Like Slade, however, he realized he wasn't getting any younger. And the instant, unexplainable connection with Megan had lit something inside him. Maybe that explained why just the word 'wedding', let alone the ceremony itself, wasn't making him break out in hives.

The members of Team Charlie had all brought their uniforms with them, determined to shine with spit and polish for the event. This was the first time he had worn anything except jeans and T-shirts, or slacks when they went out some place a little more uptown. It pleased him to see the admiration in Megan's eyes. And something else. Not just heat or desire.

He shifted his eyes from her to the front of the tent in Slade's side yard where their team leader stood waiting beside the justice of the peace to be united with the woman he loved. Next to him his ranch manager and friend, Teo, stood with great and obvious pride, as best man. Slade looked relaxed and happy as he waited for Kari to come down the aisle, more relaxed than Beau ever remembered seeing him.

He marveled at the whole thing. A year ago, if anyone had asked him, he'd have said the chances of Slade Donovan getting married to anyone, ever, were worse than slim to none. Slade's motto had always been to go it alone in the relationship department. In fact, Beau had been convinced none of them on their team would ever get married. They just didn't believe, any of them, that they could find women who would understand and accept the life of a Delta Force soldier. Marc Blanchard's brief, disastrous marriage hadn't done anything to change their minds, either.

But then Kari Malone had come back into Slade's life and things had changed, along with his priorities. Not that he'd lost his focus as the leader of his Delta Force team. That was a sure road to suicide. No, Slade was a lot more disciplined than that. Nothing affected his attention. If anything, Beau thought it sharpened it. Because now he was fighting on a personal level, defeating the bad guys to keep this country safe for the woman he loved with everything he was.

It wasn't until that fateful party, when Slade and Kari had reconnected after five years, that Slade had realized she was the reason no other woman held his interest for long.

Then, when Kari had been kidnapped by her stalker, the team had gone into action to save her, because now she was a part of their little family. Beau was amazed that after that, Slade hadn't tried to lock her away whenever he left town. Except Kari Malone stood toe to toe with him and gave it all right back to him. Just the right kind of woman for him.

As they waited for Kari to make her entrance, Beau again glanced at Megan, who was seated beside him. She looked so gorgeous, dressed for today's event, that she took his breath away. Her rich blonde hair, instead of being pulled back into its usual ponytail, fell in a smooth sweep to her shoulders, like sunshine. The light-blue dress she wore brought out the color of her eyes and set off her tan. The soft material draped with an easy flow along her curves and Beau was seized with a desire to tear it off her and run his hands over every inch of the body he'd come to know so well. He had to concentrate very hard to keep his dick from standing up and begging for attention.

Like Slade, he'd never been looking for anything more than hot and casual. It startled him to realize that even in the short time they'd been together, he was thinking of Megan as someone way beyond that. More than her sense of humor, or her ability to challenge him when she thought he needed it, or her wit and intelligence, there was something there that connected them, that gave him peace when he was with her, a peace he'd never found before. Ever.

Whoa, boy! Don't get carried away by this wedding scene here.

But deep down, he knew that wasn't it at all, and the sudden intensity of it frightened him a little. He had no idea how Megan felt. Not even a hint. They'd both been very careful to stay away from anything that smacked of relationship commitment. But that feeling that had surged through him a moment ago wasn't going away. He was going to be very cautious here. He knew the disaster of jumping into things without thinking. His teammate, Marc Blanchard, was a perfect example of that. But he was damn well going to give it a lot of thought while he was here, because he didn't think he could stand the idea of her with any other man.

She hadn't said much today but he knew she was upset that her latest story for *Sportsweek,* a story about illegal betting that she'd worked on for month, had been relegated to Page Three while Linda Alfonso had hit Page One yet again. He'd like to go down to the *Sportsweek* office and beat the shit out of Gus Kendrick, but this was Megan's battle to fight. He knew she would not thank him if he got involved. He'd just have to put extra effort into making her feel special.

Anyway, he was pretty damn sure this series she was working on would knock everything else off the front page if it turned out to be what she thought.

Megan leaned over and whispered in his ear, "You look like you're wrestling with some heavy thoughts over there."

He turned to her and winked. "Just thinking about you, sugar." He took her hand and squeezed it.

He was thinking about how good it felt to touch her, to sit with her like this, when she nudged him. He looked up to see that everyone was on their feet.

"The bride," she whispered.

And here came Kari on the arm of her boss, Bexar County Prosecuting Attorney Kip Reyes, looking like a dream walking, her face glowing with happiness. It was obvious to everyone that she and Slade had eyes for no one but each other. When Kip stopped at the archway Slade's cowboys had set up and she held out her hand, everyone laughed when Slade grabbed it and pulled her close to him for a kiss.

"You've got enough time for that later, Donovan," one of his friends hollered.

"Never enough time," he shot back, but he moved so Kari was standing beside him as they faced the justice of the peace.

As Beau watched the couple exchanging their vows, he wondered if Slade had had any second thoughts. *How did he know this was the right one for him?*

Beside him, Megan rose and pulled him to his feet.

"Pay attention," she ordered then began clapping.

Beau looked to the front of the tent to see Slade and Kari in another kiss, one that he was sure would set the tent on fire. He began clapping, too, and soon he and the rest of the team were whistling and making loud jokes. Slade lifted his mouth from Kari's and grinned at them.

"You all are just jealous," he joked, and brushed one more soft kiss across the lips of his bride.

That's the damn truth, Beau thought, and gave himself a mental jerk. *Am I jealous? Why?* He was very happy for Slade and Kari, but for the first time in his life he wanted something like that for himself.

Maybe.

The new bride and groom hurried back down the center aisle of the tent, laughing, amid a shower of rice.

"Kari said they aren't doing a receiving line," Megan said as they followed the crowd out of the tent.

"That's right. Slade said the bar would be open at once. You ready for a drink? I sure am."

She chuckled. "Weddings scare you that much, soldier?"

He pulled her around to face him and stared into her eyes. "Maybe not as much as they used to."

She looked at him, her eyes filled with questions. She opened her mouth to say something then shook her head and tugged him along with her.

"Don't tease me, soldier," she joked, and tugged him along with her.

"Maybe I'm not teasing," he whispered to himself. Then he tucked the thought away for a time when he could look at it with his brain working and not his dick.

Then it was time for the wedding celebration. Slade had ordered a second tent set up in his huge yard, with a full-service bar and enough food to feed two armies.

"I think he invited everyone he knows in San Antonio," Megan whispered to him.

"And then some. That's okay. He deserves this."

"And they are so good together. I've gotten to know her and I like her. A lot."

"Me, too," Beau agreed.

They chatted with some of the people they'd met at the Huttons' party, and spent some time with Trey and Marc and their dates. Beau did his best to conceal his curiosity about the woman with Marc, who had been isolating himself for so long. Christy Alvarez was a petite, dark-haired woman with a tentative smile and a soft voice, who stuck to Marc like glue. Beau would give every nickel he had to know more about her. He just hoped maybe she was someone who could finally pull Marc out of the dark place where he'd been living since the destruction of his marriage.

They were standing to one side, sipping their champagne, when Megan tugged his sleeve.

"Oh, look! Kari's getting ready to throw her bouquet. It must be almost time for them to leave."

"I can't believe they stayed around this long. Come on." He folded her hand in his and tugged her over to where the small crowd was gathering.

Slade brought a chair into the center of the floor and helped Kari to stand on it.

"We want to thank all of you for coming here today and sharing this wonderful moment with us." Her eyes were shining as she gazed over everyone standing in front of her. "I wish for all of you the same happiness Slade and I have found with each other. Ladies, this is a good luck bouquet so get ready to catch it and follow in my footsteps."

She turned around on the chair, being careful not to fall, counted to three and tossed the bouquet over her shoulder. Megan had taken a step back, but the flowers headed in their direction and bounced off Beau's chest. Without thinking, she reached out to keep them from falling to the floor. With her fingers closed around them, she stared up at Beau, not sure how he would react. There was a look in his eyes that she wasn't sure how to interpret. Heat and something else. For a long moment they stood there, just looking at each other.

At last Beau cleared his throat. "Nice flowers."

Megan burst out laughing. "That's a loaded comment which I am going to ignore."

They waited just until Slade and Kari boarded the helicopter for Teo to ferry them off on their honeymoon. Beau stood with Megan, waving goodbye along with the rest of the guests, until the helo was just a speck in the sky.

"Ready to hit the road?" he asked.

"You bet. But do we need to hang out with the rest of your team at all?"

He chuckled. "I see plenty of them as it is. Besides, they indicated they have plans." Then he frowned.

"What's the matter?"

"I just wish I knew where Marc was off to. He's been such a basket case for so long. I just don't want him hiding out in some bar getting blitzed."

"Should you check with him again?"

He shook his head. "He told me in a very polite voice to mind my own business, so that's what I'm doing. I hope he's hooked up with a woman, and that it's someone who appreciates him and takes good care of him."

"You told me what happened with his marriage and his ex-wife. Women like that should be shot."

"And we'd all line up to do it. Anyway, he's gone and so is Trey, so we're cleared for takeoff." He glanced at the flowers she'd been holding all this time. "We should take those someplace and put them in water so they'll last, don't you think?"

"Yes. We should."

He brushed his lips over her cheek. "Then let's get you home and take care of it."

Beau barely took time to say goodbye to Trey and Marc before hustling her to the car and hauling ass out to the highway. Megan glanced sideways at him, sensing a fine tension thrumming through him, every muscle on controlled high alert. He'd been like that almost from the moment they'd arrived at Slade's ranch for the wedding. She couldn't figure out if it was because the wedding made him nervous, or at least the thought of it, or maybe made him horny. But he'd said little since they hit the highway and she didn't know whether to be happy or nervous.

"Slade and Kari looked so happy." She figured she needed to break the intensity building between them, an intensity she didn't know was good or bad.

"Yes, they did. I never thought Slade would make a commitment like this. He was such a loner, his one focus on Delta."

"Maybe all this time he was just hoping he'd find Kari again. Have her back in his life."

"Having hot, anonymous one-night sex isn't all that usual for any of us, I am somewhat ashamed to say."

Megan couldn't help laughing. "You and at least half the male population in the world."

"Don't think much of us, do you?" *And why should she?* he thought. The athletes she covered no doubt approached relationships of any kind much the same way dedicated soldiers did.

"Just being realistic."

He paused, choosing his words. Something was going on here between them, something new. He didn't know if it was too much wedding or what and he didn't want to say the wrong thing.

"Maybe I can change your mind," he told her in a soft voice.

She laughed again, but there was a thread of uncertainty beneath it. "Getting serious here, Beau? That's not your style."

"I might be getting ready to change my style."

When she didn't answer, he just let it hang. He didn't even have his own thoughts in order. All he knew was something had hit him at Slade and Kari's wedding, a feeling of unwanted isolation and the idea that he might be missing out on something good gripping him.

At last thank the lord they were at her townhouse. He was still examining his brain while he parked the car, then they were inside.

"Let me just deal with these flowers," Megan told him and headed for the kitchen.

He might have to throw the damn flowers away if she took too long.

She had just finished arranging them in a vase when he came up behind her, spun her around, threaded his fingers through her hair to hold her head in place and kissed her. She had been expecting something hot and hard, but instead she got just a soft brush of his lips over hers. She closed her eyes and tipped up her face a little, hoping he'd increase the intensity of the kiss next time.

Instead, he drew the tip of his tongue across the seam of her mouth, licking the tender surface as if tasting an ice cream cone.

Which might be what she'd need if she got any hotter. How was it this man took her from zero to burning in just seconds? And not just her mouth. Her blood felt liquefied, heated as it splashed through her veins and her pulse was hammering away in triple time. She had to squeeze her thighs together to control the throbbing between them.

Beau slid his mouth over to her ear and whispered, "You just do it to me every time. Every damn time. I think you've bewitched me."

"Mmmm," she hummed. "That would be nice."

"Megan?" His voice was soft against her cheek.

"Yes?" She wished he'd stop talking and do other things with his mouth.

"I—" He stopped. "I want to take all your clothes off. Right now."

A little warning bell rang way in the back of her brain, but she blocked it out. Whatever he had been planning to say, if it wasn't good she could wait a long time to hear it.

"Okay," she whispered.

He lifted her in his arms and carried her to her bedroom, placing her on her feet beside the bed. He stood there for what seemed like an eternity, just looking at her, his eyes seeming to bore right into her. He reached out with one hand and ran his fingers in light strokes along the line of her jaw, a touch so sensuous it sent her liquid coursing into her sex, signaling her readiness in the slickness of her flesh.

Just that touch, nothing more. And the heat burning in his eyes.

A shiver raced along her spine and she had to force herself to focus or she would have collapsed at his feet.

Never taking his gaze from her, he undid the tiny buttons that marched down the front of her dress. He flicked open the bottom one, right at the waist, before lowering the hidden zipper of the skirt.

"Why did you have to pick something to wear that takes a genius to remove from you?" Beau growled.

"The better to tempt you," she teased.

"I'm tempted plenty, and that's no lie."

It took a lot of control for her to stand there while he worked his way through the maze of buttons until at last he eased the dress from her body. A shiver skated over her at the devouring look in his eyes. She had to squeeze her thighs together to contain the insistent throb in her sex, a pulsing that thrummed through her body. When he ran his tongue over his lips, all she could think of was how much she wanted him to run it over various parts of her body.

Impatient, she reached behind herself to unclasp her bra, but Beau pushed her hands away.

"Let me." His voice was low and rough. "I want to do this."

He slid his hands around to unfasten the hooks then eased the straps of the bra down her arms. The moment he pulled it away from her and tossed it to the side, her nipples hardened like diamonds. The hungry look in his eyes increased the reaction.

"Gorgeous," he whispered and cupped both breasts in his palms. Locking his gaze with hers, he slipped his thumbs back and forth over the hardened tips.

Megan sucked in a breath. *Your mouth*, she wanted to shout. *I want your mouth on them.* She had held nothing back with him right from the beginning, so attracted to him that she was open to just about anything. But, today, something stronger and more volatile seemed to be simmering between them. It thrilled and scared her at the same time.

When Beau put his mouth on first one then the other of the beaded tips of her breasts, she folded her hands into fists and dug her nails into her palms. She felt the tug and pull all the way to her core, a moan of desire whispering from her mouth. When Beau knelt before her and eased her tiny bikini panties down her legs, she had to brace herself on his shoulders for balance.

He helped her step out of the flimsy piece of lace and silk but insisted she leave on the high heels she'd worn to the wedding.

"One of my fantasies is to fuck a gorgeous woman wearing nothing but those sexy heels."

"I can't believe you haven't done that before now." The words came out in a breathy little tone.

He looked up at her, that same intense hunger in his eyes. "Never met the right woman before."

While she was still digesting his words, he trailed kisses up the inside of one thigh, pausing right at her sex to blow a puff of air on her well-trimmed mound before traveling his mouth down the other leg. Megan wasn't sure how much longer she could remain standing. The need building inside her made her weak and shaky. She wished Beau would take off his clothes, too, so she could run her hands over every inch of his incredible body.

But in the next moment, he placed his mouth right over the lips of her sex, then trailed the tip of his tongue through her slit.

Oh, God!

She dug her fingers into his shoulders, afraid she would collapse to the floor. When he looked up at her, the sight of his mouth wet with her juices ratcheted up the intensity of the need racing through her. When he rose to his feet, stroking her skin from her hips to her breasts, she moaned again.

He lifted his hands to cradle her cheeks in his palms. The look he gave her was so intense she wondered why she wasn't incinerated right where she stood.

"I'm planning to take my time today, Megan, and enjoy every single inch of this body in as many ways as I can."

"Take off your clothes," she whispered.

"Doing it right now."

He lifted her, nudging her to wind her legs around his waist, as he drew back the covers on the bed and placed her against the pillows. He studied every exposed inch of her as he toed off his shoes and socks and got rid of his slacks and shirt.

She frowned when he kept on his boxer briefs. "I want to see you," she breathed. "Touch you,"

"And you will. Soon."

He climbed onto the bed with her and after one hot, hungry stare began trailing hot kisses again, from each ankle to hip bone, across the swell of her abdomen, and up the valley between her breasts. Each brush of his tongue woke up tiny nerves on the surface of her skin and set them sizzling until she felt as if an electric current was running over her.

She touched as much of his body as she could reach, loving the feel of his roped muscles and warm skin. The hard thickness of his cock pressed against her leg and his warm breath heated her skin. She tried to signal him with her hips where she wanted his hands and his mouth, but it was obvious he had his own agenda and did not plan to divert from it.

"Slow," he breathed against the hollow of her throat. "Very slow. Remember?"

She wasn't sure slow was even in her vocabulary any more. Just as it had from Day One, his touch set off a craving inside her, a need stronger than any she'd ever felt before. And today, for whatever reason, there seemed to be a sense of desperation in everything Beau did.

He placed a soft kiss at the hollow of her throat before beginning the journey of his mouth down her body, again placing soft kisses on every bit of her flesh until he reached her ankles. Then, kneeling between her thighs, he spread her legs and rested them on his thighs to open her wider to him. Anticipation surged through her, the muscles in her inner walls flexing in need. He touched her flesh with the tip of his tongue before bending to his task in earnest.

Megan had to fist her hands to hold on to her control, digging her nails into her palms as he licked the outer lips before sliding his tongue inside. He had a hot, magic, wicked tongue that set off a trembling inside her. She tried to push herself against his mouth but his strong hands held her in place. Everything faded away except for the feel of his mouth and intense craving it ignited inside her.

When he pinched her clit, hard, her climax hit, bursting from deep inside her to explode against his mouth. Immobilized as she was, the shudders were intensified, shaking her from the inside out, and it seemed to go on forever.

At last, the spasms slowed then subsided, as he eased her down from her high, still coaxing the last response from her with his very talented mouth. When she was at last reduced to a limp mass of nothing, Beau moved up her body, his lips wet and glistening with her cream. He smiled at her as he pressed his mouth to hers, sharing her taste with her.

"Better than anything else I've tasted," he murmured when he lifted his lips from hers. "I'm not sure I'll ever get enough of it."

"I hope you never do." The minute the words were out she wanted to smack herself. She and Beau had never talked about more than the here and now and she should shut up before she turned him off.

"Doesn't get better than this," he drawled, ignoring her remark, for which she was grateful.

Enjoy the here and now, she told herself. *Worry about anything else later.*

"Those look like some heavy thoughts." Beau was lying on top of her, catching his weight on his forearms and brushing strands of hair from her damp face. "If you're thinking like that, I must not be doing something right." He nibbled at her chin. "Maybe I need to try harder."

"Maybe," she whispered, her spent body beginning to recover at his words and the tone of his voice.

It seemed like mere seconds before she was craving him again. He used his mouth and hands on all her sensitive places, testing her readiness with his fingers as he slid two of them inside her hot, wet sex. In an instant, her muscles tightened around them and she tried to move her hips to ride them.

"Damn, Megan," he breathed. "I wanted to take a lot of time pleasuring you today, but you just do it to me. I'm not sure I can hold off much longer."

"Don't," she whispered. "Don't hold back. I need you inside me."

Right this minute, she wanted to add. She needed that intimate connection where his cock filled her and they rode the wave of a climax together.

"Damn," he whispered again. But then he moved back to yank off his boxer briefs.

His cock sprang free so swollen, the head so purple, Megan had to push herself up and wrap her hand around it. The vein that spiraled around it pulsed in her hand and she squeezed, stroking up and down until Beau tugged her hand away.

"Later," he growled. "We'll get to that later."

He reached into the nightstand drawer and fished out one of the condoms she kept in there. Megan was astonished that his hand trembled as he sheathed himself. *What is going on here today?* Everything seemed to be more intense, more intimate, more…something.

She stopped trying to figure it out when Beau placed his hands beneath the cheeks of her butt, lifted her and drove into her with one hard, swift thrust.

Oh, God!

Was it possible his cock had grown bigger just since yesterday? He filled every bit of her channel, his movement scraping her sweet spot and lighting a fire deep inside her. If she'd thought she needed time to recover from the other orgasm, she was out of her mind because there she was, ready to pull the trigger again.

She wrapped her legs around him, locking her ankles and digging her heels into the small of his back. He drove into her again and again, his balls slapping against the curve of her ass, the soft hair of his chest rubbing against her sensitized nipples. He pulled her into the rhythm, in and out, forward and back, again and again and again. He filled every millimeter of her, heating her from the inside out. Just as before, everything faded away except the two of them riding a hard rhythm as they reached for the edge of release.

"Now," he growled, pressing his body against her so he rubbed her clit with every movement of his body.

The word flipped a switch and she exploded, spasming around him and milking his throbbing, pulsing cock. Nothing mattered except hot flesh clenching around him as she drew every bit of cum from him. She squeezed him with her inner walls, draining him, convulsing around him until she had nothing left.

She closed her eyes, letting the feeling of fulfillment wash over her as she tried to even out her breathing and the staccato beat of her heart. Releasing her ankles, she let her legs fall to the side, although she wanted to keep him locked inside her forever.

Forever? For real?

With an effort she tamped the intrusive thoughts and concentrated on just the intense satisfaction gripping her.

"You didn't go to sleep on me, did you?" Humor tinged Beau's voice as he kissed her eyelids and her mouth.

"Uh-uh." She just wanted to enjoy this feeling of...whatever it was, more than sex...for a little while longer.

"Megan?" He whispered the word as he sprinkled light kisses on her forehead and cheeks.

"Mmm?"

"I..." He paused. "This..."

What is he trying to say? Is it good or bad?

"Whatever it is, this is okay," she told him in a soft voice. She knew he wasn't good with words. "It's all good."

He buried his face in the curve of her neck. "Better than good. Much, much better."

And just how am I supposed to take that?

Chapter Five

"Oh, God. Oh, I hope this turns out not to be what I'm afraid it is."

Megan stared at the screen of her laptop. It was Sunday morning and they were recovering from the most intense night of sex Megan could ever remember. Something was happening and she was afraid to look too hard lest she destroy it before she figured out what it was. Beau had gone out for bagels with all the trimmings and now they were sitting side by side in her oversized bed, each with their laptops, and Beau was helping her with the research for her series. She was doing searches for three athletes aged thirty-five or older who had in the last two weeks been lauded for incredible seasons.

"What?" Beau set his laptop aside and leaned over to read from her screen. "What's wrong, babe?"

"Look." She pointed to an article she'd pulled up. The headline read *Tennis world loses shining star*. "Jessie

Moran was an icon for women athletes approaching forty. Her success inspired so many of them."

"She passed away Friday," he pointed out. "They got this article out plenty fast."

"The advantages of the Internet," Megan told him. "Someone sneezes and in seconds thousands of people on social media are saying *Gesundheit*. The worst of it is, half the time the information is incorrect, because whoever put it out there hasn't taken the time to check it out."

"Well, that sucks. Don't they care about accuracy?"

Megan shook her head. "Just about getting it out there first. This is from a blog that isn't always so careful, so I'm going to check the news outlets and ESPN."

"I'm surprised you didn't go there first."

"You want the truth? It was an accident. I was just doing a broad search for recent deaths of athletes and this popped up." She pulled up ESPN and *damn!* There it was. The story on Jessie's sudden death.

World shocked at sudden death of Jessie Moran.

Beau read over her shoulder. "It says she had just come home from practice and was consumed with an extreme thirst. Her sister, who was visiting, said she drank three glasses of water very fast, as if she was dehydrated. Then she clutched her chest and dropped to the floor. She was dead by the time the paramedics got there."

"Another so-called heart attack," Megan commented. "Tony G's death was also attributed to a heart attack. I've been trying to do research on the other two athletes I heard about and see what their cause of death was."

"Give me their names." He closed the window he had up on his screen and opened another. "Let me see what I can find out."

She gave him a sideways look. "You would do that? I know you said you'd help me but—"

He held up his hand and for a moment she thought irritation flashed across his face.

"I'm not a techno-idiot, you know. When you have downtime and nowhere to get to and nothing to do except keep training, exploring technology helps to pass a lot of time." He began typing on the keyboard. "And I do have a college degree."

He tossed the statement out in such an offhand manner that Megan didn't know if she should act surprised or matter-of-fact. She was stunned to realize how little she knew about him except for surface information.

"I, um..."

"It's okay, sugar. I don't hand out copies of my diploma." The carefree hotshot was back.

Now Megan wondered how much of it was a public shield for a very private person. Who was the real Beau Williams behind the sense of humor and the incredible sex? What struck her was the sudden need to know more, maybe everything, about him. She hadn't been looking for anything more than friends with benefits, for as long as it lasted. It was safer that way. Long-term relationships never seemed to work for her.

"You could have mentioned it when we were in the getting to know you stage."

He shrugged. "I got a degree. It is what it is."

"Okay, now I want details." She put her hands over his to stop him typing. "Where and for what?"

He was silent for so long she began to wonder if he was making something up.

"MIT. Mathematics."

Now she was stunned beyond belief. "And you became a sniper?"

He turned his head to look at her. "Megan, what I do is very important, and knowing mathematics is very useful in calculating things like wind factors, distance, a lot of variables. Besides, MIT has one of the best ROTC programs in the country, believe it or not. I applied for a four-year scholarship and was accepted. It's how I was able to go to college."

She wet her lower lip, choosing her next words with great care. "You know, as much as we've talked about a lot of stuff, we don't know all that much about each other."

"You're right." He set his laptop to the side and turned to her. "We should fix that, too. Not right this minute, but later. Maybe over a drink on your patio, because I want to know every single thing about you. And I'll tell you anything you want to know about me."

"But—" She stopped, trying to phrase this so he wouldn't get pissed off.

"Why? Is that the question?' He cupped her chin and looked hard into her eyes. "Maybe it's Slade's wedding or maybe I'm getting older or maybe we hooked up at the right time in the right place. But I don't want this to be just shits and giggles, Megan. I want to see if we have something here that's more than just a good time."

She was trying so hard to read his expression. "You've been thinking about this since yesterday, haven't you? I felt it when we left the wedding."

"Yes, but it wasn't just the wedding. On this last deployment, I thought about Slade and Kari and how they were going to make this work, which with a Delta is very difficult. And for the first time I realized I had a hidden emptiness that you were filling without me even recognizing it."

Megan stared at him, her heart all of a sudden trip-hammering. "Wow. I mean, Beau. Wow."

His hand tightened on her chin. "If you don't feel the same thing, if you don't want to see what we've got underneath it all, tell me right now. Because we can go back to having fun and off-the-charts sex if that's all you want."

She drew in a deep breath and let it out in a slow exhalation. "You have your reasons why you've avoided relationships up until now. You alluded to Delta force as an obstacle and I never asked any more questions. But I haven't had the best luck with relationships. A lot of men are threatened by a woman in what they perceive as a man's job. And they don't like strong women, either. So I — "

He touched his fingers to her lips. "So we've both got baggage. Okay. But let's give this a chance, Megs. We'll take it slow. We'll have separations here that may wear on you and your job can take you away at inconvenient times. But you are the first woman I've wanted this with. So — "

Now it was her turn to touch her fingertips to his mouth.

"Yes. Just — yes." She shifted her laptop so she could put her arms around him. "Yes," she repeated.

Were those flowers some kind of sign? A portent of the future?

She pressed her mouth to his in a kiss that carried all the emotion she could put into it. When she broke the contact, she stroked his cheek, loving even the overnight scruff he still had.

Beau's smile was hot and tender at the same time.

"We'll get into details later," he promised. "Lots of details."

Megan forced back the wave of sexual hunger that surged through her. That would come later, too, but she felt they had crossed a threshold into a new phase of their relationship. It was both scary and satisfying, but how could she not embrace it?

"Does this mean I can order you back to work?" she teased.

"If I can give the orders afterward."

The look in his eyes told her just what he meant.

"Okay." She pulled her computer back into her lap. "Let's see what we can find out about the two deaths before Tony G's."

Half an hour later they had pulled up and bookmarked articles about a football player and a major league baseball player. In both cases the cause of death was listed as a heart attack.

"There's no specific geographic locale," Beau commented. "And so far we haven't found more than one athlete in any sport mentioned."

"That's what I'm finding," Megan agreed. "Either these are all isolated incidents — which I don't think is true — or the athletes are selected with great care to use whatever is causing this. Okay, let's try some other search parameters."

They worked side by side for another hour, splitting the sports and using every search engine they could find. At last, Megan leaned back against her pillows, rotating her head to get the crick out of her neck. Then she looked over at Beau, who had his eyes focused on something he was reading on his screen.

"It looks like you found more incidents."

He nodded. "I did. Four more. What about you?"

"Three." She blew out a breath. "On the one hand, it seems like so few for all that work. On the other, I'm happy we didn't find more. And there could be more that our search engines would find with different parameters."

"Or there could be deaths where the listed cause is different or not listed at all," he pointed out. "But seven is nothing to be sneezed at, Megan. It's a significant number, especially for something like this."

"Yeah." She raked her hands through her messy hair. "If the numbers were a lot higher it would already be a national or even international incident. The international world of sports would be rocked back on its heels."

"No kidding." He stared at the article on his screen again. "This guy played Australian football and was celebrating his forty-first birthday after his best season yet. The writer says his stats for the season were off the charts."

"Did you check for autopsies on the ones you found?"

"Of course. I told you I'm no dummy." He glanced over at her and grinned as if to take the sting out of his words.

Megan spared a very brief moment to wonder how many people knew the reality of how intelligent this man was, and if his brains had been a blessing or a problem growing up.

"I know. So what did you find?"

"Autopsies were requested in two of them, but not in the other two." He frowned as he scrolled through bookmarked pages. "Okay. On the other two the families did not request them. No reason given either way."

"Tell me something. If your husband or boyfriend or significant other or son or whatever dropped dead without warning, wouldn't you want to know why?"

Beau nodded. "But I'm not the average guy here, either. I question everything because in Delta that's what we're taught. Question everything but what the brass sends down."

"All my stories are the same." Megan clicked over to a previous page. "Athletes hitting their stride at a time when they should be retiring. Having banner years. Healthy. In great shape. Then, without warning, they drop dead. I don't know why this isn't a red flag."

"Because the events are so isolated and spread out across the sports world that no one ties them together," Beau pointed out. "These athletes all get regular physicals, too, so if they're taking something, it is either one hundred percent undetectable or masked by something else. If it were me and they had recent physicals with no heart problems detected, wouldn't that in itself would be suspicious enough to request an autopsy?"

"Like I said, there are always reasons why that doesn't happen. And I plan to find out what they are." Megan pushed her laptop aside and swung her legs over the side of the bed. "I have to take a break. I'm getting a headache, not from the searches but from the enormity of what this might be. I need a shower, too." She looked over her shoulder. "Coming?"

Beau burst out laughing. "Before the shower or after?"

She giggled. "Either or. Take your choice."

He was out of the bed and beside her in seconds, dropping a kiss on her neck. "Maybe both, if you're lucky."

Then he swooped her up in his arms, nuzzling that same spot again. "We'll get back to the project later."

"Wait— What—"

But he didn't give her a chance to say anything else, plunging his tongue into her mouth and licking the soft, sensitive skin as he carried her into the bathroom.

* * * *

Manny Rushmore shut down the treadmill and wiped the sweat from his face with the towel around his neck. The equipment recorded his heart and pulse rate and he checked them every time. Since what had happened with Tony Gagliardi, he was even more conscious of his numbers. He'd even gone so far as to have a full physical, even though it wasn't on the schedule.

"You're healthier than ever," Bert Danvers, the team physician, told him. "I wish everyone was in such good shape. Even more so, if you'll pardon me, at your age."

Manny shook hands with him, relieved at all the test results. He just wished he could get rid of that little niggle of fear that wouldn't let go of him. Of course, he could always stop the vitamins, the one thing new introduced into his system. But they made him feel so damn good. Better than he had in a long time. The one side effect he could find was an unquenchable thirst. Even now he pulled a bottle of water from the fridge in the workout room he'd set up in his house and chugged almost the whole thing.

I'm making problems where there aren't any.

And making himself crazy. It was unfortunate that two athletes in his age bracket that he had a personal relationship with had died in such a shocking manner, without warning. But he couldn't let it spook him. They might have had problems he knew nothing about. Yeah, that was it.

"You all finished, sweetheart?"

Julia jogged down the stairs to the workout room, a vision in pink shorts and a pink and white T-shirt. She often worked out with him, telling him she was determined to keep herself in shape.

'Your shape's just fine,' he always told her.

'And I plan to keep it that way,' she teased back.

"Hey, before I forget. The fridge in the workout room is almost empty of Special Water. Do I need to arrange for more? We can pick it up while we're out today."

"Already taken care of," she assured him. "Delivered and in the garage. I just hadn't taken any downstairs yet."

"I'll do it before I shower."

Each day he asked himself how he'd gotten so lucky where she was concerned. How many men had a woman who was gorgeous, smart, funny and devoted all the way to them? Or who would put up with the crazy schedule of a professional basketball player? All the traveling and training and practice could wear hell out of a relationship. But Julia was just incredible. She ran a great graphic design business that occupied her when he was on the road and allowed her the time to spend with him when he was home.

He opened the little fridge in the workout room to get a bottle of his favorite water and took out the last one. He uncapped it, tilted it and drank it without taking a breath. The icy liquid cascaded down his throat, lubricating his parched body. He'd been drinking a new kind of water that had been recommended to him, one that was supposed to have extra electrolytes in it to replace those burned off with his exercise. Without it, he was susceptible to muscle fatigue, dizziness and nausea. It was also supposed to boost the elements of his special vitamins. It wasn't available anywhere except through one company and cost a bundle, but as far as Manny was concerned, it was more than worth it.

He didn't have a game tonight and Julia had told him she was taking the day off from her computer so they could have some together time.

"You look good enough to eat." He grabbed her before she could climb the stairs and pressed a kiss to the back of her neck, forcing himself to stop from licking the tender skin behind her ear. He could spend the entire day ravishing his wife's body, but today he wanted them to do other things. Things they didn't often get to do. Memorable things, although he wasn't sure what was more memorable than sex with his wife.

She chuckled. "Maybe after lunch. Go take your shower. The food will be ready when you're finished. You did say we were going out to have fun, right?"

"Uh-huh." He'd been seized with a sudden urgency to ravish her in every way possible, as if he'd never get enough of her. And when had he ever felt that way about a woman?

Never, his brain answered, *so don't screw it up*.

Chapter Six

Megan hadn't planned to go into the office that day. She had a list of things to research for her 'secret' project and she felt safer doing it at home. However, Kendrick texted her that he was having a staff meeting to discuss new deadlines and review assignments. Then he added that he needed two fluff pieces by yesterday and she should get them done while she was there so he could check them right away.

"Not 'can you write these while you're here'," she complained, "but, in effect, get your ass in here and after the meeting, crank these out. He might as well have said I'm the one person low enough on the totem pole to do them."

"Just do it," Beau said. "Go in, go to your meeting and crank this shit out for him. Don't let Kendrick get pissed off at you for any reason. Whatever itch he has where you're concerned, don't give him a reason to scratch it. When you get everything together for the series on older athletes, maybe we'll put it out for bid."

Megan snorted. "He'd have a stroke for sure then."

"Tough shit." He cupped her chin and lifted her face so he could brush a kiss over her lips. "By that time we'll hold all the cards. You can do a lot better than him, honey. Believe me. Besides, his attitude seems to be getting worse every day. I don't know how he holds his job."

Beau had been with her twice when she'd stopped in to get something from her office desk, and Kendrick had cornered her for some insignificant thing or others.

"I told you before. He's in tight with the publisher."

He made a face. "Well, that sucks."

"Big time." She leaned into him, soaking up his strength and heat. "What would I do without you?"

"We're not going to find out." He nipped her lower lip. "I called Trey and I'm going to meet up with him. His lady is tied up with clients until later today but she scored some passes for us to the health club where she lives. So you go on ahead to work this morning. Then we can meet up for lunch and have some fun this afternoon. That work for you?"

"It does." She nodded. "If the fun is for public consumption, you could ask Trey to hang with us until it's time for him to meet Kenzi."

He kissed her again. "Have I told you how special you are? If I haven't, let me tell you now and show you later."

She smiled against the pressure of his mouth. "I'm all in for that."

Neither one of them had mentioned the bridal bouquet since the wedding, although the flowers sat in gorgeous display in a vase in the living room. She supposed that was good news, because if he'd been irritated about it, he'd have spoken up. *Nothing shy about Beau Williams.*

That kiss kept her going all morning. Kendrick almost never bothered her unless he had junk work for her to do, but today after the meeting he was all up in her space. She'd better get these two pieces out in the next hour. Had she followed up on any of the stuff he'd sent her about the high school all-star game? Had she done anything about why the Mustangs' schedule was all screwed up?

She didn't bite back at him the way she wanted to, or tell him she'd just gotten his email five seconds before. Instead she gritted her teeth because it gave her a chance to use the resources the magazine had online, like access to LexisNexis. She had used multiple search parameters, searching for athletes in the thirty to forty-five-year range who'd had stellar years and died without warning. After two hours, she had found just three more and they were spread out worldwide. Not quite the concentration she was looking for. *Am I chasing a shadow here?*

Then she wondered if it was possible that whatever was causing the unexpected deaths had been distributed on an international level on purpose. There had been no autopsies in any of the deaths. Whichever physician had pronounced them had attributed death to natural causes. Some of them had even said it might have had to do with the athletes pushing so hard to play above their normal level that their bodies had just given out.

According to one doctor, "*Many of these tragedies are the result of athletes being willing to sacrifice their health — sometimes without knowing — while following no-pain, no-*

gain programs in a futile attempt to surpass their previous level of play."

Megan could see that as one possibility. She did notice that in three of the instances a post-mortem blood test had been run to rule out PEDs and it had done just that. But that didn't mean that there wasn't some other substance they'd been using, one that metabolized so fast it left no trace. She kept coming back to that, stuck on that concept. That meant she either had to prove she was right or find evidence she was wrong. And look for another answer.

She sat back in her chair and stretched, twisting her head from one side to another to relieve the strain. When she glanced at her watch, she realized with a start it was just past twelve. Beau should be calling any minute to ask her where she wanted to meet for lunch. The thought had no sooner popped into her head than her cell chirped at her with the ring she'd set for Beau.

"You all done getting hot and sweaty?" she asked.

"For the moment." He lowered his voice. "I plan to do it again later but not with Trey. He's not quite my type."

She laughed. "I can get on board with that."

"Listen, Trey's got a restaurant on the Riverwalk Kenzi wanted him to check out. It just opened a month ago. You up for Cajun food?"

"Sounds good to me. I've heard of it and it got pretty good reviews. I can walk to it so I'll meet you there in, what, fifteen minutes?"

"About that." He paused. "I know you can't say anything much, but how was this morning?"

She gave a very unladylike laugh. "About the way you would expect. I think he gets worse all the time."

"I wish you'd quit that damn job," he growled. "Go to work somewhere the boss isn't a Neanderthal."

Megan sighed. "I hear you. It's just that this publication has such great visibility. If I have a hit story here, I think I can write my ticket any place else."

"If the story you're working on turns out to be what you think, you don't need to launch it on *Sportsweek*. Editors will be lining up for you."

"Maybe. Meanwhile, I'm tougher than he is." She began to shut down her computer. "Anyway, enough about Kendrick. I'm on my way to the Riverwalk. And don't forget Manny Rushmore's party tonight."

"After," he told her.

She frowned. "After what?"

"After the private hot and sweaty workout."

Megan laughed. "I won't forget."

She disconnected the call and reached for her purse just as Gus Kendrick filled the opening to her cubicle.

"You off somewhere?"

"Lunch. Did you need me for something?"

"Just wanted to tell you we got good feedback on that interview you did. I have a couple more for you if you're interested."

Damn straight I am. "Of course."

"Okay. I'll send it to you in an email. Take a look and let's put a schedule together."

Well. Would wonders never cease? I'll be sure to tell Beau about this.

"Thanks."

All the way to lunch she bounced a little on her feet. Maybe things were changing at *Sportsweek*. Maybe she wouldn't have to shop her story after all.

* * * *

The party was in full swing at the Rushmore house by the time she and Beau got there. Manny had hired a valet parking service for the evening, which eliminated the hassle of finding a place to park.

"Do we ring or what?" Beau asked.

"No. Just walk in. They leave the door unlocked at parties like this."

Beau frowned. "Aren't they afraid of unwanted guests?"

Megan laughed. "Wait until you see the greeters. They are legendary."

She opened the door and they walked in and were met at once by two men in tuxedos who left no doubt what their job was. They were pleasant, smiling, greeted them with deference and asked for their names.

"Megan Elliott and Beau Williams," she answered.

One of the men scrolled through a tablet he was holding until he found what he was looking for.

"Welcome to the party. Enjoy yourselves."

"That was pretty damn smooth," Beau murmured in her ear as they moved into the thick of the crowd. "Does he always have bodyguards?"

"For events like this, yes. Party crashers are a plague on celebrities."

"They're so smooth," he told her.

Megan nodded. "They have to be. Rough bouncers wouldn't work in a situation like this, not with the crowd Manny and others like him move in."

She noticed a table just to the right of the entrance to the living room, one that was piled with gifts, so she added the one she'd brought from Beau and herself.

"Hey, Megan!" Manny broke away from the people he was talking with to greet her. "How about a hug from my favorite sports writer?"

"Always." She exchanged a squeeze with him. "Happy Birthday, Manny."

"Thank you, sweet thing. And Beau. My man." Manny gave him a fist bump. "Glad you could make it."

"Wouldn't miss it," Beau told him.

Although he tried to conceal it, Beau was pleased was that the basketball star remembered him and greeted him like a friend.

"Well, there's plenty of food and drink." Manny waved his hand around the massive living room and toward the patio, visible though the open French doors. "Have at it. Oh, and Megan?"

"Yes?"

"The profile you did that was in *Sportsweek* caught the attention of a bunch of the guys. Don't be surprised if they try to corner you about one for them." He leaned a little closer. "And I'll be looking for mine."

"No problem," she assured him, even as she tried to figure out how to turn the non-assignment into an approved article, an interview she'd done for her own research.

"See?" Beau murmured in her ear as Manny moved away. "I'm telling you, sugar. If this story you're researching turns out to be what you think, it will be a blockbuster that you can take anywhere."

"From your lips…"

They had started toward the bar when she felt thick fingers closing around her arm. Startled, she tried to jerk it away and turned to see Barry Maier, a sports attorney she'd had more than one clash with, glaring at her.

"Take your hand off her." Beau's voice was low and lethal. "Now."

Barry frowned but removed his hand. "This your watchdog, Megan? You have so many enemies you need one?"

"Go back in your kennel, Barry." She wished he'd evaporate.

"This party's just for Manny's friends," he snapped. "The door's that way."

Megan nodded. "That's why we're here, Barry. Because we're his friends. We got a personal invite."

"I'll have to speak to him about that," he snarled.

Beau had moved even closer to Megan. "You're the same jerk who hassled her at the last party we were at together." Beau's voice was still low, even and lethal. "I see you haven't learned any manners since then."

Every nerve in Megan's body vibrated with suppressed anger. She was damn sick and tired of Barry Maier's attitude and his penchant for embarrassing her in public.

"Watch who you're calling a jerk." Barry glared at him then glanced at Megan. "If you think you're getting a story out of Manny — or any of my other clients — you're dead wrong, so you can just get the hell out of here."

"What's going on here?" Manny's soft voice broke into the conversation. "Barry? What's the problem?"

"The problem is I don't like gatecrashers, in particular those who write nasty things about my clients."

"We've been over this before," Megan reminded him. "If you don't want me to write negative things about your clients, tell them to behave themselves."

"Problem here, Manny?" Julia Rushmore joined the group, a concerned look on her face.

"No, darlin'," Manny assured her. "Everyone's good." He looked at Barry. "These people are my guests. You may be my attorney, but that doesn't give you the right to hassle my guests."

"Just protecting my clients," Barry grumbled.

"If you don't protect them with a little more diplomacy," Julia said, "you might find them taking their business elsewhere."

Barry opened his mouth to roar again, but Manny closed his fingers over his arm and tugged him out of their little group. Whatever he whispered in Barry's ear must have worked. The attorney glared at them but allowed Manny to lead him to another part of the room.

"I'm so sorry." Julia smiled at everyone. "Barry needs to polish his social skills. Come on, let me get you a drink." She winked. "That always helps. And, Megan, you have a lot of fans here, so be prepared to be bombarded."

"I can handle it." She grinned at Beau. "I travel with my personal bodyguard."

They had just turned away from the bar with their drinks when a tall, lean man walked over to them.

"Hey, Megan. Barry chewing on you again?"

She gave a half laugh. "Isn't he always? It's a good thing I don't scare easily. Beau, meet Jason Aponte, an associate in Barry's office."

"For my sins," he laughed, shaking Beau's hand. "And a great fan of Megan's."

"I hope you have a better disposition than Maier does," he said. "Otherwise I don't know how you hold on to any clients."

"Almost everyone has a better disposition than Barry." Jason grinned. "In the office, we call him Barry the Bear because he growls like one."

Beau chuckled. "Good description."

"Listen." Jason turned so his back was to the crowd, fished a business card out of his wallet and slipped it to her. "I know you have the office number, but here's my direct line. If you need to contact any of our clients, just give me a call. I work with Barry and I can facilitate things for you."

"Thanks." Megan slipped the card into her tiny purse. "Most of the time I go through the agents, though."

"I understand, but sometimes it helps if it comes from us. I deal with the agents more than Barry does and it's rare that I can't arrange whatever is needed." He smiled. "We like good publicity, Megan. And if it's bad stuff, we need to know so we can handle it."

"Okay, then." She grinned at him. "I can get behind that. Truth be told, I might be calling you this week. I have a couple of names in your stable on my list for a story I'm doing on the success of the older athletes."

Jason cocked an eyebrow. "More like the one on Manny? I know you didn't do that one, but —"

"Yes. More like that. The fans eat that stuff up."

"Give me a call. Let me know what you need and I'll set it up."

"Thanks very much. I appreciate it."

"Nice guy," Beau murmured as they moved away from the bar. "A lot better than Barry the Bear."

"No kidding."

"You haven't met him before?"

Megan shook her head. "But I'm glad he gave me his card. I'd like to meet with him alone and sound him out about his aging clients and what he thinks is up with then."

"Don't get too explicit with him," Beau warned her. "You don't want to tip your hand."

"Don't worry. I've learned to be very careful."

Someone called her name and she turned to say hello to a special events planner she'd gotten to know well. After that the evening passed in a blur. Her intention had been to show up, leave the gift, wish Manny a happy birthday and head out. Somehow they got caught up in one conversation after another. It seemed everyone had something to say about the premature death of Tony G.

When she heard his name drift from the little knot of people standing next to her with drinks, she nudged Beau in that direction and eased herself into the group.

"It was a damn shock," a tall blonde said. "I understand his poor wife almost had a heart attack herself."

"Fuzzy Smith was there," someone said. "He'd stopped by to leave something for Tony. Said the man had gone for his usual run first thing in the morning, came home, drank about a gallon of water real fast and dropped dead."

"That's just so terrible," the blonde commented, sadness edging her words.

Next to Megan, a man she recognized as Chris Draken, the owner of a popular sports bar, shook his head.

"Not terrible," he corrected. "A disaster. Tony G was a master of his game and an icon for aging players. He showed them you were never too old to excel in your sport."

"Trolling for tidbits, Megs?" a masculine voice said in her ear.

She jerked at the sound and turned. Fred Weirman had a very active sports blog and she often ran into him at different athletic events. For a while, he'd been persistent about asking her out but then had had to take the hint that she didn't date anyone in the business.

"Nice to see you, too, Fred. I could ask you the same."

"Always. You know me." He inclined his head toward Beau. "The new man in your life?"

Before Megan could say a word, Beau wrapped his arm around her and pulled her against him.

"That's right." There was no mistaking the possessive tone of his voice. He held out his free hand. "Beau Williams."

"Fred Weirman."

Megan swallowed a smile as she watched the two macho males in a handshake contest. Beau released his grip at last and curved his lips into the hint of a smile.

"So you know Megan, do you?" He might have been smiling, but there was no mistaking the steel in his voice.

"Just as a professional colleague." Fred grinned and held up his hands. "That's all, I promise you. Right, Megan?"

She nodded and swallowed a laugh. "You can stand down, Beau. Fred and I have never been more than friends."

"Glad to meet a friend of hers, then." But he kept his arm in place around her.

Fred cocked an eyebrow. "So I guess you were listening to the gossip about Tony G's death."

She tilted her head. "You've heard it, too? People speculating about the situation?"

"Uh-huh." Fred shoved his hands into his pockets. "On the one hand, I've covered Tony G for a long time. I can't see him taking anything that would harm his body. On the other, something had to cause that sudden heart attack. He kept himself in top shape."

"Has anyone spoken with his wife? She has to be devastated."

"I understand after the funeral she left town with her sister and brother-in-law for the usual undisclosed location. Can't blame her."

"Me, neither." Megan waited to see what else he'd say. Fred was plugged in to a lot of people and caught a lot of gossip.

"Fuzzy Smith's been telling people something just wasn't right about the whole thing. Be interesting to get his take on it. Maybe it's a story you ought to follow up on, Megs."

Megan was tiptoeing around this. No question about it. She wanted information, but she didn't want anyone to realize she might be conducting her own investigation.

"I might give him a call. Maybe try to talk my boss into letting me do a follow-up piece on his obituary."

"If you come across anything," Fred told her, "give a shout. Maybe you could guest on my blog."

"Sounds good. Thanks."

But whatever she found out was going a lot higher and wider than Fred's sports blog.

As they wandered from group to group, it seemed everyone at one time or another was discussing Tony G's shocking death and speculating about what had caused it.

"Very healthy," everybody kept murmuring. "Such a shock. His poor wife."

Throughout the evening as conversation swirled around them, Megan paid careful attention to everything that was said without adding any comments herself, but she filed away each tidbit of opinion. Tomorrow she'd spend some time with her laptop and see what she could dig up about the man, his history in sports and how he'd played during the past year.

They applauded along with everyone else when the birthday cake was brought out and joined in the raucous version of 'Happy Birthday'. Manny blew out the candles and gave his wife a big kiss. Megan waited an appropriate length of time after that to ease toward the door to make their goodbyes.

"Remember." Fred Weirman materialized at her side. "If you find anything hinky about Tony G's death, be sure to let me know. I'll give it primo space."

"There's nothing to find." Barry's loud, annoying voice broke in from beside Megan. "No one needs to go digging around where there's nothing to dig. Jealousy and rumors, that's all you'll find."

"Wasn't he one of your clients?" Weirman asked.

"Yes, and I plan to protect his legacy and the privacy of his family, so don't stick your fucking nose in their business."

Megan knew she should keep her mouth shut, but she just couldn't help herself. "If there's nothing to find, Barry, why the big defensive act?"

"I know how you do things, missy," he snarled. "You poke and prod until you get something you can build into a big fat lie. The gossip about Tony G tonight was just that. Gossip. You stay the hell out of that business."

Megan dug her nails into her palms to keep from swearing at the man. "Asking questions is what I do," she reminded him, keeping her voice as even as possible. She'd hold on to her temper no matter what. "I'm just doing my job."

"Not about my clients," he growled.

"If there's nothing to find out, what are you so over the top about?"

Barry insisted on moving right into her space so he was almost nose to nose with her.

"Because part of what my clients pay me for is protecting their privacy. I told you before and I'll tell you again. Stay the fuck away from them. I mean it."

"Barry, leave it alone." Jason Aponte moved up next to the man. "She's right. This is just what she does, and she does it well."

"Thanks, Jason." She said the words without taking her eyes away from Barry.

"Come on, Barry." Jason touched the other man's arm. "Pull in your horns."

Barry yanked his arm away, shaking him off. "Don't fucking tell me what to do."

Megan could see now that Barry must have been hitting the bar all night. His skin had turned ruddy and his eyes had a slight wild look to them. Beside her, Beau tensed. She reached for his hand, squeezing it, signaling him to do nothing. She'd handle it.

"Barry, maybe we should discuss this when you're a little calmer."

"I'm not *discussing* anything with you." He stressed the word. "You just listen to me. I know your boss real well. Don't you go asking questions where there are none to ask, or you might be looking for another job. You hear me?"

Megan had to control the urge to smack him.

"She's got other fish to fry," Beau told the other man in a voice that sounded as if it came from an ice chest. He gave her shoulder a squeeze. "Come on, Megan. Time to get out of here."

She held on to her temper until they reached the car.

"Why did you drag me away from him?" she asked as Beau held the door open for her.

"Because you have better things to do than argue with that asshole. But more than that, he looks like someone who's dangerous when he holds a grudge. I still remember how he acted at the Hutton party. Pure jackass. You need to be very careful with him, darlin'."

"He's just a big blowhard making a lot of noise," she protested. "Trust me."

"And *you* trust *me*," he told her. "I've known plenty of men like him. If he thinks you're doing him damage, he's worse than the devil."

"I'm going to find out for sure if these athletes are taking something that kills them but doesn't show up in a routine autopsy," she protested.

"And just how do you plan to do that? Try to make them redo the autopsy? You know how much chance you have of that."

"I have this hunch that Barry might be in the middle of it," she told him. "That's why he was so over the top tonight."

"How do you figure that?"

"I couldn't find out from everyone, but all the players I checked were represented by Barry."

"And you know that because?"

"Because I searched everywhere for every scrap of information, every article ever written, every notice ever published, and made a list of the ones where Barry's name is mentioned." She heaved a sigh. "It's such a muddle."

"What about the ones where you couldn't find a connection?" Beau shifted in his seat.

"I'll find it sooner or later. Maybe I'll talk to Jason Aponte about who they represent in this age group and run a few names past him."

"You be careful," Beau warned. "If there *is* something going on, you don't want to put yourself crosswise with them."

"I'll be careful. I promise." She nibbled her lower lip. "Maybe if I could find enough evidence pointing to it..."

"Don't get in a bad situation with the wrong people while you're doing this," he warned. "You never know what people will do to protect themselves, even more so when there are unexplained deaths."

"I'll be careful," she promised. "But you heard everyone tonight speculating about Tony G. I started researching other athletes who've died the same way after Tony G's death. That's why I got the meeting with Manny, although my hook is super new stats for aging players. And I'm going to contact others. If they turn out to be Barry's clients, he'd better be prepared for me to keep moving forward."

Beau reached for her hand, lifted it and kissed her fingers. "Just take care, please? I don't want to lose you when I've just found you."

Just found me? Does that mean he sees this as more than a temporary play period? Stop it, she told herself. *Don't count chickens that aren't even in the coop yet. Just enjoy this.* She let out a slow breath and tried to relax. Barry Maier always made her blood pressure spike. Beau was right. She needed to watch herself where he was concerned.

"I'll be careful. I promise." *But I'm not giving up on my story, period.*

"Okay. Fine. And that's all we're going to say about that tonight. I have other things on my mind for when we get home."

At his words her pulse ratcheted up, her nipples tingled and deep inside her the need he always ignited began to spread through her body. She couldn't wait.

Chapter Seven

Beau could almost see steam still coming from Megan's ears when they walked back into her townhouse. Although she had been quiet during the drive home, her rage was a palpable thing. She had controlled herself at the party, drawing her professional cloak around herself, but the minute they'd left, that cloak had disappeared. He could tell by the way she held herself that she would have liked nothing better than to cold-cock the bastard.

He was damn enraged on her behalf himself. Given half a chance, he'd have dragged Barry the Obnoxious Bear outside and beaten the shit out of him. But he knew that would never fly with his spitfire. He was glad that the long years of discipline helped him maintain his control, because that was what was called for right then. In the short time he and Megan had been together, he'd learned this was not a woman who liked having a man speak up on her behalf. Not unless it became a real necessity.

Inside the townhouse, she headed for her bedroom, her posture rigid as a stick. After tossing her purse onto the dresser, she turned to face him and just stood there, fists planted on her hips.

"Damn that asshole." She spat the words out. "Just damn his fucking hide."

"Harsh words from a sweet mouth," Beau teased, determined to defuse her anger.

"Not harsh enough," she protested. "Maybe I should cut off his balls."

"Ouch!" Beau gave a mock shudder and made a show of cupping his hands over his junk in a protective gesture.

Megan's mouth twitched as she fought a smile. "Not you, stud. I'm not foolish enough to cut off my nose to spite my face, if you'll pardon the pun."

She turned away from him and kicked off her shoes. The lines of her body still shrieked anger even though he could see she was making an attempt to tamp it down. If he didn't get her to relax, she'd never sleep tonight.

He came up behind her, swept her hair to one side and pressed his lips to her neck in a soft kiss. When she started to shrug him away he closed his teeth in a gentle bite on the tender place where her neck and shoulder met, then licked it with a delicate swipe of his tongue.

"I can think of a lot of other more pleasant things for you to do with my balls." He blew a gentle stream of air on the place where he'd licked, then swiped his tongue over it again. This time, instead of a shrug, she shivered, that delicious sign of pleasure he'd come to recognize.

"Is that a fact?" She leaned back to him just a bit.

"Uh-huh. But first I want to make sure you're relaxed so you don't get confused about what to do."

"Relaxed? Just how do you propose to accomplish that, Dr. Beau?"

"I think Dr. Beau has just the ticket. He prescribes a hot bubble bath to soothe the nerves. Together."

She gave a short laugh. "Dr. Beau in a bubble bath? That will be the day."

"You mock me?" he teased. "Those are fighting words, darlin'. I have yet to meet a bubble bath I can't conquer."

Megan giggled and leaned into him. Pressing his advantage, he swept her up in his arms and carried her into her oversized bathroom with the extra-large soaking tub. He stood her beside the tub while he turned on the taps and tested the temperature of the running water. When he looked around, Megan was watching him with her mouth quirked up in a half grin.

"Is this supposed to make me forget what an insufferable ass Barry the Bear is? Fat chance."

Beau glanced at her. "We will not mention that name in this room. The only B word you can use is for bubble as in bubble bath. Or in Beau. Now, come on, let's do this."

He grabbed the jar of pink bath salts he'd seen each time on one corner of the tub and shook a generous amount into the water.

"You're taking a pink bubble bath with me? For real?"

He chuckled. "Isn't pink supposed to be an erotic color? Figured I'd try it out."

The moment the bath salts hit the water a thick, sparkling pink foam covered the entire surface. While the tub continued to fill, Beau lowered the zipper at the back of Megan's dress, using the tip of his tongue to trace a line following the progress. She shivered at the contact, and just that little wiggle made his cock swell and press against his fly. God, he wanted to be inside her wet heat more than he wanted to breathe, but tonight he would not rush it. She was tense, angry and everything in between. Time to show her he could be more than a rutting bull in bed.

He eased the sleeves of the dress down her arms and, with a light touch, pushed it past her hips to the floor, balancing her while she stepped out of it. Next came the bra, a nothing bit of silk that he tossed aside. Sliding his hands around to her front, he cupped her breasts in his palms, giving them a gentle squeeze while he rasped his thumbs over her nipples. They hardened at once under his touch and she sucked in a tiny gasp. When he pinched the pebbled buds, she gasped again.

He gave her shoulder a gentle bite before sliding his hands down to her hips and the upper band of her tiny lace and silk bikinis. When he crouched, he took the panties with him, down to her ankles, then banded his arm around her to balance her while she stepped out of them. Still resting on his heels, he turned her around and pressed his mouth to her sex, nibbling the pouty lips and running his tongue between them.

"Ahhh." Megan gripped his shoulders for balance, closed her eyes and exhaled a slow breath.

"Like that, do you?" He grinned up at her.

"You know I do."

"There's more where that came from, but not until after the bath."

"Are we doing this together?" She looked down at him. "I wouldn't think a bubble bath, not to mention one with pink bubbles, was your style."

He rose, cupped her face and nibbled her lower lip. He'd bathe in purple if it relaxed her, and what was that all about? His long-time rules seemed to be fading.

"You'd be surprised what my style is where you're concerned."

The pulse at the hollow of her throat accelerated. "If so, one of us is overdressed."

"Just for a moment." He tested the water then turned off the faucet. In the next second he had shucked his clothes and added them to the pile of hers while she pulled her hair up on top of her head and fastened it with a clip.

"You might lose your man card taking a bubble bath," she teased, as he lifted her into the tub.

"It will be more than worth it."

He lowered himself into the tub, still holding her, and when he was situated, he settled her between his thighs. Once he had her where he wanted her, he pressed the button that turned on the jets. And the water began to bubble in earnest.

Stroking her arms and nuzzling her neck, he coaxed her to lean back against his chest. When he slid his hands around to palm her breasts, she let out a tiny sigh.

"It's all good, Megan," he breathed in her ear. "Just relax and let me take care of you."

He could sense her internal struggle as she fought to hold on to the bitter feelings that she harbored. But his soothing strokes and caresses, the little nips and kisses on her neck and shoulder, the gentle squeezing of her breasts began to do their work. He rolled the pebbled tips of her nipples as he continued his assault on her senses. The bubbles churned around them, the pressure of the jets pulsing against them beneath the surface of the water.

Her body pressed back against his, her muscles more lax than they had been. Time to move things along. Easing his hands down to the inside of her thighs, he nudged them apart until they rested on either side of his legs. He pressed his knees against her until her thighs opened wide and he could slip his hands down over the plane of her stomach to the mound of her sex. With a very gentle touch, he slipped one finger between the swollen flesh and stroked up and down the length of her slit.

She tried to close her thighs, to press them against his hand so she could trap his fingers, he knew, but she couldn't fight the pressure of his knees. He murmured in her ear as he rubbed her flesh, telling her how sexy she was, how he loved to fuck her. How hot it was when he slid his cock inside her and the walls of her gorgeous pussy gripped him so hard. He whispered how he couldn't get enough of her, telling her every filthy thing he wanted to do to her.

Soon she tried to wriggle her hips, to press her ass down onto his shaft and trap it between the cheeks of her buttocks, but he had her so immobilized her movement was very restricted. Kneeing her legs even farther apart, he leaned forward for a moment, taking her with him, while he redirected the stream from one of the jets.

He knew by her gasp and the slight jerk of her body the exact moment the pressurized water hit her opening. When it did, he touched her clit with the tip of a finger, making her twitch again. But he banded one arm across her waist, holding her in place against his body, his legs keeping her knees apart.

"Does that feel good, spitfire?" He crooned the words in a soft voice. "Does it make your sweet little pussy ache for more?"

He kept up the erotic flow of words while he rubbed her hot little nub and the jetstream of water pulsed into her core. Soon she was making those sexy little moans that turned him on and made his cock hard as steel. And speaking of hard, it was nestled in the cleft between the cheeks of her buttocks, demanding entrance to her rear channel. He had to grit his teeth to keep himself under control. This was all about her, about Megan. His own satisfaction could come later.

Beau moved the arm holding her waist just a little higher up on her body so his hand could reach her breast. When he pinched her nipple, she moaned and wriggled her butt against him. That didn't go far in helping him keep his cock, now begging to plunge into her anus, under control.

He kept up the dual assault on her senses, watching for the signs of impending orgasm that had by now become familiar to him. When her muscles tensed and her breathing ratcheted up, he knew she was close. Increasing his strokes on her clit, he licked the rim of her ear and bit down on the soft flesh of the lobe. That pushed her over the edge and she convulsed in his grip, hips jerking, little cries of pleasure drifting form her mouth.

The release went on and on until at last the spasms eased and she leaned back against his chest, limp and spent. The water continued to bubble around them, a punctuation to the sound of her rasping breaths.

"Did that take your mind off things?" He nuzzled her ear.

"Some things." She sighed. "But others…" She tried to squeeze her thighs together again.

Beau pressed his hand over her pussy and gave a gentle squeeze. "Are you saying there's still something missing?" he teased.

"You know there is."

He laughed when she almost growled. Then he relaxed his legs so she could press hers together. From the bottle he'd placed on the ledge of the tub, he poured liquid soap into his hand and stroked it down her back. When he reached the curve of her ass he trailed two fingers through the hot crevice, pausing to press against the sensitive opening there.

"One of these nights," he growled, "I'm going to take you back here. Count on it." He added more soap to his palm. "But right now, I don't want to let this bubble bath go to waste."

He bathed her with easy strokes, paying careful attention to every part of her body while again whispering in her ear every erotic thing he planned to do when they got out of the tub. He knew the orgasm had aroused her more than satisfied her. She still trembled with unmet need when he set the water to drain and lifted them both out of the tub.

Using a towel he yanked from the rack beside the tub, he dried her with careful strokes. Then he sat her on the edge of the tub, towel wrapped around her, while he took care of himself. When he was finished, he carried her into the other room, tossed away the towel and placed her on the bed. He took a long moment to just stand there, drinking in the sight of her.

Of all the women he'd been with — and he'd be the first to admit there had no doubt been far too many — none had ever affected him like this. It wasn't one individual thing but rather the entire package. She was smart, sexy, feisty, mouthwatering to look at and a tiger in bed. He'd have to watch himself, because he was on the verge of breaking Beau's Rules For Women.

Would it be so bad? Look at Slade. He's all in.

He shook himself out of his reverie, because right now he had other things on his mind. Like the fact that his dick was so hard it was begging to slide into Megan's hot sex, filling her and riding her to an explosive climax. He reached into the nightstand drawer where he'd stashed the condoms, yanked one out and sheathed himself with hands he was stunned to see were trembling. Then he climbed up between her legs and pushed them back at the knees, exposing all of her soft, wet pink flesh to him.

"I'm a selfish bastard." He bent forward and licked one of her nipples. "I had full plans to take you to paradise tonight and keep you there for a long time. Do all those things I talked about."

"I think you already took me there once." Her voice was unsteady. "I'm not sure I could take much more. I think we need to get down to business."

He laughed, a sound edged with rough need. "You read my mind. I planned to take it nice and slow tonight, but I think I'm at the edge of my limits here."

"We already did it nice and slow." The pulse at the hollow of her throat beat in a wild staccato. "Now I want fast."

"Then hang on, because it's gonna be a wild ride." He nudged the head of his cock at her opening.

"Oh!" Megan sucked in her breath, heat flaring in her eyes.

She tried to push her hips at him, but with his hands on her knees, pressing them back so she was wide open to him, her movement was restricted.

"Like that, sugar? Here's more for you." He used every bit of his control to ease into her with a slow, steady movement, when what he wanted was to just push deep inside her with one hard thrust.

Hold back, hold back, hold back.

But then, at last, he was inside her all the way. Her tight walls gripped him like a vise, squeezing his shaft until he was sure his eyes crossed. Keeping his gaze focused on her, he began what should have been a slow climb to satisfaction. *Yeah, right.* The feel of her surrounding him, the sexy little noises she made, the heat in her eyes — they all made slowness impossible. He'd been on the edge of the ledge since the bathtub anyway.

Bracing himself, he sped up the tempo, thrusting into her, then retreating, then pushing hard again. He never broke eye contact with her as he drove into her again and again. He knew all the little signs that she was nearing her climax and he gritted his teeth to hold his own back until she was ready.

God, make her ready soon.

Then they peaked together, an earth-shattering explosion that shook them both. She pulsed around him as he emptied himself into the thin latex, and, at last, the cyclone abated. He braced himself on his arms as he leaned forward and brushed a kiss against her lips. He didn't want to move, but he knew he'd better get rid of the condom stat.

"Be right back," he whispered against her mouth. He withdrew from her, lowering her legs as he did so and giving a gentle rub to her thigh muscles. In seconds he was back, sliding into bed next to her, curling her so she spooned into him and pulling the covers up over them.

"Mmm," she murmured when he wrapped an arm around her waist and cupped a breast in his palm.

"Hope that got rid of the uglies from Barry the Bear, darlin'."

She paused then murmured, "Barry who?"

He chuckled to himself, pulled her tighter against him. The moment her breathing evened out he closed his eyes and let himself drift off into what turned out to be the most erotic dream of all time.

* * * *

Alex Zahn stood beneath the shower spray and let the stream hit his body full force. Today's sprint had been hard, but he'd made it. Competing in marathons took a great deal of endurance and a lot of training and he didn't stint on any of it. A lot of sponsorship money was riding on the next race, another twenty-six-mile marathon, and he wanted to be in the best shape possible.

Last year he'd been sure he was done for, except for the shorter sprints. Trouble was, there wasn't that much money in them — his longevity in the sport was shortening, so he wanted to sock away as much as possible. But then he'd been steered to what he called the magic bullet and, as if he'd had extra shots of adrenaline, he ran like he'd competed ten years ago. He couldn't argue with that. And he felt so much stronger, so much more fit.

He'd worried a little, the past two weeks. How long could he keep this up? *There has to be a limit my body will reach, right?* But no, he followed directions, ate the way he should and kept on running, scoring trophy after payday after trophy. He didn't even get as winded as he used to.

"Hey, Alex." The voice of his live-in girlfriend, Jocelyn, came from the bedroom. "You in there, sweetheart?"

Alex shut off the shower, slid open the big door and poked his head out.

"That you, Joss?"

She walked into the bathroom, her tank top and shorts showing off the figure that always made his mouth water, and grinned at him.

"It better be," she told him, "or you're in big trouble."

"How about sharing this humungous shower with me?" He wiggled his eyebrows.

"Not today, you dirty old man. Besides, you're already showered."

He grinned. "You can't ever be too clean."

"I just wanted to remind you about that interview for *Runner's Magazine* at four." She handed him a towel. "I'm done with the ladies, so I can go with if you want."

Jocelyn, a breast cancer survivor, spent a lot of time with a local group raising money for an organization that worked with victims of the terrible disease.

"That would be great." He wrapped the towel around himself and knotted it at one hip. "You can help me tame the beast."

"Don't tell me he horned in on this." Jocelyn sighed and shook her head.

Barry Maier, Alex's attorney, had flown in with some new contracts to review and invited himself to the meeting. Alex had to admit the man was second to none in getting the bucks for his clients, despite the fact that he had a personality like a wounded animal.

"You know Barry." Alex headed into the bedroom to dress. "If there's a smell of publicity, he wants to be there to get his name in lights."

"Doesn't he realize it's his clients who get the publicity? That it's the reason why he can negotiate those big buck contracts?"

Alex shrugged. "Who knows what he realizes? If he didn't do such a damn good job of keeping everything in order for me, I'd replace him. Listen, babe, could I bother you to get me a bottle of water?"

"Of course." She frowned. "You sure have been drinking a lot of that these days. Are you okay?"

"I'm fine. Just thirsty. I ran a short sprint just before and that always makes me crave water."

"You know thirst is one of the first indications of diabetes," she told him.

"I'm fine, Jocelyn." He reined in his impatience. "And I'm not diabetic. I just had a complete physical last month, remember? The doctor said I was fine."

"Okay, okay." She threw up her hands. "Forgive me if I'm just concerned about your health."

He reached out and pulled her close to him. "And I'm glad of it. Makes me feel special to have you worry over me."

She looked hard into his eyes. "I just love you, Alex. I don't want anything to happen to you."

He patted her butt. "Then get me my water, woman, or I'll be dying of thirst here."

The thirst problem was a recent thing, more severe than he was used to having after working out, but he just chalked it up to getting older and the needs of his body changing. He wouldn't believe it had anything to do with the new addition to his regimen. He was excited about being a part of something so revolutionary, something that would give other athletes in his age group and beyond the ability to play longer and better.

He'd just noticed it of late, so maybe it was only a temporary thing. He hoped. He turned on the television to watch while he finished dressing. He flipped to the sports news channel in the hopes of catching the results of the marathon in Athens. He hadn't been able to fit it into his schedule, although he would have loved to compete against the reigning champion, Linus Misko.

"...shocked everyone," the reporter on screen was saying. "You can see the ambulance and the emergency crew behind me here, and the Athens police out in force to maintain crowd control."

Alex stared at the screen. "What the hell?"

"Repeating, star Greek runner Linus Misko died of an apparent heart attack at the finish of today's event. As expected, he was the first to cross the finish line. After rehydrating, he hugged his fiancé and stood to pose for pictures. Before the first shutter clicked, he collapsed on the ground. All efforts to revive him have failed."

Alex was frozen to the spot, struggling to breathe.

"What's wrong?" Jocelyn, who entered the room during the announcer's recap, hurried to his side. "What's the matter?"

He pointed to the television set. "Did you catch that? If not, rewind it and play it back. Shit!"

A tiny thread of fear wriggled deep inside him. *Rehydrating? How can that have anything to do with this?* Athletes were always doing that. It wasn't out of the norm at all.

Unless his body required more fluid than usual.

He pushed the thought from his mind as soon as it popped into it. His own need for water hadn't increased that much. Most of the time he checked it off as the rising need of an aging body. At fifty-one he was part of a small group — and growing smaller — of what he liked to think of as mature competitors. When his wife of twenty years had passed away, he had upped his competitions as a way to run out his grief. He'd met Jocelyn at a run benefitting cancer survivors and she had given him new life. But just of late —

No!

No, don't do that. He was fine. Great, in fact, if a little more thirsty than usual. But he couldn't deny that Linus' death had shocked him.

"Alex." Jocelyn rested her hand on his arm. "You don't know what conditions he might have been battling, what his situation was. Don't read anything into it. Please."

"Yeah, you're right." But he couldn't drag his eyes away from the television screen.

"Come on." She smiled. "You've got a hot interview this afternoon. I want to watch you be a star. And you can tell them all about how after you hit fifty you began to run even better."

That was the damn truth. He just couldn't tell them why.

Chapter Eight

The sun had just come over the horizon when Beau left for his usual morning run. Megan thought about lounging in bed, but the conversations from the night before kept replaying in her mind, the ones about Tony G more than others. And, of course, there had been that little verbal altercation with Barry, or Barry the Bear, as Beau was now calling him. So instead of relaxing, she was at her computer with a cup of coffee, even more determined to find out if something out of the ordinary was happening with the older athletes.

Her plan was to work while Beau went for his run, then shut down for the day. But she was so engrossed in her research she almost didn't hear him when he let himself into the townhouse. Now, showered and dressed in jeans and T shirt, he was standing behind her drinking from a glass of orange juice and reading over her shoulder.

"Find anything good?" he asked.

"I got to thinking about what Barry said last night."

"You shouldn't think about what Barry says at any time," Beau pointed out.

"I know, I know. But I thought about it this morning and wondered if he's trying to hide something." She pointed at the screen. "I used different parameters and did a little more searching to see if I had missed any deaths and if they were clients of his firm." Megan stared at the list, tapping a pen against her chin. "I widened the search boundaries and found some names I missed the other day. I recognize them from conversations."

"And all of these are recent deaths?"

"Well, within the last year." She rotated her neck, easing the muscle strain working at the computer always produced.

"Damn!" Beau shook his head. "Either bad luck or bad timing."

"And nothing about what happened raised any eyebrows," she went on, "which puzzles me. Didn't anyone say, gee, what's happening to these athletes?"

"If they passed all the usual tests," Beau pointed out, "and they made it through their physicals, why would anyone question anything? How'd you come up with this new list, anyway? I thought you searched everywhere the other day."

"I started again with a search for athletes in a certain age group who died within the past twelve months. I eliminated those I already had on my list and looked for athletes who were reported to have died from a logical cause. Overexertion. For a football player, a hard hit that caused internal problems. Stuff like that. Names I bypassed on the first round." She put down the pen and picked up the glass of ice water next to her. "It's not all that long, thank goodness. Ten more people. But it's a significant number, considering the circumstances."

"No shit." He glanced at the parameters she'd written in a notebook lying on her desk next to her. "Ages thirty-five to fifty-five? Are there many athletes still competing after they passed fifty?"

She nodded. "More and more, it seems. It used to be for the most part the long distance runners who beat the age barrier. Now almost every sport seems to be covered. Football, basketball, baseball, hockey, skiing. And the athletes are from all over the world."

"Does Barry have clients in all these places?"

"Oh, yeah. I knew about a couple of them, but just because the magazine has done profiles on them."

"The Bear sure gets around." He pulled over the ottoman and dropped down onto it. "I didn't realize his practice is international."

"Yup. He's all over the place." Megan sat back in her chair, stretched her arms and flexed her fingers. She'd been promising herself to start taking breaks every hour when she worked, but she just got so involved in what she was doing that she lost track of time.

"So what's next?"

"Okay. I've got my notes from Manny's interview, but I need to ask him a few more questions."

Beau tossed her a quizzical stare. "Like?"

"Like is there anything special to which he attributes his continuing athletic success? Then I need to bend Kendrick's arm for the go-ahead to develop it into a series."

Beau frowned. "Are you going to tell him what your focus is?"

"Are you kidding?" She gave her head a vehement shake. "He'd pull it from me faster than you can reload your rifle."

"But it's your story. Your idea. Your research."

"Doesn't matter. If he knows I suspect something's not quite right, he'll want to give it either to Linda or one of his vaunted male writers."

Anger flashed in Beau's eyes. "He needs to understand you get the same respect as everyone else. You're a damn good reporter. You heard how Manny sang your praises."

Megan snorted a laugh. "That doesn't always matter. Never to Gus Kendrick. But I'm going to make him give it to me."

"Yeah?" Beau lifted an eyebrow. "Just how are you planning to do that?"

"First of all, no one else on the staff will want to do Golden Oldies. And I can tell him I made the contacts, I have the notes, I have the go-ahead from the athletes who are expecting to be interviewed by me. And if he doesn't like it, I'll just take my idea to someone else."

Beau's smile warmed her heart. God, she was so lucky to have him here, for however long that was. "Damn straight. We'll just tell him he can shove his attitude and his fucking magazine right up his dictatorial ass."

Megan burst out laughing. "What I wouldn't give to say it just like that."

"Have you ever asked him why you get the short end of the stick all the time?"

"Of course. He hands me a plum assignment to shut me up. The thing is, Gus knows when he needs an article with in-depth research I'm the go-to person. He throws me a bone every time he thinks I might take a hike."

Beau spun her chair around so she faced him, and cupped her cheeks.

"Okay, here's what I say. Let's give Kendrick one shot at this, but just one. If he hems and haws and says something about giving it to someone else, at that point you take a hike. Megan, I'll bet there are plenty of high profile sports publications whose editors would give their left nut to have a story like this."

She leaned forward and brushed a soft kiss on his lips. Just the slight contact sent a shiver slipping through her. "My hero. What can I ever do to reward you?"

A dirty laugh rolled up from deep inside him. "I'd say hot, erotic, filthy sex would be a good start."

Oh, God!

In an instant, her nipples hardened and the pulse in her sex thrummed an insistent beat. She was certain if she touched herself between her thighs, she'd be sopping wet. How was it he was always able to do that to her in no time at all? For a brief moment, she wondered how she'd handle it when their time together was up — and she had no doubt they'd reach that point sooner or later. He said he wanted to explore their relationship further but she also knew he had never been a long-term guy. Would this time be different?

Just enjoy it while you can.

"Hey." His soft voice broke into her reverie. "Where did you just go?"

She gave herself a mental shake. "To a tropical isle where we're having naked sex on the beach."

Beau burst out laughing. "Don't tease me. I'll be hard for the rest of the day." He leaned closer. "And most of the night."

She ran her tongue in a slow sweep over her bottom lip, a habit she knew made him hornier than hell.

"Maybe we can arrange something." She pressed her mouth to his then gave his lower lip a gentle bite.

Beau gripped her upper arms with his warm fingers, holding her in place.

"Damn straight we will." Then he sat back. "But first, let's take care of this project. When we get naked, all I want on your mind is me."

"Well, then." She cleared her throat. "Let's get on with it."

"What's next on your agenda? And what can I help with?"

"You have your laptop, right?" She hit the key to wake up her own computer, which had gone into sleep mode.

"In the bedroom. I'll get it. What are we looking for?"

"You saw the names I came up with. They're scattered all over the world. The one thing many of them have in common, besides an outstanding performance year for their age, is the fact Barry represents them. I discovered that by doing some complicated search procedures. My question now is, how did the others become part of this?"

"Babe, you don't even know a part of what yet."

"Right, right, right. I'm aware of that. But it's something, Beau. Something that caused their unexpected deaths. I can feel it." She stared at her screen, as if it would give her the answers she wanted. "Damn. I wish we could get copies of the autopsies."

Beau frowned. "You think they were poisoned or something?"

"Or something. Maybe. I don't know." She shook her head. "I might be reaching here. Why would anyone poison these athletes? No, not poison. Too well dispersed with no real common thread to cause it." She looked up at Beau. "Here's a wild idea. What if they're taking some kind of performance enhancer?"

"Megan, these athletes are tested for PEDs all the time. If they were using anything, it would show up in those tests."

"But what if this is something that doesn't show up in routine testing? Some kind of thing that mimics a heart attack? Something you'd find in an autopsy if the coroner knew where to look."

"Why are you so positive about this?"

She stared at her computer, still focused on the screen. "Because I can't find any other logical explanation. If it happened with a just a couple of athletes, I'd say it's an anomaly. But with this many? Nope. Something's going on. And who knows how many more are out there that haven't shown up on my searches?"

"Don't get yourself in a jam with this stuff," he cautioned. "I don't know a lot about what goes on under the covers in athletics, but I do know it can involve dangerous people."

"I promise to be careful." She hated the little flip her heart did at his concern and had to remind herself it didn't mean anything more than one person looking after another. "I wouldn't know how to go about getting copies of autopsies, anyway. And a lot of places have laws about who can see them."

"No doubt with good reason."

"I know, I know."

He scooted his chair closer to her, close enough that she inhaled the intoxicating scent of the soap he used. Her pheromones woke up and began tap-dancing through her body. Most of the time when she was into a story, nothing else could tempt her. Of course, that was before Beau Williams had dropped into her life. She had to dig deep to stay focused, a very unusual phenomenon for her.

"Meg." He took one of her hands in his. "I want you to be very careful with this. Tread easy wherever you go because I have a feeling there are some very nasty people involved in this. Whatever this turns out to be."

"I will." *For the most part.* Treading easy wasn't part of her makeup, but for him, she'd make an effort. "Believe me, I know what kind of scum can be involved in these things. I've seen more than enough of the underbelly of athletics."

"I'll bet you have." He shook his head. "I hate that you ever have to set foot into that stuff."

"Me, too. I hate that it even exists." She blew out a breath. "Anyway. We should also widen the parameters of the search. For one thing, I want the names of all of what I'm calling the Golden Athletes. Those at an age when their skills should be decreasing rather than increasing. That's the gist of the story I'll pitch to Kendrick. I just won't mention what I think is the real angle."

"Okay." He dropped a soft kiss on her lips. "Let me get set up and you can tell me what my specific assignment is."

"Bring your stuff into the dining room." Megan unplugged her laptop and carried it and her notebook out of the room she used as a home office. "There's room for both of us to work there."

Less than ten minutes later, they were set up and she'd poured fresh coffee for both of them.

"I think we should stick to North America for this first search," she told Beau. "Even though there were similar deaths all over the globe, let's not make this unmanageable."

"So what are my particular parameters?"

"Look for women thirty-five and older who have without warning had miraculous playing stats. I've just found men. If this is a male-oriented phenomenon, then I redesign the parameters."

"And if it is?"

"Then that could change the whole thing. So let's start with the fifty states first, then widen the search to Canada." She opened the search engine on her computer. "Best-case scenario is this is contained to a small group of athletes. Otherwise, we have a problem that goes far beyond a good story."

They worked in silence, each concentrating on their particular tasks. An hour passed. Then two.

"Well," Beau said, breaking the silence, "I have an answer, but I'm not sure if it's good or bad."

"Let's have it." Megan leaned back in her chair and fiddled with her ponytail.

"I tried a bunch of different key words, phrases, whatever. Unless there's a global media conspiracy to hide this, I can't find any female athletes who had their best year then dropped dead of a supposed heart attack."

"So." Megan picked up her pen and tapped it against her fingers. "Whatever's going on, we're looking at just the male athletes. I know, I know." She held up her hand. "I'm stating the obvious, but I had to hear how it sounded."

"So where does that lead us?"

"We need to list every one of them, their sport, their team if it's a team activity and the stats for the best year. Which, by the way, we expect will be their most recent one."

Beau nodded. "I can do that. Simple. What's on your plate?"

"I'm going to see what I can find out about the male body and what would make it respond with superhuman effort, without leaving a trace." She sighed. "Then I'm going to pull up the performance histories of the male athletes whose deaths we know about and chart their stats. See when they began to exceed their age-imposed physical shortcomings."

"You do this all the time?"

She nodded. "For every article."

Beau shook his head. "And here I thought *we* spent the most boring hours learning and memorizing minute things."

"Not quite the same," she told him. "If you guys don't have every bit of information locked down in your brains, someone or several someones could get killed. For reporters, the worst thing you can do is get caught with incorrect facts in a story. But if that happens, all they'll do is hang you by your balls." She chuckled. "Or other parts of anatomy if you aren't a man."

"Ouch!" He made a show of cupping a protective hand over his crotch.

"Right." She smiled at him. "Don't worry. You won't be on the front line."

"Maybe so, but I don't want any part of your delicious anatomy abused by a knuckle dragger."

"So noted." She winked. "Let's get to work."

Megan had no idea how much time passed before she at last sat back, flexed her fingers and blew out a breath. "I think I'm done for the day. My brain aches."

"I hear you." Beau looked up from his laptop. "I'm just about finished, too. Man. These statistics are eye-poppers."

"Very bad or very good?"

"Depends on how you look at them." He glanced at his screen. "These guys must be pumped up on something to achieve stats like this, that's all I can say. No one else even comes close to them, and I'm talking guys much younger than them."

"So there *is* some kind of chemical involved." She nibbled the end of her pen.

"I'd say the chances are pretty damn good. So what next?"

"Next, we combine all our notes into one electronic folder which I save on both my computer and a flash drive. Then I decide who I'm going to interview next. I also want to talk to the surviving family members of those athletes like Tony G who died."

"Okay, I'm emailing my stuff to you right now." A few clicks of the keys and he went through the process of shutting down his laptop.

"Thanks."

"And your boss?" he asked. "What about him?"

"Just to be up front about this, I'll ask to meet with him Monday morning and lay it out for him." She shrugged. "But if he turns it down or says he's going to give it to someone else, I am well and truly out of there. Oh, and taking all my notes and information with me, since it's my story. I dug it up and I did all the research."

"Will he get nasty?"

"Maybe. But it doesn't matter, because if he does, I am so gone out of there."

Beau reached for one of her hands and squeezed it. "Want me to go with you?"

She shook her head. "It's a nice gesture on your part, but I've been fighting my own battles here for a long time. I can handle it. There's one more thing I want to check before we call it a day."

"What's that?"

"I want to find out, if I can, how many of these clients are also Barry's." She dropped her pen on the table and rubbed her faced with both hands. "I have to be objective about it, too. I don't want to be on a witch hunt just because I dislike the ass."

Beau grabbed one of her hands and closed his strong fingers over it. "Maybe Jason what's his name can help you. He did say if you needed anything from the firm to contact him."

"Aponte." She sat up straight. "Good suggestion. I can sell it as a series on golden superstars and ask him which ones are clients of the firm. I have no doubt he'll salivate over the chance for publicity." She kissed the hand that was holding hers. "Very smart of you."

He grinned. "I am more than just a boy toy, I'll have you know."

"I do know, but please don't lose that side of you." She winked. "I'm not through playing."

"Maybe you could take your toy into the other room and play with him for a while," he teased. "Then I think we can treat ourselves to lunch on the Riverwalk."

"Sounds like a plan to me."

The moment she shut down her computer, he swept her up in his arms and headed toward the bedroom. His mouth was firm on hers, his tongue hot as it swept inside. By the time they reached her bed, she couldn't get her clothes off fast enough.

Chapter Nine

The man sat in Java Joe's, a nondescript coffee shop despite its glitzy name, studying the screen of his tablet while sipping from his cup of extra-strong black coffee. He'd had a miserable weekend, people calling him about Tony G and asking him if there was any more information on what had caused the heart attack.

By Sunday afternoon, he'd wanted to throw his phone in the pool and take a long vacation somewhere. Too bad he couldn't. The drawback of his situation. He was right in the middle of this mess even without Felix's special project.

Fuck.

That was the one word he could think of as he read for the tenth time the obituary for Linus Misko. A sick feeling filled him as he studied the details. Someone had snapped a picture of the man lying in the roadway, and of course the media had paid big bucks for it. *No privacy in today's world.*

The news had shocked him, just as it had stunned everyone else. They had just begun running projects with the man three months ago and had been working with his agent on a raft of new ones. His outstanding performance had been the impetus for that. A month ago, the runner had completed a marathon that killed everyone else's time. Now he was dead.

Fucking damn!

He fiddled with his coffee cup, drumming his fingers on the table in an impatient tattoo. He had called Felix and demanded the man leave his lab and come meet with him at once. He was on his second cup of coffee — not good for a man who already was on edge — when at last Felix walked into Java Joe's. He glanced over at the man and dipped his head a fraction while he got his own order.

"Okay, Mr. Over the Top, what's so urgent I had to leave what I was working on and haul my ass over here to meet with you?"

"Linus Misko. That's what's so urgent." The man turned his tablet around so Felix could see the news bulletin about the runner's death. "You insisted you'd fixed whatever the problem was with this stuff."

"This *stuff*" — Felix emphasized the word — "is going to make us a fortune, as you well know."

"What I know right now is that it's killing our test subjects. If someone puts all the pieces together, we'll be in deeper shit than we can imagine." He raked his fingers through his razor-cut hair. "Fuck."

Felix leaned forward so his head was closer to the man's.

"Now you listen to me. These assholes are being very well compensated for participating in this trial. As if they didn't have enough money already, we've arranged the little nest eggs you insisted on that appear to be compensation for personal appearances. They went into this with no objections, salivating to find a way to extend their careers and go out with a bang."

"They didn't bargain for death." The man took a slug of his coffee and made a face when he realized it was just lukewarm.

"You knew there were risks," Felix reminded him. "We discussed this at great length. The athletes knew it, too, but they want something to prolong their glory years."

"I know, but…" He raked his fingers through his hair again. At this rate he'd be bald before this was over. "I just never figured it would be this fatal. I thought maybe one or two athletes might get hit by it, but Felix, we're losing almost everyone."

"Not everyone." Felix's voice had an edge to it. "The new formula is working even better and we haven't lost anyone from it."

"Yet," the man pointed out.

"And if I'm right, we won't." Felix curved his mouth in a tiny smile. "Relax. We'll be good to go with this one."

"We'd better be." The man scrubbed his hands over his face. "At the office, people are already whispering about what's happening to our clients, and they don't know the half of it. Tony G's death tops everyone's conversation, but then they mention a couple more names. I guess just the ones they're aware of."

"And you're keeping it that way, right?" Felix's tone had hardened.

"Of course," the man snapped. "It's not hard. Our client base is scattered all over the earth, so they seldom come into the office. It also helps that I use law firms in different countries to facilitate things." He shook his head. "Let's hope none of them start connecting any dots."

"Then you just have to make sure that doesn't happen. Listen." He closed his fingers in a light grasp over the man's wrist. "We are almost there. I have reworked the formula to take care of its, ah, shortcomings. There should be no more mishaps."

"Mishaps?" The man looked at Felix and ground his teeth. "You call all these deaths mishaps?"

"Calm down, you idiot." Felix pitched his voice even lower. "You were all excited about this when I proposed it to you. Bigger endorsement contracts for your clients, more money for you, not to mention, your share of the profits on our little miracle creation. So pull up your balls and act like everything is wonderful. Be solemn when necessary and encouraging to all your clients. A couple more tweaks and we'll be home free."

"We damn well better be."

"I have just as much to lose here as you do," Felix reminded him. "Maybe more. My whole career could blow up in my face."

"Mine, too, asshole. It's not just you with a reputation out there on the line."

"Then we'd better make nothing goes wrong. What about that idiot reporter?" Felix asked. "Is she going to be a problem?"

"I can handle her." The man curled his hands into fists, digging his fingertips into his palms. Thinking of Megan Welles always got him riled up. *Stupid bitch, always complicating my life.*

"I'm counting on it. You said she's been contacting some of the athletes who are having great years. Does she know they're connected to you? We could lose everything if she digs hard enough and pulls all the loose threads together."

"I said I'd take care of it." The man tossed back the rest of his coffee, grimacing at the taste of the cold liquid. "And I will."

"Then do it. And don't call me again. I'll reach out when I have something for you." He stood, glared at the man for a moment then left, tossing his cup into the trash on his way out.

The man sat there, his stomach churning, bile burning his throat. He was no penny-ante shyster, for God's sake. He was a key player on the scene. That was why Felix had come to him. *But fucking damn.* He seemed to be the one taking all the risks. If one more athlete died, Megan Welles could start digging deeper and they'd all be screwed.

What he needed to do was put in a casual call to each of the clients in this test program, shoot the shit with them and check on their physical well-being. Get the latest medical reports. Be sure they were all on track and nothing was hinky about their conditions. And while he was at it, assure them that the unfortunate deaths of some athletes of late had nothing to do with them.

He rubbed his abdomen, where a familiar burning sensation had ignited again. Ulcers, he was sure, and reached into his pocket for the antacid tablets he carried all the time. Was the promise of all that money worth it?

Fuck, fuck, fuck.

* * * *

"I need to call Barry the Bear's office." Megan pulled up her contacts list where she kept everyone's number.

"I thought you were staying away from him?" Beau reminded her. "Things with him could get very ugly."

"No kidding." She shook her head. "As a matter of fact, it's not Barry himself I'm calling. I'm going to take your suggestion and ask Jason Aponte to meet with me. We met him at Manny's, remember? He said if I had questions or wanted to contact any of their athletes to let him know."

"I do. He seems like an okay guy. Wonder how he stands it working for such an asshole?"

Megan grinned. "Maybe we should ask him."

"We? Are you saying it's okay for me to go with you?"

She winked at him. "I figured you weren't about to let me out of your sight, anyway."

He pulled her into his arms, pressing her against his body.

"You got that right." He wound her ponytail around his hand and tugged her head back. "He may not be as over the top as Barry the Bear, but I don't trust anyone from that firm."

"I think he's a good guy, though. Anyway, you can dissect him with your sniper's eye and tell me what you think.'

"What is it you're looking for from him?"

"I want to interview his aging players who are having such stellar years. I'll tell him it's for that series I made up, Golden Oldies in their Gold Star Year or whatever. He said I could go direct to him for stuff like this and it's easier than hunting down individual agents. But I have to know if he's sincere, whatever he says, or he's just blowing smoke at me."

"It must be nice having a job where you don't have to hike into the office every day."

She nodded her head. "Don't you know it. But the very nature of what we do means we're out gathering material and covering events most of the time. We just have to check in with the office in case Kendrick wants to talk to us, or in my case, shout. And, of course, we're always available on our cells."

"Tell me something." He tugged her head back again so he was looking right into her eyes. "How come Gus Kendrick has such an enormous hard-on for you? And I mean that in the totally non-sexual way."

"I should hope so." Megan sighed. "I'm sure it goes back to when I was first hired. He was pressured by the publisher who was pushed by a friend. I wasn't chosen by Gus himself and he's always resented it."

"Even though you do a great job?"

She shrugged. "Even though. I just do my best to ignore it most of the time. And avoid him as much as I can." Then she sighed, a tiny whisper of breath. "But I will have to go into the office to pitch the series."

"You planning to tell him everything you suspect?"

She shook her head. "Not on your life. Like I said, I'm taking the Golden Oldies angle until I have my facts in place."

"Okay. Make your call, then."

He cupped her cheeks and lowered his head until his lips were a scant inch from hers. "Then I think we should shower before we get dressed."

His words ignited the flame inside her that always simmered when he was around, and sometimes even when he wasn't.

"I don't want to be late for my appointment," she teased him.

"Then you'd better make it a late lunch." He brushed his tongue over the surface of her lips.

A little shiver skated over her body. "I'll do that."

Jason was free and agreed to meet at one-thirty.

"Later is always better," he assured her. "Smaller crowd, better service, less noise."

They agreed on a restaurant and she hung up.

"Shower time," Beau reminded her.

Megan looked at her watch. "We've got two hours. Think that's enough?"

He laughed. "No, but I'll make it do."

* * * *

Manny Rushmore hit Stop on the treadmill, drew in a deep breath and let it out. He looked to his left where his teammate, Carl Sanchez, had just finished his stint and powered down.

He and Carl had been together since high school. They'd both entered the University of Texas as top freshmen recruits. Both had compiled outstanding college records and both had been taken in the first round of the NBA draft their senior year. Then Carl had been drafted by Houston and Manny by Seattle, but five years into their pro careers, luck had landed them both on the Austin team.

Knowing the fluidity of professional sports and the fact that everything could change in an instant, they'd both built homes in San Antonio, where they had grown up and where they had many ties. During the off-season, they socialized together and often worked out together at the well-outfitted gym Manny had installed in his house.

"You about ready to call it quits for the day?" he asked, wiping the sweat from his face with the towel around his neck.

"You know it." Carl stepped off the other treadmill and grabbed a towel from the nearby bench. "I think I'm getting too old for this stuff."

"Not a chance." Manny clapped him on the shoulder. "We'll be getting over on all those kids for a good long time yet."

"Maybe you, Manny, but not me. My body's telling me it's time to slow down. Maybe even get out altogether." Carl shook his head. "I swear, I don't know how you do it. Run up and down the floor, make those high shots, outpace the kids. It makes me tired just watching you. What's your damn secret?"

For a brief moment, Manny was tempted to tell him, but he banished the thought as soon as it popped into his brain. He'd get in big trouble for doing it, or worse yet, cut off from the program altogether. So instead he just shrugged.

"Good genes, I guess."

"You guess?" Carl laughed. "Come on. I know your family, remember? They consider racing the light at the crosswalk exercise for the day."

"Well, whatever. I'm just giving thanks and hoping it lasts a while longer." He opened the door of the fridge and pulled out two bottles of the special water he drank, tossing one to Moe.

"What kind of water is this?" Carl frowned at the label.

"Just something I got turned onto. It's supposed to have all these extra vitamins and minerals in it."

"So is this your secret weapon?"

Manny chugged half the bottle before answering. "I don't know. Maybe it helps." He grabbed another bottle and finished it off just as fast.

"Jesus, Manny. You'll be peeing like a racehorse if you keep that up."

Manny shook his head. "No, I won't."

"Then you must have kidneys bigger than a house." He stared as Manny grabbed yet a third bottle. "Hey, bro. You're going to float out of here in a minute. I'm not kidding."

But Manny's mouth was still dry as the Sahara as he uncapped the liquid. More than usual, he thought. Tilting his head back, he emptied the bottle in five large swallows. As he tossed the empty into a trash basket, he noted how rejuvenated he felt, how energized even after all the exercising he'd just finished. He was about to tell Carl when it hit him, a sharp chest pain so excruciating it stole his breath.

"Manny?" Carl took a step toward him. "You okay there?"

Manny tried to tell him no, he fucking wasn't okay, but then the intensity of the pain ratcheted up even more. The last thought to ever register in his brain as he fell to the floor was that the fucking program was killing him.

* * * *

Jason Aponte greeted them with a smile, shook hands with Beau and settled himself across from them in the booth. He waited while the waitress took their drink orders, then sat back and looked from one to the other.

"I appreciate the invite to lunch, Megan," he told her. "And, Beau, good to see you again. But I'm guessing this has to do with our conversation at Manny's birthday party more than a social get together."

Megan nodded. "You said if I had any questions about any of the firm's clients or requests for interviews to go direct to you."

"That's correct." He paused while the waitress set glasses of ice water in front of them. "I don't have to tell you that Barry is, shall we say, difficult to deal with. And I'm happy to help you with whatever you need. Good coverage for our clients is always essential."

"I don't know if you'd consider this good or bad." She took another sip of water, gathering her thoughts. Beneath the table, Beau gave her thigh a reassuring squeeze. "I've been researching for a series I'm pitching to my boss called Golden Oldies Still Hot, or something like that. I want to write about the aging players who for no apparent reason are having the best years of their lives."

"There are some outstanding players, that's for sure." He studied her face. "And the reason you called me is because some of them are ours."

"A significant number," she pointed out. "I'm interested in how they are doing this. Is it a different diet? New exercise program? Better vitamins? My reporter's nose tells me it has to be something. If it was just one athlete, I'd say there goes a miracle. But there are enough of them to pique my interest."

"I can understand that. But I can assure you, if there was something like that going on, we'd want to shout it to the world and try to patent it."

Megan lifted an eyebrow. "So there isn't?"

He paused, as if to choose his words with great care. "Not that I'm aware of. Just the usual stuff. I'd say these athletes are just sticking to it better than some others."

"Can you tell me what they might be doing that other athletes should incorporate into their own regimens?"

Before he could answer her, the waitress returned to take their orders. Megan wanted to kick her for showing up just when Jason had between about to tell her something. Maybe. At last, with business taken care of, she nudged him again toward the topic.

"You were about to tell me about the programs your clients follow," she prodded.

He shrugged. "Not in any detail. Each one has his or her own. Many of them work with trainers and they don't share information. I can tell you that the agents who represent our joint clients are focused on having them take special care of themselves. And we also got lucky."

"Lucky?" Megan frowned. "In what way?"

"We represent people who we think have that little extra dollop of talent that every athlete looks for. That's what makes them have the kind of year they have, even though they might be close to retirement. It's a psychological thing."

"Is that what Barry tells you?"

He shook his head. "He doesn't have to. We all know it."

Megan looked at her phone and made a show of scrolling through her notes. She wanted to frame her next question with very great care.

"I bring this next thing up, Jason, because I know you'll give me an honest answer."

"Uh-oh." He looked at Beau and grinned. "Should I get ready to duck?"

Beau chuckled. "Where Megan's concerned, I always anticipate trouble. Just kidding," he added, when she elbowed him in the ribs. "I can say this. That she's always straightforward, whatever she asks."

"Okay." Jason looked at her again." Let's have it."

"Some of your clients might have spectacular endurance and talent, but it also seems as if a lot of them are dying out of the blue in recent months. Do you think it's because, with the program they follow, they're pushing themselves beyond their limits and their bodies give out?"

Megan watched Jason for any tell, any indication that there was something going on here she should push for. But either he was very good at control or he thought she was misinterpreting the situation.

"Megan, we do our best to make sure our clients take the best possible care of themselves," he assured her. "This may sound crass, but they're worth their weight in gold. We go out of our way, along with their agents and coaches or trainers, to make sure they don't do just that."

"I had to ask," she pointed out. "Otherwise I wouldn't be a good reporter. Now. Can you set me up to interview some of them?"

"Depends on who you want to talk to." He studied her over the rim of his water glass. "You don't have some ulterior motive here, do you? Because that would cause a problem for both of us."

She held up her hands. "No hidden agenda here. My readers are interested in how these superstars are so super at their age, and if they are taking good care of themselves. I have a lot of older readers. They focus on stuff like that, looking for things to adapt to their own lifestyles."

"Okay, I get it. I had to ask, though, because — "

Whatever else he was going to say was lost when both of their phones chimed at the same time. Megan answered her call and what she heard stole her breath. When she looked across the table at Jason, she was sure he'd gotten the same message.

"Manny Rushmore just dropped dead at home." She struggled to get the words out.

"That was my secretary telling me the same thing. She says it's all over television."

Megan woke up her tablet, logged in to the restaurant's Wi-Fi service and pulled up the app that would let her access the news. And there it was, on the local ABC affiliate.

"...responded to a nine-one-one call to the home of star NFL player Manny Rushmore. What we're hearing is the man dropped dead without warning after finishing a normal workout session. Teammate Carl Sanchez, who had been working out with him, made the phone call. That's all the information we have at the moment, although there is already speculation on social media that he died of a sudden heart attack like some other well-known athletes have done in recent months. We will bring you more updates as we get them."

"I have to go. Sorry about lunch, Megan." He slid out of the booth.

"No, no, go ahead. I'm sure his wife will need you."

"And I'll bet the office is a madhouse." As he spoke, his phone chimed again. He looked at the screen and nodded. "Speak of the devil. Okay, gotta dash."

He already had the phone to his ear as he raced out of the restaurant.

Megan looked at Beau. "Is it okay with you if we skip this, too? I've lost my appetite and I want to start reaching out to my contacts."

"I already figured as much." He tossed a ten-dollar bill on the table then helped her out of the booth. "Don't worry about me. I can scrounge. Let's get you home so you can work."

"Thank you."

But they had just retrieved her car and he'd slid in behind the wheel when his own cell rang. He looked at the screen.

"Shit."

Megan looked over at him, sure this couldn't be good news.

"What is it?"

"A text from Slade. Let me read it."

"Slade? But he's on his honeymoon." She frowned. "Kari's going to kill him for texting when he should be paying attention to her."

"Yeah, well, welcome to Delta Force. Honeymoons and personal disasters fall by the wayside when command calls."

She waited, holding off on her own calls until she knew what the situation was.

"Well?" she asked when he blew out a heavy sigh.

"Duty calls and all that shit. He's even having to cut his honeymoon short. Can you take me to the ranch? Teo's picking up him and Kari and the call's out to the others. We have a mission that's a top priority." He threaded his fingers in her hair and pulled her face close to his. "I am so sorry, babe. I hate leaving you with this mess going on."

"It's okay." She'd make him believe it. She'd known what his situation was from the first day. "I walked into this with my eyes wide open. Go work for Uncle Sam. I'll be fine."

"You damn well better take care of yourself." He said the words in a fierce voice. The he took her mouth in the hungriest, most demanding kiss yet.

"I promise. Now get this car started so we can get your gear and get you to the ranch. You drive, I'll make my calls."

She didn't want to let herself think how much she was going to miss him. Swallowing a sigh, she punched in the number of her contact at the television station.

"Jan? It's Megan Welles. What the hell is going on?"

Chapter Ten

"Are you listening to me?" Felix's voice was cold and uninflected. "We have to shut this bitch down. Get rid of her if we have to."

The man was sitting in his car in the parking lot of Java Joe's, the place where he and Felix met when they needed to. He'd wanted to return this call where no one would see him or overhear him, and no one he knew ever came here. At Felix's words, he gripped his cell phone so tight he was sure it would crack. In point of fact, he wished it was Felix's neck that he would snap without another thought.

"I'm assuming by we you mean me?" he asked, although he knew the answer.

"Of course, I mean you. Cleanup is your job."

Because you always panic and make a fucking mess out of it. I'd like to clean you up, you bastard. This is your fault.

"Are you there?" Felix's voice poked at him. "Do not hang up on me."

"And do not give me orders that cannot be carried out." He swallowed. "I can't believe how stupid you are, for someone who's supposed to be so smart. Do you have any idea what kind of disaster would follow if we got rid of Megan Welles?"

"Do you have any idea what kind of disaster she's already causing for us? She's after our athletes."

"Felix, you asshole. We can't just get rid of someone who is so visible in this situation. So she's hot on the story of the so-called super athletes. As long as no one lets the cat out of the bag, we're good. And I can control her access. Besides, the publicity these pieces would generate would help our bank accounts. Killing her would just let people know she was right."

The man waited through the silence at the other end of the connection.

"I asked about her," Felix said at last. "What if in fact she's after a story on the athletes who died without warning? It's not such a leap. Everyone says she's like a bulldog when she gets hung upon a story. We don't need that."

"Have you been asking questions?" The man leaned his head back and closed his eyes. *Kill me now.*

"Will you just leave it to me?" He blew out a breath. "There's no connection to us at the moment and there won't be. Besides, if *Sportsweek* decides to go down that path, they'll assign one of their guys to it. Gus Kendrick is the world's biggest misogynist. I don't think he ever heard of equality of the sexes or political correctness."

"She makes me very nervous. I don't want her nosing around. If a hint of this gets out, I could lose my very lucrative job."

"If a hint of this gets out, we could all be in jail," the man pointed out. "Don't you think I know it? What the hell do you suggest? I'm busy as a cat covering up shit reassuring our clients that they aren't in any danger and no one has a vendetta against them. I'll just remind them not to give her any hint of what they're participating in."

Silence.

At last, Felix said, "I guess I'll just have to keep an eye on her myself. I don't trust this situation. We have too much money involved to take any chances."

"I don't want to have to tell you this again. You stay away from her. I'll make sure our athletes don't give her a sniff of anything." The man wasn't sure he could commit murder himself.

"Either you figure it out or I will. Listen. We're so close to the finish line here I can smell it. We can't lose it all now."

"And you're sure you've got all the bugs worked out?" *God. If only.*

"This last test run will let us know for sure. You've got the distribution all set?"

The man nodded, even though Felix could not see him. "We're set."

"Fine. Then let's make sure that Welles bitch can't do us any harm before she destroys us."

"I don't know how many times I have to say this. Stay away from her. Did you hear me?"

But the call had disconnected. The man stared at his cell, a mixture of anger and dread swirling in his system. Every time Felix had ever decided to take things into his own hands, disaster had followed. *Why the fuck did I get involved with him again, anyway?*

Because of the money. It's always about the money.

Sighing, he climbed out of his car and walked into Java Joe's. He had calls to make, but before he got back in his vehicle he needed coffee, large, strong and hot.

* * * *

Even on the bumpy truck ride to the city of Kabul, Beau kept reliving that week in Megan's townhouse. He didn't have too many expectations where women were concerned, but Megan had seemed different. And he couldn't get away from that invisible connection that tugged something deep inside him. Was he misreading the whole situation?

Enough! Do your job. Worry about her later. Pay attention to your job now.

Using his discipline, he blocked everything else from his mind as they drove at a slow pace through the streets to the prearranged drop for the truck. He couldn't afford to be distracted until the mission was complete.

Kabul, the three-thousand-five-hundred-year-old capital of the province of the same name, lay wedged between the Hindu Kush mountains along the Kabul River, in the eastern part of Afghanistan. In the war on terror, focused on defeating the Taliban, it had been the scene of many suicide bombs and attacks on Americans and, tonight, Delta Force Team Charlie was hoping to prevent yet another attack on a compound that housed many Americans working for civilian defense contractors.

Team Charlie had reviewed and analyzed the intel provided by a contact who assured them his information was reliable. A cell of ten terrorists was planning a mass suicide bombing of the compound that, if accomplished, would not only kill a huge percentage of the people housed there but also destroy the construction work that had been accomplished so far. Without the workers, the rebuilding could not go forward and what was already in place would crumble in neglect.

Team Charlie's job tonight was to take out the cell, eradicating each and every man, and to do it in a way that would not create a stir on a street of crowded apartment buildings. Not an easy task at all.

Beau had spent two hours on the range at Bagram, on the base where they were temporarily assigned that they shared with the Air Force. He'd taken painstaking care to make sure his rifle was sighted and had worked with Trey focusing on a variety of targets. Slade and Marc had made the arrangements for transport for the twenty-five miles from Bagram to Kabul. At last, at the 'go' signal, they had loaded up in a beat-up truck and headed to Kabul.

Each man was hyper-alert, knowing danger could pounce on them at any moment. They were dressed to blend in with the city's population, and practiced by this time at moving in the strange clothing. With their weapons and other equipment concealed beneath the voluminous robes, they made their way through the city to their destination.

If they missed anything, it was sunglasses in the brightness of the day. Shades marked the wearer as American, or, at the very least, a suspect European. So they spent very little time in the daylight, concealing themselves in the spots marked for them until nightfall when they could move with silent ease.

Their info had pinpointed the location of the apartment where the cell met as well as the time and date of the meeting when they would gather to arm for their attack. Their contact had arranged to get them into an empty apartment across the street where they could wait and watch. Beau and Trey were posted at the window while Slade and Marc hovered outside in the alley between buildings. Their job was body disposal, silent and swift. The men would arrive one at a time which made their job that much easier.

"Target one approaching."

Slade's voice crackled in the receiver in Beau's ear. He blinked and focused on sighting through the scope. Yup, there he was, walking with rapid steps down the almost deserted street. Trey called out coordinates as Beau inhaled a deep breath, let it out and pulled the trigger.

Puff!

The man crumpled into a heap. Slade and Marc emerged at once from the alley and hauled him into that space between the buildings. The few people on the street scurried away as if afraid of seeing anything. *Good*.

Beau flexed his shoulders and set himself to ready for the next target.

Everything went like clockwork. In less than thirty minutes, they'd taken out the entire cell, the bodies had been stashed behind the garbage in the alley and Team Charlie had blended into the night. Moving with great care, they made their way out of the city to the point of exfiltration, waiting with practiced patience until the chopper dropped out of the sky to pick them up.

In the cabin of the helo, they bumped fists. Another mission completed successfully. This one had taken longer than expected, but Slade had used his shortened honeymoon to twist some arms and get some extra leave for them as soon as they got back.

"Ten days," he told the team. "Use it wisely, because then we have a long stretch before we get any again." He looked at each of them. "Don't count on this until the ink is dry, but I requested we be reassigned to Fort Sam. I think for all of us that's a good move."

He looked at each of them in turn and one by one they nodded. Beau noticed that even Marc dipped his head in agreement. For his part, he couldn't fucking wait to get back to Megan. They had been off comms the whole time, their personal cells shut down, no texting or emailing, and he was about to go out of his mind with worry. He had needed every bit of learned discipline to focus on the job and shut Megan out of his mind.

She was savvy, experienced and not given to taking unnecessary chances, and thank the lord for that. He trusted that she'd be smart enough not to put herself in a dangerous position. They had no idea who was behind this—whatever *this* was—and he just hoped she'd wait for him before dipping her toe in dangerous waters.

And that brought another thought to mind. Megan Welles was the first woman ever—and there had been plenty—who made him want more than sex and a few laughs. He *liked* her, admired her, enjoyed her company out of bed as well as in, which was something brand new for him. He'd always believed he could never be faithful to one woman, always be married to Delta Force until—*Yeah, until what, jackass? Until you're old and cranky and no one wants you?*

But he hadn't seen himself sharing that part of his life with a woman, until Megan. He'd take it slow, be very careful, but for the first time he could see himself with just one woman, a woman who could fulfill all his needs.

The moment they landed back at camp, he grabbed both his cell and his laptop. First he texted Megan to see if she could talk.

Can you Facetime?

He held his breath until the answer came back.

Yes. Give me five to get set up.

"Debrief in fifteen," Slade told him as he passed by him.

"I'll be there."

He set up his laptop, logged on, and five minutes later there was Megan's beautiful face staring out at him from the screen.

"Hey, soldier." She grinned at hm. "Got time for a kiss?"

"The minute I get home," he growled. "A kiss and a hell of a lot more."

"Did-did everything go okay?"

He'd told her he couldn't share details with her, but he knew she worried for his safety.

"Yes. Mission completed."

"Good."

He could see her relax. "How goes it with your project? What's the skinny with Manny Rushmore?"

"Oh, my God, Beau." She pushed a stray hair back from her face. "Everyone is going nuts. The team owner has called down the wrath of God on everyone. Barry's on the warpath. Poor Jason is having to field his calls because Barry won't talk to the media or anyone except the team owner and Manny's immediate family. It's a big mess."

"Has anyone started to connect the dots to the other deaths?"

She shook her head. "But I'm digging into each of them as much as I can, contacting their families, all that stuff."

"Have you, uh, talked to Kendrick about it yet? I imagine he wants to give it to one of his top dogs."

She snorted a laugh. "You would have loved that conversation. He was making loud noises about doing a series on the whole thing. I told him I'd already been working on it. I did all the research and I have all the contacts. He then told me in his jackass way to give them to him. He was putting one of his guys on it. It was—get this—beyond my experience."

"Good thing I wasn't there. I'd have smacked the shit out of him." Anger was growing in him even now.

"Simmer down, soldier. I took care of it myself. I told him flat out I'd done all the work on my own time and if he didn't give me the story, I'd take it to someone else."

"Good for you." Pride swelled inside him. "I'll bet he wasn't happy."

"No, but If I had to guess it's because he knows he's got no choice."

"Hey, Surfer Dude." Trey Williams hollered at him from the other side of the tent. "Briefing time."

Beau gritted his teeth. For the first time he hated that nickname. He was even planning to talk to Slade about changing his call name.

"Right there," he shouted back. Then he looked at the screen. "I've got to go, babe. I should find out soon when we'll be back and I'll text you."

"You do that. I'll be waiting." She blew him a kiss, then the screen went dark.

He hoped to hell they were getting out of there damn soon. He had an insistent need to hold her naked body in his arms and kiss the life out of her, then make sure she was being safe working on this story. Maybe he'd find out at the meeting.

* * * *

Megan leaned back in her desk chair and blew out a breath. She massaged her cheek muscles, stiff from the effort of maintaining a smile and a cheerful expression. The very last thing she wanted to do was give Beau Williams a hint of what was going on. She knew he was, as they say, mission weary, and she didn't need to give him things to worry about when he was thousands of miles away.

But holy hell!

Beau had been wheels-up out of there for scant minutes when the media had exploded with the news of Manny Rushmore's death. It had been the topic of conversation no matter where anyone went. The websites had been jammed with the meager information given out and paragraphs of speculation. Every sports news site had devoted major space to it.

There had been speculation that it might in some way be tied to Tony G's unexpected death, but no one had included data on any of the others that Megan had discovered. There had been a lot of speculation about older athletes pushing themselves beyond their limits and their bodies at last giving out. She was sure the people behind whatever this was were patting themselves on the back and doing everything they could to perpetuate that myth.

She'd opened a massive can of worms with all her questions and phone calls and requests for interviews. With Manny's story front and center every day, no one was willing to discuss anything about anything with her. She was frustrated but did not intend to give up now. Not after the toe-to-toe match she'd had with Gus Kendrick, refusing to turn over her materials and threatening to go someplace else. One thing she could say about her boss—he might be an asshole and missing any people skills, but he had a nose for a hot story and could read a threat to lose it. She had the story, the series, but she knew she'd be under a microscope and if she didn't deliver, she could kiss her career goodbye.

If the past ten days had been any indication, she was pulling someone's string. No doubt about it. First there had been the texts to her cell phone, one each day for three days.

There's no story here. Move on.

Don't be so nosy or you might lose your nose.

She'd almost chuckled at that one—it sounded so much like an old-time gangster movie. But then she'd remembered this was real.

Be very careful. Accidents happen all the time.

She couldn't imagine anyone doing anything to her. Too many people would ask questions, and Kendrick would put a real bloodhound on the story. And while she'd brushed off the first two, by the time the third had showed up, she was curious. She'd typed in *Not to me* and hit Send.

Unable to send flashed at her on the screen.

What the hell? She'd tried again, with the same result. Okay, so whoever this joker was he was blocking her. If she got another text, she'd figure out what to do.

She'd tried calling Jason Aponte, but his office had said he was just accepting the most urgent calls for the moment. Was there something someone else could help her with? She'd left her name, but she had little expectation of hearing from him. She was sure he and Barry and whoever else was involved were tied up with everything relating to Manny Rushmore.

In the morning, she conducted two telephone interviews with athletes in other locations. Her budget wouldn't stretch to cover her flying all over the country — or the world — so she'd managed to set these up long distance. One was a Skype call, one a Facetime. Neither had been as productive as she'd like.

They both told her if she wanted any further contact to go through their agent and gave her the number. She'd had the feeling, though, that her questions made them nervous. She wondered if she'd get the same reaction from any others she tried to contact.

She hadn't had any texts since the last one, but she figured maybe they thought they'd scared her off. Would they know about the recent calls she'd made?

She had some errands to run and stopped for lunch at a busy café that had Internet service She was lucky to score a booth in the back so she could eat and do some additional research. There was little commonality in the agents so she was working on the attorney angle. *How do I find out who represents these people?*

When her number was called for her order, she lowered the lid on her laptop and went to pick up her food. She was sure it would be safe for a few minutes and, after all, it was in a booth tucked out of the way. But when she returned, the computer was gone and a note left in its place, written in red ink.

The next time it could be you who disappears.

She looked around, panicked, her heart beating a sudden, loud tattoo.

"Did you see anyone come near my booth?"

She asked the question of the people seated at the closest table, but they just shook their heads and went back to eating their lunch. She raised her voice, hoping to be heard over the general bubbling of conversation.

"Anyone see someone take something from this booth? Anyone at all?" When no one answered her, she shouted the words, hearing a touch of hysteria in her voice. "Please. Anyone? Did you all have your eyes closed? Damn it. Someone took my laptop."

Arnie Something—or—other who owned the place came over from behind the counter and took hold of her arm.

"You need to stop shouting. Please. You're disturbing the customers."

Megan yanked her arm away. "Someone in this damn place stole my laptop right from this booth, you're damn right I'm shouting."

"No one in here would steal anything. This is not a place where people like that come to eat."

"People like *that* eat anywhere," she snapped. "We need to call the police."

And didn't that just turn into a three-ring circus, Arnie protesting, even threatening and the customers watching with avid curiosity. It seemed to take forever until a uniformed cop showed up. He took statements from her, from Arnie and from anyone looking for their five minutes of fame, but it was a useless exercise. Everyone had been so engrossed in themselves and the people they were with that no one had paid the slightest attention to her booth.

At last, frustrated, she thanked the cop for showing up and asked for a copy of the report so she could file with her insurance company. She was still riding the wave of anger when she bought a new computer and took it home to set up. It wasn't until she was sitting at her desk, downloading everything from her Cloud — *and thank the lord for that* — that the deadly meaning of the message hit her.

The next time it could be you who disappears.

Her hands began to shake enough that she had to curl them into fists and dig her nails in her palms to stop it.

Breathe. Deep breaths.

She finally stopped shaking, but the sudden reality of fear, of the cesspool she could be digging into, didn't leave her. She had turned back to setting up her laptop when her phone chimed with an incoming text. She smiled when she read it.

Catching an overnight flight. Home tomorrow. Will text what time.

Tomorrow! Yes!

Pick you up at the ranch?

Of course!

Although she was sure he'd be in macho male protective mode, she was glad that Beau was coming home. Pictures of them together flashed through her mind, and they reminded her not just of the wild sex they indulged in—it was the way they *got* each other. Understood each other on an elemental level. She could be herself with him, her feisty, sometimes aggressive, confident self without worrying that she was infringing on his masculinity. She'd battled that with most of the men she dated.

But Beau was different. Maybe it was because as a Delta Force soldier nothing threatened his masculinity or his self-confidence. He'd seen and done it all and was still alive to talk about it—or not, since so much of it was secret.

And the sex? Beyond off the charts. He took her to places in bed she'd never dreamed of and made her feel as though she was the only female in the world. Every night since he'd been gone, she'd had the same dream—a naked Beau flat on his back in her bed, one hand fisted around his cock, another cupping his balls while she licked the purple head of his shaft and stroked him to completion. The pulse in her sex set up a hard throbbing at the thought of being naked with him again, of doing just that. Her nipples tingled, eager for his mouth. With an effort, she shut down the erotic fantasy that began to play out in her mind.

And everything else aside, she'd be damn glad to have Beau back with her. He'd be able to help her make sense of all the information she'd been collecting.

And be my bodyguard, too.

She hadn't thought in this job she'd ever need one, but with everything boiling out there and people threatening her, the situation had changed.

She chewed on her fingernail for a moment while she reread Beau's text. Then she pulled up a number on her speed dial. Maybe she could take care of two things at once.

Chapter Eleven

It was Friday morning by the time they landed in San Antonio. Just like the other times when they arrived in the city closest to Slade's ranch, Teo Rivera picked them up in the ranch's shiny black helicopter. But this time they landed at Fort Sam Houston, rather than the civilian airport. Slade had worked his magic to get permission for the helo to land there on an army facility, no doubt because of the success of their recent mission. The team piled into the bird with their duffels and Teo ferried them the short trip to the ranch.

When they landed, the team deferred to Slade, their leader and a new bridegroom, whose wife was waiting for him in the yard, the wind from the rotors blowing her hair and the soft skirt she was wearing. Beau, who was right behind, had paid no attention to the landing whatsoever. He had texted Megan their approximate arrival time, but she hadn't replied and he wondered what the hell that was all about.

Then he jumped from the helo, looked up and there she was, the sexy woman with streaky blonde hair who pushed all his buttons. He forgot about Marc and Trey, who'd sat behind him in the cabin, Teo shutting down the bird, Slade and Kari wrapped in each other. Forgot he was still in dirty fatigues. Forgot everything but the vision standing in front of him. He dropped his duffel, gathered her into his arms and kissed her as if his life depended on it.

And maybe it did.

Her mouth was hot and welcoming and he thrust his tongue into it as deep as he could. *God!* She tasted like every kind of sin. His cock swelled and pushed against the fabric of his cammies, demanding attention. It wanted her mouth, too, and Beau didn't blame it. He thrust his fingers into her hair, capturing her head and holding it still while he plundered her mouth. He broke the contact only when he needed to breathe. When he lifted his head just a bare fraction, he saw the same heat in her eyes he knew was alive in his.

"Let's go home." He murmured the words against her lips.

"I vote for that."

A sound pierced his consciousness, one he became aware of when the wolf whistles Trey and Marc were directing at them got through to him.

"Pay no attention," he told Megan. "They're just jealous. Can we go now?"

"Should we say goodbye to Kari and Slade?"

He turned his head sideways and scanned the yard. "I believe they have business elsewhere. They're gone."

"Then so are we."

Megan waved as he pulled her toward her car and threw his duffel in the back seat while she climbed in under the wheel.

"It's a damn good thing you have a console in this car," he told her as she pulled out onto the two-lane highway.

"Yeah? And why is that?"

"Keeps me from climbing all over you while you're driving and maybe running us into a ditch."

She laughed and the sound was sweet music to his ears.

"A little horny, are we?"

"Babe, I am way past horny. Way past needy. Can you say desperate?"

She glanced at him, a quick flick of her eyes. "Beau, is there something going on here I should know about? Something that happened on this mission to make you so frantic?"

How do I say this without scaring her off and without her thinking I'm giving her a line? Without ever having said anything, they both knew this was more than a passing relationship, but they hadn't given it any form yet. He'd wondered more than once if the wedding bouquet she'd caught was still alive and sitting in her living room. And what she thought when she looked at it. He was equal parts excited and frightened when he thought of the possibilities.

"There's not much time to think out there in Noplace," he began in a slow voice. "It's all about the job. The mission. But—"

"But?" she urged.

"But in the very few minutes I had to myself, I kept thinking about you, and wondering if you missed me. And if things between us would still be good when I got back. And that after all these years, at last I had found someone I want more than a hot fuck and a quick goodbye with."

Now it was her turn to be silent.

"Megan?" Uncertainty crept into his voice. "Want to forget I said that?"

"No." Her mouth curved into that sexy smile of hers. "No, I'm thinking I wonder what I could possibly have that would put that in your brain."

He ran his fingers along her arm. "When we get home, I'm going to tell you, then I'm going to show you, if it takes all night."

"All night, huh?" Another smile.

"You know it." And he was going to ask her for chapter and verse about Manny Rushmore, what she'd found out and what was happening with her series. And if anyone was giving her a hard time.

Megan had so many conflicting emotions churning around inside her she wasn't sure if she could control them all. Fear for her situation with the story. Need for Beau. Confusion about the actual status of their relationship. But right then, hot desire swirled through her body, stiffening her nipples and soaking her panties. She couldn't wait to get home and get naked with him, then figure out how to keep him from locking her in a safe room until the whole dying athletes thing was resolved.

One thought kept chasing through her mind, a thought she squashed in case she was building herself up for a letdown.

Is this my forever, at last?

They had just made it inside the townhouse when he pulled her into his arms and pressed his mouth to hers.

If she'd thought the kiss at the ranch had been hot, that was nothing compared to this. Incendiary to the ultimate level. His tongue was a hot, wet flame probing her mouth, licking every inner surface, and his teeth scraped against her tongue.

His body was hard against hers and the swollen thickness of his cock pressed into the soft flesh of her belly. When he slid his hands down her back to cup the cheeks of her ass, pulling her against him, she wrapped her legs around his waist and pulled herself close to him so his shaft was imprinting itself on her sex.

"Wait!" He tore his mouth away from hers.

"Wait?" She blinked, confused. "For what?"

"For us to get our clothes off. I want to lick every inch of your naked body, fuck you blind then do it all over again."

"God, Beau. Let me catch my breath a sec." She tried to loosen his grip on her.

"No breath catching." He did back up and drop his arms, however, but just so he could pull her short-sleeved sweater over her head. His gaze dropped to the swell of her breasts and he leaned forward a little, tracing the contour with his tongue.

A shiver skated over her skin and she dug her fingers into his upper arms to hold herself steady. She started to unbutton his shirt, but he brushed her hands away.

"You first. If I don't get you naked in ten seconds, I might lose my mind."

She wanted to protest and tell him she needed to see him in all his magnificent flesh, too, but he was already tugging at the rest of her clothes. She kicked off her flats just as he tugged down the zipper on her jeans and yanked them off, along with her bikini panties.

He just stood there for a long moment, staring at her, his eyes eating up every inch of her naked flesh. She was stunned to see his hands shaking as he ran them over her shoulders, down her arms, over to her breasts, which he cupped in his warm palms. His gaze locked with hers as he whispered his thumbs over her nipples, now hard and pebbled with desire.

"Naked," she whispered. "You. Now."

And that fast he was out of his clothes and his boots and stood before her, tall and proud, his body ridged with muscle, his cock full and swollen. They stood there in the foyer in the midst of their discarded clothing, naked, and the lust was so strong Megan could smell it.

"I'm not doing this standing here in the foyer," Beau told her, and swept her up in his arms.

With long strides, he carried her into the bedroom, yanked back the covers on the bed and sat her on the edge. Then he knelt in front of her, a faint trembling in his hands as he nudged her legs apart, sliding his thumbs up her inner thighs until he reached the lips of her sex. He touched the lips with his thumbs, pressing them open enough so when he lowered his head, he could press that very educated tongue to her hot, greedy flesh.

At the first contact, her inner walls clenched, the spasm rocketing through her. He did it again but then, when she tried to open her legs even wider for him, he rose and lifted her, placing her full on the bed with her head on the pillows. Then he positioned himself between her legs and lowered his head to take her mouth in a greedy, soul searing kiss. She could taste herself on his tongue, the intimacy of it setting every nerve ending on fire and sending spasms of need through her body.

Beau took his time exploring her body, kissing every inch of it just as he'd said. He sucked her nipples, grazing them with his teeth then soothing them with his tongue. He molded his fingers to her breasts, squeezing them, while he kissed his way down to her navel and drew circles in the indentation with the tip of his tongue.

Megan threaded her fingers through his hair, twisting it to give her a firmer hold and attempting to push his head down even farther.

"I thought you said you were in a hurry," she breathed, her body screaming to feel him inside her.

"I was," he murmured against her hip, "but now I'm afraid if I rush things, I'll miss something. My fantasies are what kept me sane on this last mission."

"Is that right?" With a tremendous effort of will, she managed to push him off her body and onto his back so she could kneel beside him.

"What—" He tried to rise, but she pushed him back.

"My turn. I've been needy and greedy, too. And I want this to last longer than five minutes."

She closed her fingers around his very erect cock, giving it a gentle squeeze and sliding her hand up and down in one slow stroke then another.

"Megan." Her name was like a plea. "What are you doing?"

She wet her lips and smiled at him. "I thought that was obvious. I'm satisfying a need that's crept into my dreams every night while you've been gone. You think men are the only ones who have sexual fantasies?"

His lips curled in a sensuous smile. "You have dreams about me, Megs? Hot dreams?"

She nodded.

"Wet dreams?" he persisted, his voice ragged with need.

Again she dipped her head.

"Tell me about it." His laugh had a rough edge. "But make it quick because when you touch me, my self-control goes all to hell."

She moved her hand faster and, as she increased the pace, she slipped the other hand between his thighs, cupping his balls in their velvety sac, curling her fingers in a gentle squeeze.

"Jesus!" The word whispered from his mouth.

Heat flamed in his eyes, a flare of need, and she leaned down to swipe her tongue across the soft skin on the head of his dick. He jumped when she did it, so she did it again, this time eliciting a long, deep groan from him. Then, inhaling a deep breath, she opened her mouth and took him inside.

Oh, God!

The skin was so soft over the hard length of him, and his taste was all male, an aphrodisiac that made her sex throb, her nipples tingle and every part of her body ache to take him inside her. She set up a steady rhythm, her mouth and her hand working in cadence to draw out the maximum pleasure for him. She wound the strands of her hair around his fingers, gripping them and moving her head this way and that to show him how she needed to adjust her mouth.

She twisted her tongue around him so she could lick him with each up and down movement. More groans, and a slight lift of the hips to urge her to take him deeper. She obliged, as turned on by the whole process as he was. She inhaled the masculine scent of him, reveled in his taste and absorbed the feel of him.

"Megan!" His voice was raspy. "God. Sweet Jesus."

She knew he was close by the way he gripped her hair harder and pushed himself up toward her mouth. She breathed hard through her nose, increasing her pace and gripping him tighter.

Then he exploded, his cum shooting into her mouth, filling it, coating her tongue and the inside of her cheeks. She squeezed his balls as she pumped harder, drawing every last drop from him. At last, when she was sure he was depleted, she slid her mouth from his cock and moved her hands away.

Beau loosened his fingers in her hair, smoothing the strands against her head. She smiled at him, licking her lips, and he groaned again.

"Have mercy, woman. When you do that, my dick wants to fuck you, and right now it's all out of energy."

She bent over him and pressed her mouth to his.

"Now we shared our tastes together. Blended. Right?"

He nodded and something flashed in his eyes, a flare of possession, but then it was gone almost as soon as it appeared.

She rested her head on his chest, waiting for him to recover, to get his breath back. Impish, she licked the sweat from his chest then trailed her tongue over his nipples.

"Think you'll get me going again so soon?" he asked, stroking his hand up and down her arm.

"I don't know. Think you've got what it takes?"

Before she could blink, he'd pushed himself upright and turned her so she was flat on her back. His face was so close she could feel his breath on her cheeks and smell their combined scent on his lips.

"Oh, I've it and more, babe. You just teased the tiger."

He pulled her arms over her head, braceleting her wrists with the fingers of one hand while he trailed the other along her cheek. Just a whisper of a touch that woke any nerves still not screaming for attention. He palmed her breasts, giving them each a gentle squeeze before turning his attention to her nipples, pinching each one to the sting of pain. But the pain, instead of turning her off, sent streaks of heat straight to her dripping sex, already hungry for his fingers, his tongue, his shaft.

And all the time he had his gaze locked with hers, reading the truth of her in her eyes. From the first time they met, she'd never been able to hide any part of herself from him. She didn't know what that meant for their future, but for right now the reward of laying herself bare to him was worth it.

By the time he finished teasing her nipples, they were so sensitive just the puff of air when he blew on them was enough to make them harden even more. It was almost impossible for her to lie still as he moved his mouth from her breasts to her belly, picking up where he'd left off before. Every touch of his lips, every lick of his tongue made the need in her grow stronger and hotter.

She wanted to squeeze her thighs together to control the pulse beating so hard and strong inside her, but Beau was now lying between them as he worked his way down to her pussy. His tongue was like a thin flame dancing over her skin, lighting her nerve endings wherever it handed.

By the time he worked his way down to her thighs, he had to release her wrists. When she tried to reach down for him, he just growled at her.

"Hands over your head and keep them there."

A heady thrill of sexual awareness rocketed through her. This was the first time she had seen this masterful side of Beau and it excited her. She reached over her head and linked her fingers to keep her hands in place.

Beau trailed tiny kisses over her belly down to her mound, where he peppered little bites over the curve of her skin. He took so long to get to the good part she wanted to scream at him to hurry, hurry, hurry. She wanted his hot, wet tongue in her slit, lapping at the sensitive skin and swirling around her throbbing clit. She wanted him to thrust it inside her and fuck her with it until she screamed from the pleasure of her orgasm.

And he knew it, damn him, which was why he was taking his good old sweet time.

He blew a soft stream of air on her sex before closing his teeth on her swollen nub in a gentle nip.

"Aahhh."

The moan of pleasure wafted from her throat. She tried to press herself against his mouth, a silent plea to do more, faster. But Beau pressed his arms on her thighs to immobilize her while he took his pleasure. The assault on her senses continued as he licked every inch of her slit before thrusting his tongue inside. Her swollen flesh clamped down on it, riding the hunger and need bubbling up inside her. With her hands clenched together over her head, she was at his mercy and he took full advantage of it. Everything he did with his educated tongue made her hotter, greedier, more desperate for release.

It hit her without warning, rising up from deep in her body, her inner walls clenching around his tongue over and over as the orgasm grabbed her. She pressed her thighs against his shoulders to anchor herself, riding out the release until the tremors eased, leaving her sweating and — unbelievably — still wanting more. Wanting Beau. Inside her.

"Now," she pleaded, her voice raspy with need.

"Not yet." He looked up at her from his place between her thighs, a dirty grin on his face. "I'm not done yet. Come on. One more."

"With you inside me," she pleaded.

"Soon," he promised. "After you give me one more here."

No matter how she protested, he went back to work on her with the same hunger. He used his mouth and fingers, paying careful attention to the inflamed flesh of her outer lips and toying with her now ultrasensitive clit. When he slid two fingers inside her, she tried hard to push herself down on them, but he still held her in place with his body.

She wanted to scream in frustration, even as she strained to reach that pinnacle again. Then, as he curled his fingers inside her hot pussy, touching *that* spot, there it was, her body shuddering as the tremors grabbed her. She rode his fingers, pushing herself down on them as best she could until the last one faded.

She was just catching her breath when Beau levered himself upon his knees, eased her arms back down to her sides and took her mouth in a hot kiss.

"Now," he told her.

He reached into the nightstand drawer for one of the condoms he kept there and rolled it on. She was mildly surprised to see his cock already recovered and swollen, thick and heavy. He lifted her legs and pressed them back so every bit of her was exposed to him. The orgasms had taken the edge off a little, but her need for him was still so strong.

He stopped for a moment, his gaze locked with hers, the head of his cock at the entrance to her sex, every muscle in his body rigid with the strain of control. Then, with one swift stroke, he thrust inside her. He filled every inch of her, his thickness pressing hard into her sensitive inner muscles.

His eyes never leaving hers, he moved with a rhythm already so familiar to her. In, out. In, out. Slow at first then faster, until her entire body rocked with every movement. She climbed the slope with him, the orgasm driving up from deep within her body. He shifted her until her legs were over his shoulders, opening her to him even more.

He increased the tempo, driving into her harder and harder and her entire body was focused on the feel of his thick shaft in her hot sex. Everything else faded away, until—until—

Yes! There it was! The explosion roaring up from deep inside her, shaking her, blotting out everything except this man, this moment and the sensations racing through her.

Megan had no idea how long it went on, but at some point the shudders subsided and their bodies were limp. Beau eased her legs down but still stayed connected to her, their sweat-slicked bodies glued together. She didn't know whose heart was pounding so hard or whose breath was making that rough sound as they fought to draw air into their lungs.

At last, he lifted his head and placed a kiss on her lips that was so gentle she wanted to cry. They'd had plenty of sex since the night they'd met, but this was somehow different. *Special.* There was a connection that went beyond the physical, one she didn't want to think too

much about right now. Instead, she just let herself enjoy
how good they were together.

Chapter Twelve

Megan wanted to prepare dinner, a sort of welcome home feast, but Beau said no deal.

"I didn't wear you out enough?" He grinned, kissing her forehead. He was still trying to sort out what his real feelings were for her and how to handle them. For the first time in his adult life, he had allowed himself to care for someone — care with every part of himself — and it scared the shit out of him. Not including, of course, the fact he had no idea of the depth of her feelings.

"I think I might have enough energy left over to cook," she teased.

"Let's save it. You've used up enough already. I vote for pizza and beer."

After she'd placed the order, they showered, doing their best to stick one hundred percent to soaping and rinsing each other. Downstairs, as he passed through the living room, he noticed the bridal bouquet was still hanging in there. Was that some kind of signal?

Because he might be able to deal with the R word — relationship — but the W word — wedding — still scared the crap out of him.

Better figure it out pretty soon. She won't wait forever.

And isn't that just the damn truth.

But first they had to deal with her current situation.

When the food and drinks arrived, they carried it out back to catch the last rays of the sun and the early evening breeze. While they ate, she gave him all the details on everything that had happened while he was gone. He absorbed everything she told him, nodding now and then, until she got to the threats and the stolen computer.

"I don't think I like any of this." Beau took a swallow of beer and set the bottle back on the table. Megan's recounting of events had given him a very unsettled feeling. "And I don't think you should be running around out there by yourself."

"You can run around with me while you're home," she pointed out. "I can't back off from this story, Beau, not when it's getting bigger by the day."

"I'm home for ten days again," he reminded her. "I wish it was more so I could protect you."

Yeah, protect her. Right. Bad choice of words where Megan's concerned.

Maybe he could lock her in a closet when he had to leave, although if Slade's request for reassignment to Fort Sam came through, he might be able to work things out.

"Then we'll just have to figure out how to wrap it up in that time."

"Megan, I don't like that business with the texts. It's obvious they blocked you from texting back. It could be because they were dumb enough to use their own phones, but my best guess would be they used burners. It means we're not dealing with your average asshole here."

"But the texts have stopped," she reminded him. "I haven't had one in more than a week now."

"Because they upped their game. They stole your laptop and left you a stronger message. I'm not happy with this at all."

"My computer is password protected."

"First of all, I don't think they give a rat's ass about what was on your hard drive. Or even your Cloud, assuming they could hack your password." Beau took a swallow of beer before continuing. "My best guess is they were just trying to send a message, the one they left you. That you could be gone in a blink of an eye without anyone even seeing what happened."

For a moment, panic flashed in her eyes as she caught the reality of what he said. Then it was gone and she was hard-assed Megan again.

"I promise to be careful."

Beau started to say something then shook his head and seemed to swallowed whatever it was. "We'd better find the answers in a hurry, then."

"Isn't that what we're trying to do?" She sat back, took a bite of pizza and chewed, a thoughtful expression on her face. "I know there's something we're missing. Something everyone is missing, but I'm damned if I can figure out what it is."

He was just as baffled as she was. On the long plane ride overseas and back he had turned everything over in his mind, again and again. The one conclusion he could come to was that each of the athletes was taking something, but what the hell was it? What could they have taken that did not show up on an autopsy?

"There's no other reasonable explanation for what's happening," he told Megan as he shared his thoughts with her. He blew out a breath. "Especially with Manny. Damn! His death shocked me more than anyone's, I think."

"I know. Me, too." She sighed. "Everyone's all over that one, too."

"Well, you pulled someone's tail with all your questions. I'm sure they did an autopsy on him, right?"

She nodded. "I was thinking I would ask Kari to see if she could get a copy for me. In Bexar County, they're a matter of public record. I could request one myself, but since I have no idea who is looking over my shoulder, I'd rather not be that visible about it."

"Good idea. Let's call her and ask." He reached across the table for one of her hands. "Then we're going to make a list of everyone involved with all of these athletes. What we don't know yet we'll figure out how to get. And we'll make a plan to get to the bottom of this. Remember, no one's connecting all the dots except us."

"Because I am looking at it from a different angle. If I went to the police with what I know right now they'd tell me I should be writing movies, because this was too unrealistic."

"Then we have to find something to convince them. Now, go on. Call Kari. See what she says."

"I'm sure she's busy welcoming Slade home," Megan joked.

"You can always leave a message on her cell, or I can call his. They have to get out of bed sometime."

* * * *

"I wanted to meet here rather than the office," Kari said, "because we didn't need anyone asking questions at this point."

It was the following evening and they were seated at the kitchen table at the ranch. Slade had passed out cold drinks for everyone and told them Teo was barbecuing dinner.

"I'm just grateful you were willing to do this," Megan told her. And she was. Very much so. It would be a huge break if there was something here that they could get their teeth into. They very much needed something, because right now all she had was an accumulation of facts and a lot of suppositions.

"You piqued my interest. If there is something here everyone is missing, we need to find it. I made copies for all of us." Kari handed out a folder to everyone.

While she had taken the day off yesterday to welcome Slade home, she'd still taken their phone call. Today, when she was back at work, she'd texted Megan that she had the autopsy report and they should all meet at the ranch around six.

Slade looked up from his folder. "How about taking us through this, Kari?"

"Sure. I spoke with Ben Stokes, the medical examiner, and asked him a lot of questions so let me pull up my notes." She tapped her tablet to bring it to life.

"Did he ask you why you were asking for this?" Beau asked.

"He was curious, but he was also a big fan of both Manny Rushmore and Tony G and was pissed off that no one was looking beyond the obvious cause of death, a heart attack. He asked to be kept in the loop."

"No problem," Megan agreed, "once we have something. Right now it's all just a big bunch of speculation."

"Well, let me go over this and tell you what he said." She swiped her finger on the screen. "They didn't find any of the usual symptoms of a heart attack — blocked arteries or evidence of ventricular irregularity. I didn't know what that was, either," she added as Beau opened his mouth. "Ben explained it to me. It's when the electrical system to the heart malfunctions. Blood flow to the brain can be drastically reduced and death can follow in an instant."

"Does he think that's what happened with Manny?" Beau wanted to know.

Kari nodded. "He thinks that's a distinct possibility." She swiped the screen again, then turned to the second page in the folder. "Take a look at the lab analysis. They tested for everything, including PEDs, although there is no prior evidence of him taking them."

"So, they didn't find a thing?" Megan persisted.

"Well, yes and no."

Beau frowned. "What does that mean?"

"It means he found one thing that is a sort of an anomaly that might or might not be something."

Slade burst out laughing. "Way to beat about the bush. Okay, what's a maybe, maybe here?"

"They found a high concentration of caffeine in his system. There's a question of how he got it. Some energy drinks were found in his house, but not enough to do that kind of damage unless he drank them all at once."

Beau studied the report in front of him. "Was there anything else? Did he drink a lot of coffee? Other caffeinated drinks?"

"That's still being investigated," Kari told him. "Julia's done her best to answer questions, but she's pretty much of a mess. The cops collected everything from the house that might be a source, including the generic meds in his medicine cabinet. It's going to take a while to test them all, though." She paused. "Beau, you're turning into a first-class assistant here."

He closed the folder and with a casual movement draped an arm around Megan. Slade give him an odd but knowing look. *The hell with it.* If by rare chance — and in his life anything like this was rare — this turned out to be something beyond a good time, he wanted his team to know he was establishing his claim.

Claim? Really, you Neanderthal?

"I want to give Megan any help I can. I think she needs to tell you how far she's gone in her research and some of the things that have happened as a result of that."

"Beau." She turned her head to look at him, "I don't know —"

"Babe, Kari's the law. She needs to be aware of this."

"But what if I'm wrong?"

He shook his head. "My gut tells me you're not, and when Kari hears what you have to say, she'll agree with me."

Kari looked at them both with a quizzical expression on her face. "Tell me what?"

"Go on." Beau squeezed Megan's shoulder. "See what she says."

By the time Megan had finished explaining about her research and the results and the threats she'd been receiving, Kari had gone from interested to concerned to angry.

"Megan, you're putting yourself in a lot of danger. If what you suspect is true, there have to be some powerful people behind this."

Beau was glad to hear Kari say that. "That's what I keep telling her. I know her cell number is out there so anyone can get it, but she was blocked from replying. Someone had her laptop stolen, in such a way that it escaped everyone in the restaurant."

Kari nodded. "And I say again, they aren't penny ante people."

"I don't know, Kari." She nibbled her lower lip. "I thought one of those threats sounded like something out of a bad movie."

"That could have been deliberate," Beau pointed out.

Kari nodded. "Plus whoever did this blocked you. That means he is either using burner phones or the dark web to get an untraceable account, or any number of things. All of which point to more than some casual idiot deciding to flex his muscle."

"And swiping your laptop?" This from Slade. "That was done by someone who knew what he was doing, not by some street thief who saw a good thing. It's all part of the same plan to scare you off."

"Well, it didn't work," she told them. "I'm not giving up on this. There's something very wrong here and it's produced incidents even on an international level. Athletes from places like Greece and England and Australia. And if they aren't stopped, who knows how many other athletes will die from whatever this is."

Beau chose his next words with great care. He didn't want her thinking he had no confidence in her, but he was damn concerned for her safety. "I agree with you, but maybe it's time for you to take a step back and let the people who do this for a living take over."

"Are you kidding?" She glared at him. "Do you see anyone investigating now?" She looked at Kari. "Is there any kind of inquiry going on into this? Anyone looking past what seems to be the obvious?"

Beau hoped Kari would tell her at least someone was looking into it, but the prosecutor shook her head.

"Despite what the four of us think, there's no real evidence for them to do so. Beau, if Megan hadn't gotten the idea in the first place and started digging, we'd all be sitting here writing Manny Rushmore's death off as a very sad event."

Damn it. She's right.

"What if Megan takes everything she has to the appropriate person and lays her case out for them?"

Kari shook her head again. "They'd tell her it's all supposition and her theory is farfetched. First of all, there is no single thing tying them together. No single sport. Not even a single agent."

"But!" Megan leaned forward in her chair. "Some of them have the same attorney. Barry Maier."

Slade lifted an eyebrow. "The Bear?"

Kari burst out laughing. "Whoever gave him that nickname has him pegged, for sure."

"You know Barry?" Beau asked.

"Everyone knows Barry. He's a brilliant attorney with the personality of a wounded tiger and all the finesse of yesterday's garbage."

Beau chuckled. "That's him all right. Like a bear with a thorn in his paw."

Kari's face lost every trace of humor. "Megan, I can't see Barry getting himself mixed up in something illegal. That's not his style, but on the off chance that he is, be very, very careful. He'll destroy you before he has his second cup of coffee. How did you get this information, anyway?"

"I connected most of them to him just by digging through articles and things. But I'll bet if I contacted the families of other athletes who died, they'd —"

Kari held up her hand. "Don't even go there. Those families could be very touchy. They could also contact Barry to get you off their backs and all hell could break loose."

Beau was beginning to wonder what it would take to rein Megan in and still help her with her story. "I second that."

Megan shrugged. "I can't do nothing. Who knows how many more will die? And for what? A few more months of playing time?"

Kari tapped her tablet and brought up a blank page. "Let me see what I can do on my end. I can contact the medical examiners in other cities and ask for autopsy reports, if there are any."

"Can you do that?" Megan asked. "Without anyone knowing?"

"Kip Reyes lets his prosecutors pretty much run their own ships, as long we don't get in trouble and don't make waves. I'll just fly well under the radar."

Beau relaxed a fraction at her words. His problem would be keeping Megan from haring off on her own in twenty different directions while she waited for the reports.

"Thanks," he told Kari. "That would be a big help."

"I can also do some under the radar research on Barry. And I can't rush it," she added, when Megan leaned forward. "Just…let me see what I can do."

Beau picked up Megan's hand and gave it a gentle squeeze. Even in that slight contact, he could feel the tension running through her. He lifted it and placed a gentle kiss on her knuckles. Slade looked at him then exchanged a glance with his wife.

Fuck it, he thought. For the first time in his life he wasn't running away from a woman. He just hoped he could keep this woman safe.

* * * *

He was in Java Joe's again, facing Felix across the booth, doing his best to get a handle on his rage. He hadn't liked getting the phone call that demanded his presence at once. In point of fact, he didn't like anyone doing the demanding except himself.

"You're falling down on the job." Felix said the words in a cold, even tone of voice.

"I'm not falling down on anything," the man growled. "If you didn't make so many fucking miscalculations, we wouldn't be in this spot."

"Will you get your shit together?" Felix leaned toward him. "And for the love of God, keep your voice down. We don't want to broadcast this conversation to everyone here."

The man looked around. "As if anyone in this rat hole would even understand what we're saying."

They had chosen this place, whose name was the fanciest thing about it, because it was a grungy coffee shop, not well lit, that catered to the lower level of the population. He wasn't even sure many of them understood English.

"We're not taking any chances." Felix took a slow sip of his coffee and stared at his companion. "What now?"

"What now? What now?" The man had to reach for his control to keep from shouting. "It's that fucking bitch, damn it."

"You said you had it under control and I believed you," Felix reminded him in a cool voice. "That's your responsibility. What's the problem?"

The man closed his hands into fists. "We have to step up our game. She isn't that easy to scare off."

"Well, of course she's not." Felix shook his head. "Did you think she got where she is by being timid?"

"Now she's got that fucking asshole soldier boy hanging around again, it won't be that easy to get to her."

"I remind you that so-called 'soldier boy' is a member of Delta Force and one of the most dangerous, lethal men in the world. You should have tried harder before he came back."

The man wanted to punch something and he'd have preferred it be Felix's face. "No one is that indestructible. I'll find a way around him."

"Yeah." Felix snorted. "Good luck to that. Even you can't neutralize a Delta."

The man had to force himself to take a deep breath. He had to find some measure of control here or his pot of gold was going to disappear before he ever got to spend it.

"He doesn't scare me. But I need to get her away from him long enough to send another message. One she'll pay attention to this time."

"You have to know enough people with the skills we need."

"I said I'd take care of it." The man had to restrain himself from shouting.

"Then do it, and soon."

The man leaned toward him across the table. "How close are we to final success with this, anyway? If we end up with any more bodies, we'll have to shelve the whole thing."

"No!" Now it was Felix's turn to fight for control. "We are not doing that, not with everything we've put into it."

The two men stared at each other for a long moment.

"Then you'd better make sure the next batch is perfect."

"And *you'd* better take care of that nosy Welles bitch."

Chapter Thirteen

"Kari just called."

Megan set her cell phone on the counter just as Beau came into the kitchen. She turned to hand him a mug of coffee.

"Yeah?" He lifted an eyebrow. "Did she come up with anything yet? We just discussed this two days ago."

"Believe it or not, yes. Not every body was autopsied, but of those that were, the medical examiners were happy to fax her copies of the results."

Beau lifted his mug and took a swallow of the hot liquid. "That was fast."

Megan grinned. "I think our girl Kari has a way with her that few people can refuse."

"I have to agree with you. So what's the deal? Do they want us to come out to the ranch? They fed us last time, so we can bring dinner."

"The fact is, Slade drove her into town today because he had some business to take care of. He's picking her up after work and I invited them to come here." She looked at him. "That was okay, wasn't it?"

He laughed. "Of course. It's your place, isn't it?"

She stared at him for a long moment, the muscles in her stomach tightening.

"I sign the lease, but I kind of think of it as our place when you're in town." She picked up her own mug and turned away from him. "Please tell me if I've presumed too much."

"Hold it."

She barely avoided sloshing her coffee when he grabbed her arm. "What?"

"That didn't come out quite right."

She focused on her mug, not looking at him. "How should it have come out?"

"It shouldn't have come out at all. It was a dumb thing to say and shows that my brain can't get rid of all its bad habits." He pulled her toward him, banding one muscular arm around her waist while with his other hand he cupped her chin, forcing her to look up at him. "I've kind of gotten to think of this as our place, Megs."

Now her stomach did a little polka, half in happiness, half in uncertainty.

"And in plain English, what does that mean?" She had to know. Up until now she'd played by the parameters he'd established the first night they were together — this was fun and temporary. Okay, maybe he was spending all of his leave with her instead of chasing after a variety of women, but he'd been very clear in the beginning that lasting relationships weren't for him.

"But that was when we first met." His voice was low and hot.

"Oh!" She tried to turn away from him, but he held her chin firm in his hand.

"Like I said, that was in the beginning. Things have changed since then." He locked his gaze with hers. "Haven't they?"

She wasn't sure what the right thing to say was. Then she figured, *what the hell. He's asking, right?*

"Y-Yes. I feel like they have. But I didn't want you to feel I was pushing you."

"Megan." The way he said her name sent heat straight to her sex. "I told you I'm not much good at these things, but you can bet that fine little ass of yours they've gone way past being just better." He brushed his tongue over her lips. "I'm finding my way here, sugar. This is all so new to me. I don't want to make a mistake. But yeah, I want to see where this goes. More than anything. Do you?"

"More than I want to admit."

He gave a half hysterical chuckle. "But I have to tell you, it scares the shit out of me."

"Me, too."

They had never gone into details of past relationships or how they'd each gotten to this state in their lives. One of these nights, if they both wanted to move forward, they'd have to get to that. But for right now this was good enough for her.

"So what are the plans for *our* condo?" He stressed the word.

It made her smile, as he hoped it would.

"I invited them to dinner. Kari will bring everything with her and we can look it over and see what we can find." She sighed. "But I do have to get to the grocery store. My cupboard's a little bare right now. I know we can get Tex Mex food at almost every restaurant in the area, but I have a couple of recipes that I'm good at, if I do say so myself."

"I think Tex Mex is good just about any time. Let's get to the store now so we have time to fool around later."

Megan threw back her head and laughed. "Our fooling around time may be limited. I have two short pieces to write for Kendrick that have to be in today."

"I'll make sure you get them done." He pressed her to his body, tight enough that she could feel the swollen length of his cock. Damn, the thing always seemed to be ready where she was concerned.

"Then we'd better take care of business right away."

Megan's townhouse was located not too far from downtown San Antonio and, as such, she had her pick of grocery stores offering the things she need for that night's dinner. Because she knew where she was going today, they agreed she would drive.

"I could kind of get used to having a chauffeur," he teased, as they pulled out of the complex.

"Yeah? Maybe I should charge you," she teased in return.

"And maybe I could pay you in orgasms."

They were still joking when she turned onto the street where the store she wanted was located and pulled up to the curb. She opened the door to get out, and without warning, a car came screeching down the street. Beau grabbed her arm and hauled her over the console just as the speeding car banged into her door, tearing it from the car.

"Son of a fucking bitch!" Beau spat the words out. "You okay, Megan?"

For a very long moment, she couldn't breathe. Then she pushed herself to a sitting position and brushed her hair off her face with a shaking hand.

"W-what was that?"

"Some fucker just tried to kill you. That's what it was."

She looked at where her door should be and started to shake. She opened her mouth to say something, but nothing came out.

Beau tugged her toward him, as much as he could with the console in the way.

"It's okay, Megs. You're okay. The car is fixable and you're safe."

She pulled in a deep breath and held it before letting it out on a slow breath. From somewhere she dug out a smile for Beau.

"I'm good. I am. Thanks for pulling me back inside." At least she hadn't fallen apart. She looked past him out of the window. "There's a bunch of people on the sidewalk. It looks like they're talking about this. We need to ask them if they remember anything about the car."

"I'm sure everyone has their own version of what happened, but yeah. Let's do it. And we need to call the cops."

"Why? The car is long gone and we don't even know who it was?"

"If for no other reason than to have a police report for your insurance company. You sure you're okay to get out now?"

"Yes. Let's do it."

People were staring at the car and jabbering to each other around her, all speaking at the same time.

"…just zoomed down the block and…"

"…aimed right for her. I…"

A million witnesses and a million different stories, she thought.

She wanted to cry for her poor car. She'd bought it a mere six months ago. But better the car than her. She saw Beau talking to people on the sidewalk and left it to him while she called the police. She figured one of them questioning people was enough. Otherwise they'd end up getting two different stories from everyone.

He was huddled with a kid against the display window of the store when a radio patrol car pulled up and a uniformed officer got out.

"Someone didn't like your car." He shook his head. "People. They never think of anyone but themselves."

"I have no idea who it was, either. One minute, I was about to get out of the car, the next whoever this was came speeding down the street, smashed into my door and raced off."

"Some yoyo in a big hurry. Or kids showing off for each other. Trying to see how close they can come without hitting."

Megan shook her head. "They missed this time, thank God."

"Did you get a license plate?" he asked.

"Are you kidding? He was gone almost before I realized we'd been hit."

"Not that it matters," he told her, "except, like I said, for the insurance. The best we could charge whoever it is with is reckless driving."

"But he tried to kill me," she protested.

"And he'll deny the whole thing, say he lost control of the wheel for a minute." He shook his head. "I see it all the time. You weren't hit so that's the best we could do."

Beau had walked up while she was talking. "I yanked her back all the way inside so she wouldn't get hit."

"Let me get all the details down, anyway." The cop rubbed the back of his neck. "There's nothing we can do without the driver, but we'll at least send you a report for your insurance company."

"That's what I told her," Beau agreed.

The cop pulled a clipboard out of his car and took a pen from his pocket. For the next ten minutes, they answered his questions while he filled in all the blanks on the report sheet. He took Megan's information and asked her if she had a fax. They could send the report to her that way.

"Yes. And thank you." She heaved a sigh. "I'd better get my cell and call to get the car towed."

"Yes, ma'am." The officer touched the brim of his cap. "Sorry for your trouble. Hope the rest of the day is better for you."

"Me, too." She leaned into Beau. "Me, too. So. Did you get any information from the gawkers?"

He snorted a laugh. "Yeah. Too much. One person said it was a brown sedan, another a black pickup, a third was positive it was white."

"Not that it matters much. You know whoever is behind the death of the athletes hired someone to do this."

"We can't be positive but, yeah," Beau agreed. "I'd say you're right. Especially after the other episodes. You've been contacting all those other athletes and I'm sure that's getting back to whoever this is."

"Barry." She said the name with authority.

"You don't know that for sure."

"So far all roads lead to him. Crap. Okay, I have a body shop that's worked my cars before. Let me call them and get my baby towed."

"Good idea. While you're doing that, I'm calling Slade."

She frowned. "For what?"

"While you were talking to the cop, I was doing business with the kid standing in front of the store." He held his cell phone up to her. On the screen was a picture of the car hitting hers. There was another one that showed most of a license plate.

"Is that the name of the model of that car?" she asked, squinting.

"Sure is. We got lucky." He snorted a laugh. "Of course, it cost me a hundred bucks."

She stared at hm. "You're kidding."

"Nope. Kid drives a hard bargain."

"We should give this to the police," she pointed out. "Call and tell them what we have."

"We will. But that cop all but said this won't be a high priority with them. So I'm sending this to Slade. Maybe his guy can find out who this is, faster than the cops."

She grinned. "His guy."

Beau chuckled. "Yeah, he's got a guy for everything. While you take care of the towing, I'm sending these to him and asking him to have his guy run the plates and make of car. What do you want to do about transportation?"

"While you find us the closest car rental place, I'll call Uber so we can get a ride there. I don't think we'll be doing any grocery shopping today. Do you suppose Slade and Kari would be insulted if we fed them Tex Mex takeout?"

"Not a bit. They'll understand."

"Then let's make our calls."

Chapter Fourteen

The man was doing his best not to have a heart attack, but he was so angry his entire body heated. He'd polished off two of Java Joe's 'Hot Shots' waiting for Felix, but what he wanted most was a double shot of Scotch.

"Okay, what is it now?" Felix slid into the booth opposite him. "You may not remember this, but in addition to our little project, I have to work for a living. I have a job that I'm expected to be at." He paused. "Not to mention paying attention to our little project. So what's got a bug up your ass today?"

"I told you not to do anything stupid." The man ground the words between clenched teeth. "I thought I made it plain that you were to leave Megan Welles alone. That I would take care of her when the time came."

"Yes. And just when is that time? In my opinion you were far too vague about it. You tell me she's after your clients yet you do nothing about it. The more she talks to the athletes, the more danger we're all in. What if they start to question the test program? Or worse yet, want to pull out?"

"Considering how long it's taking you to perfect this," the man sneered, "I'm surprised it hasn't happened already."

"So why the hell can't we get rid of her?" Felix demanded.

"Because, you idiot, the moment you go after her, she gets her reporter's nose twitching and starts digging with her virtual shovel." The man raked his fingers through his hair. "What you did yesterday was incredibly stupid. I don't know who's dumber, you or the cretins you hired. Did we not talk about this?"

Felix narrowed his gaze. "What are you talking about?"

"You fucking know what I'm talking about. The idiots you hired to sideswipe Welles' car when she was getting out of it. Now there's a police report and I'm sure she's pissed as hell. You don't think that Delta Force guy she's with is going to just let this go, either, do you?"

"But I— How did you—"

"Stop." The man held up his hand, palm out. "By the purest chance someone I know was shopping at the specialty grocery store she was headed for and saw the whole thing. They let it drop at dinner, and I almost choked on my food. I know you set that up. Don't try to deny it. I knew last time we talked you weren't going to listen to me."

Felix glared at him. "Something had to be done. They had orders not to kill her, just scare her or better yet, incapacitate her so she can't work on her story."

"And you think that will do the trick? You don't think that will make her even more determined? If so, you aren't half as smart as I thought you were. Even if she ended up in a hospital bed, she's got her damn laptop and cell phone and a determination that's like a disease."

"So, we should, what?" Felix spread his hands. "Just leave her alone and hope she goes away? Meanwhile, the while program is at risk." He glared at the man. "We've been working on this for two years. You chose every one of the test subjects with great care, athletes who would understand the risk but felt the reward was worth the chance. I won't let some reporter bitch torpedo it when the finish line is in sight."

"If you want a guarantee she'll dig harder," the man said, "then keep doing these idiotic things. Megan Welles is a bloodhound. Do you think she'll just forget about almost getting killed when her car was sideswiped? But I can make her go away." The man took another hit of his coffee. "I've known her a long time. The one thing that will distract her from this is a story she thinks is even better."

"You going to manufacture one out of thin air?" Felix's words were edged with sarcasm.

"I don't have to. There's one already brewing, a big scandal about athletes betting against themselves and figuring ways to throw a game or a match so they can win big bucks."

Felix's eyes bugged out. "Shit. Are you serious?"

"I am. I found out about it because one of our clients got caught up in it and is in danger of being thrown out of his sport because of it. I can get her interviews with the commissioners, trainers, a lot of people involved in it just as the story gets ready to break."

"But she still wants to talk to your clients. You can't prevent every interview. What if they sound like they're holding something back? You told me she's a bulldog with a story."

"I'll worry about my fucking clients and you worry about perfecting your formula." He forced himself to slow his breathing. He didn't want to die of a goddamn heart attack, not when he was on the verge of becoming richer than he'd ever imagined. "How close did you say you were?"

"I'm pretty sure this last batch has hit it." His lips curved in a rare smile. "Of course, I can't be one hundred percent positive until we distribute the stuff to your clients and monitor its use. But I have a good feeling about it."

"Your good feeling better be right. We can't afford any more deaths."

Felix's facial muscles tightened in anger. "You don't have to remind me. But we have to keep that Welles bitch off our backs until everything is finalized."

"I'll see what I can do about that, but no more asshole ideas. You stick to your part of this and I'll handle mine. Period."

When the man looked across the table, he could see the hatred glittering in Felix's eyes. So be it. They didn't have to love each other, or even like. They just had to get the goddamn project perfected and out there. He slid out of the booth and tossed a dollar on the table.

"Just. Get. It. Done," he spat and stormed out of the place.

Before he even reached his car, he was digging in his pocket for the antacids he'd taken to carrying with him. At this rate, he'd have to start buying them by the truckload.

* * * *

"Wherever you got that food from," Kari said, "I want the name and address. I thought I knew all the good Tex Mex places in this town."

Megan rattled off the name of the place, as well as the location.

"I discovered it when I was interviewing Joaquin Soto and he suggested we meet there. He says it's even better than his mother's cooking and he raved about that."

"Good to know. Thanks."

They had cleared away all the debris of the meal, and now they were sitting at the dining room table, Megan with her laptop set up and everyone with the folders Kari had handed out.

"I've clipped copies of the medical examiners' notes to each autopsy report itself. There are some interesting things here."

"Such as?" Beau was looking at the first report in his folder.

"Each of them noted an excessive amount of caffeine in the blood. Since most of these athletes limit the amount of coffee they drink, everyone chalked it up to the energy drinks that all athletes chug by the bottle."

Slade frowned. "I don't know, Kari. How many bottles of that stuff do they drink in a day?"

"It varies," Megan told him. "Every athlete I've ever interviewed, that's one of the questions I ask them. I do it because there is an ongoing debate about whether these drinks are just a substitute for performance enhancement drugs. They, of course, argue that it's not true. All of them, though, said they drink one bottle of water for every one of energy drink."

Kari looked up from her folder. "Isn't that a lot?"

Megan shook her head, tapped a few keys on her laptop and brought up an Internet page. "This site says, depending on body weight, a minimum of six. More when they are actively engaged in their sport."

"So when reports were given that in each case of death, the athlete had consumed large amounts of water just before collapsing, no one thought anything of it," Beau guessed.

"Correct." Kari nodded. "The problem here is that while some things might look somewhat suspicious, nothing threw up a red flag."

"So we still have nothing." Beau tossed his folder on the table in disgust.

"Not so. Every one of the medical examiners questioned the presence of each of these things. Four of them even noted that excess caffeine can affect the kidneys so the person needs to drink even more water to keep hydrated and the kidneys working."

Megan chewed the end of her pen. "I'll make a guess here that whatever these people are getting, there is an off-the-charts amount of caffeine in it. Any amount over four hundred milligrams is considered excessive and can have negative effects on the body."

Kari looked at Megan, a thoughtful expression on her face. "So what if the base ingredient of what we suspect these athletes are taking is caffeine in, say, three times that amount? But it's mixed with other ingredients that can either mask or balance those effects. The combination causes a tremendous thirst, so the athlete is drinking even more water than usual, but whatever else is in the formula continues to enhance the effects of the caffeine."

"Good thought," Slade agreed. "I'm no chemist or pharmacology expert, but it seems to me there'd have to be a delicate balance to achieve the right amount of stimulation and energy without putting excessive strain on the heart. Because I'm here to tell you, folks, I have an idea how they feel. Hiking through the Hindu Kush Mountains or the desert with fifty pounds of battle rattle chained to your body takes about the same amount of effort. Not knowing how hard we'll have to push the men, we try to limit the amount of caffeine and increase the volume of water."

"But if this pill or whatever it is we think the athletes are getting contains not just excess caffeine but also something to boost it," Beau pointed out, "that could be what's causing these so-called heart attacks."

They all stared at one another.

Slade broke the silence. "So what can we do about it?"

Kari sighed. "It's unfortunate, but nothing until we have some hard proof. And whatever they are taking isn't leaving enough detectable traces to say yes, this is fatal."

"So we're screwed." Beau made a rude noise. "Athletes will keep dying and Megan is square in the crosshairs of whoever is behind this."

Slade shook his head. "Not at all. We have one ace in the hole. As soon as my guy tells us who owns the car that sideswiped you today, Beau and I will pay them a little visit. I have a feeling they'll be very happy to talk to us."

"Let's hope he comes through soon."

* * * *

Megan stuck the last of the dishes in the dishwasher and turned it on. Then she turned to Beau.

"I don't know about you," she said, "but that quickie shower I took when we got home did little to wash away today's grime. I'm dreaming of a long, leisurely, luxurious one where I can wash every inch of my body."

He pulled her close to him, lowered his head and nibbled her earlobe before trailing his lips down the length of her neck.

"I'd say after what happened today, this body for sure needs some soothing hot water and a relaxing massage. But—now this is just my opinion—I think that would work better with both us of us. Don't you?"

"Mmmm." She pressed her body against his. "Sounds good to me. What exactly did you have in mind? Does that mean you'll have your hands all over me?"

His cock was so hard at the image her words conjured up it was a wonder it didn't break the zipper on his jeans. The thick length of it pressed against the soft flesh of her stomach and the curve of her sex.

"All over. Every inch." He peppered lacy kisses along her jawline. "Every. Single. Inch."

"And just how would you go about it?" She shifted her hips from side to side just a little, but enough that his shaft was demanding entrance into her body.

Jesus!

"Well, to start with, I'd remove all your clothes." He moved his hands and in a moment, he was tugging her T-shirt up over her head. Her bra followed. "Then I'd be sure to spend a moment licking each breast and taking a little taste of those sweet nipples. Like this."

He outlined each breast with the edge of his tongue before pulling one ripe, rosy tip into his mouth. Closing his teeth around it, he bit down with gentle pressure and tugged. He was rewarded with a sharp intake of breath from Megan, who arched into him. When the one bud was swollen to his satisfaction, he turned to the other and gave it the same treatment. It felt hard and sweet against his tongue and he pressed it against the roof of his mouth. He didn't remember ever being with a woman who responded without restraint, whose taste was so tantalizing and who made him want to do every filthy thing with her over and over again.

It wasn't just the eroticism of it, either. Every time they made love — *yes, soldier boy, made love* — he lost another piece of his soul to her. He'd kept it sheltered for so long that it scared the shit out of him to hand it over to someone, but he could no more deny it than he could stop breathing.

Her tiny moans as he tormented her nipples were like heated arrows shooting straight to his balls. This woman just turned him on. Pushed every one of his buttons. He wondered if he'd come in his jeans like a horny teenager before they even got to the good parts.

He eased his hands down to the waistband of her jeans, popping the button then sliding the zipper down. The silk of her bikini thong was soft against his hand but not as soft as the curls on her mound or the skin it covered. He walked his fingers down toward the crotch of her jeans, maneuvering a finger inside her panties to find her — wet! Sopping wet!

Sweet Baby Jesus!

Curling his fingers, he cupped her mound, wiggling one finger along her wet folds and rubbing it over the heated nub of her clit.

She moaned again and leaned into him, pushing her pelvis toward him as she clutched his upper arms.

When she started to rock against his finger, he added a second one and increased the tempo. *Holy mother of God! Is she going to come just from this foreplay?*

He pressed against her clit, rubbing his fingers against the swollen flesh harder and faster. And, in seconds, she was there, muscles clamping his fingers, body rocking back and forth. He banded one arm around her to support her while she moaned her pleasure and let the waves of her release roll over her. Her flesh tightened around his fingers and she squeezed her thighs together as tight as she could as she rode his hand.

And all the time he murmured in her ear.

"That's it, babe. That's the way. Let me have that hot little puss and that sexy wet flesh. Let me stroke that sensitive clit until you come just from that, just the way you did right now. You got it. Shit, you're so damn wet. I'd love to put my mouth right on those pussy lips and lick every wet inch of your sweet, sweet sex."

"Oh, God!" She moaned against his shoulder, pressing her lips hard against his hot skin.

The orgasm hit without warning. One minute she was riding his hand, the next she was tightening her thighs even more to trap it, moaning and crying his name, her sweet cream pouring into his palm.

The tension in her body eased and she leaned into him, holding on to him for dear life.

"My God, Beau." She buried her face in the crook of his neck.

"Was it good, babe?"

"Good enough to want more."

His laugh was soft and low. "Then it's a good thing we're just getting started."

He carried her upstairs to the master bathroom, stood her on the floor and slipped off her jeans and bikini panties. Then he sat her on the vanity counter.

"Don't move."

"Lordy." She sighed. "As if I could."

He turned on the water in the glass-enclosed walk-in shower, testing it for the right temperature before shucking his clothing.

"This ought to take care of any tension in your body." He crooned the words as he brushed his mouth over hers.

Then he lifted her again and walked them both into the steaming shower. She had the rain-style showerhead so the water fell in a soft caress onto their bodies. He poured body wash into one palm, rubbing his hands together to work up a good lather. Then, leaning her against one wall to prop her up, he began to apply the foam to her body. He began at her neck, smoothing the foam on her skin and working his way down her arms then back up and over to her breasts.

"You have no idea how much I love touching you," he murmured. "Your skin is like the softest silk, your nipples like ripe berries. I could suck on them all night long."

He moved his hands lower, massaging the bubbles onto her stomach and down to the curve of her mound.

"You've got the sexiest little puss." He put his lips next to her ear, talking as he slid his fingers lower, into the heat of her slit. "I can't decide which I like more, sliding my fingers into you and making you come that way, or maybe just teasing your clit until you can't stand it anymore and come all over my hand."

He paused to pour more body wash into his hand then knelt and applied it to her legs.

"Sometimes I think about fucking you with my tongue, stabbing it into you and feeling your muscles clamp around it. You've got the best taste, sugar. Better than champagne. I don't think I could choose which I like best. Maybe I'll just lay you down on the bed with your legs spread wide open, slide my fingers into you and use my tongue and my teeth on your clit, until you beg me to let you come."

He had moved his hands so they were now at the entrance to her sex. He rinsed off the bubbles on his hand so he could slip his fingers inside her and tease her clit with the other.

"Feel good, babe? God, you are so hot and tight." He added a third finger. "I just purely love finger-fucking you. Oh, yeah, that's it. Tighten those muscles around me."

He knelt in front of her on the shower floor, pressing her against the wall while he thrust his fingers in and out of her hot sex. When he added his thumb, stroking her sensitive clit, she began to move her hips, riding his hand, sexy little cries drifting from her mouth. He increased the pace, holding her steady in place with one hand while he fucked her with the other.

God. He was sure he'd never get tired of doing this.

When he looked up, he saw her head rested back against the shower wall, her eyes closed and her mouth open just a little.

"Hold your beasts for me, Megs. Cup them in your palms and use your thumbs on your nipples. Yeah, like that. Just like that."

He was afraid he was going to come just from the pleasure of watching her while her sex clamped around his hand and rode it and rode it. The first tremors of her orgasm vibrated against his skin and she was there, exploding on his fingers. He used his free hand to keep her in place against the shower wall so she wouldn't slip down.

She shuddered and rocked back and forth, those sexy little moans punctuating the spasms that clamped down hard on his fingers. He worked her until they subsided and he could ease his hand free, rise to his feet and take her in his arms. He brushed her wet hair back from her forehead so he could see her face. Her eyes were heavy-lidded, sultry, the look of a woman being pleasured and enjoying it.

"You okay, babe?"

She nodded, and breathed a sigh. "Uh-huh. Real good."

"Okay. Time to do your back."

He braced her against the wall, lathered up his hands and placed them on her shoulders.

"Did I tell you how good you taste?" He licked the side of her neck then nipped it along the nape. "I could lick you all over every single day, from your ankles to your shoulders and every other place in between."

He smoothed the lather the length of her body, moving his hands in a slow, circular, sweeping movement. He worked his way down from her shoulders to the small of her back, outlining the curve of her waist then skimming over the curve of her ass.

With his lips close to her ear, he slipped his fingers into the cleft of her buttocks and murmured, "Feel where I'm touching you? Right here?" He moved his fingers up and down.

"Mm-hmm." Her eyes were closed, but he could feel her body once again thrumming with desire.

"One of these nights, I'm going to fuck you here. Right. Here." He pressed the tip of a finger against her puckered opening, a burning low in his belly when she pressed back. "I'm going to put you on your hands and knees, lube you up real good so I don't hurt you, and fill you here with every inch of my dick. Would you like that, Megs? Hmmm?"

"Yesss." The word hissed out of her on a long breath.

"Did you ever give this up to anyone else? Has any other man fucked you here?"

She shook her head and began to rock back and forth against his hand.

God!

The thought of being the first man to take her there had him so hard he almost came while he was standing there. *Okay, enough's enough.*

He took the handheld spray and rinsed off every bit of lather, even lifting each foot to rest on his thigh while he sprayed her sweet, gorgeous sex, then did the same to her back. He sat her on the shower bench while he took his own quick lather and rinse. Then he dried them both off and carried her to the bed, arranging her on her back with her knees bent and legs wide open. Breathing hard, he yanked a condom from the nightstand drawer, ripped open the foil and rolled the latex on his throbbing cock.

"I can't wait any longer," he growled.

"Then don't," she whispered.

One thrust and he was inside her. Despite the fact that she had already come twice, she was hot and ready for him again.

"Jesus," he murmured. "Mother of God."

Placing his hands at the back of her knees so he could hold her wide open, he set up a rhythm that was hard and fast, because he knew he wasn't going to last much longer. He pounded into her again and again, telling her once more everything he liked to do to her. With her. How good she tasted. Felt. Looked. It seemed as if he'd barely gotten his shaft inside her when his balls tightened and the muscles in his back tensed.

Then they were there. Together. Shuddering and shaking, her inner walls gripping him like a vise and milking him, over and over and over. When she had wrung every last drop from him, he released her legs and fell forward, catching himself on his forearms.

He looked into her eyes, heavy-lidded but with the look of a woman who had been well and truly fucked.

I did that. And I'm going to do it again. A lot more. Very much a lot more.

He kissed her, but this time with emotion, not hunger. He was more and more convinced she was the one for him. Could he knock down the rest of the walls he'd kept around his heart and his soul and give them over to this woman?

A voice whispered in his ear *yes*, and he wanted so much to believe it.

But for right now, he got rid of the condom, slipped back into bed and spooned her against him. Even with everything going on, with the danger and uncertainty, he had a feeling he'd come home. Wrapped around her, he closed his eyes and slept.

Chapter Fifteen

Beau's cell phone chirped on the nightstand where he'd placed it before he'd climbed into bed with Megan. He looked at the screen. *Slade.*

"Don't tell me they called us back early again."

"No. Shit. Don't even say that out loud. No, I called because I have information about yesterday's so-called reckless drivers."

At once, Beau was alert. He pushed himself up to a sitting position, taking care not to jostle Megan very much.

"You did. Where are they? *Who* are they?" He rubbed his hand over his face, trying to wipe away the vestiges of sleep. "Hold on. Let me get my brain straight."

"Who is it?" Megan murmured in a sleepy voice.

"It's Slade. You can go back to sleep."

"Are you kidding?" She sat up, pulling the sheet to her breasts. "I want to know what's going on."

Of course. He knew it was useless trying to tell her anything. She had a damn mind of her own. It both aroused and frustrated him.

"Okay, shoot," he told the Delta leader. "Who are they?"

"I'll tell you when I see you. I called to ask if you guys are up for company. I'm dropping Kari off at work and I thought I might come by, fill you in and we could plan our strategy."

"Sounds good to me. Give us thirty, okay?"

Megan yawned. "What time is it?"

Beau checked the clock on his phone. "Eight-thirty."

"Wow! He sure gets an early start."

"He's driving Kari in to work and she has to be there by nine. Ever since that stalker business, when we're home, he drives her back and forth."

Megan grinned. "A little overprotective, are we?"

Beau shrugged. "Cut the man some slack. It took five years before they reconnected and they were just back together before her stalker kidnapped her."

"I think it's cute," she teased. "The big bad Delta Force leader is so in love with his wife it just shimmers around them. I'm so glad for them."

"Yeah. Me, too. He deserves it."

She looked as if she wanted to say something else but just shook her head and threw back the covers.

Beau swung his legs over the side of the bed and pushed himself to his feet.

"So, what's Slade got for us?" she asked as she shuffled to the bathroom.

"He found the driver of the car that sideswiped you. At least his guy did."

She shook her head. "You're right. He's got a guy for everything."

"I should have told him to pick up bagels or something on his way over."

"We can always go out to breakfast," she suggested.

"I don't think we want to discuss this in a public place. I'll text him."

"He won't mind?"

"No. He'll want something to chomp on with his coffee, anyway." He finished sending the text then grabbed a towel from the rack. "I'll shower in the guest bath. If I get in there with you, we'll need a lot more than a half-hour."

He wiggled his eyebrows at her and she giggled. But then he pulled her up hard against his body, her naked skin coaxing his cock to come out and play.

"It may be too late for that," she teased.

"I'd suggest a quickie, but..."

"Save it for later." She leaned in to him and gave him a hot kiss, flicking her tongue into his mouth. "Okay. Shower time."

"I'll get you for that," he rumbled.

"Oh, I hope so." She tossed the words over her shoulder before she stepped into the shower.

After a quick shower, Beau pulled on his jeans and a clean T-shirt and ran a comb through his hair. He brushed his teeth but decided to forego shaving until later. Megan was still dressing when the doorbell rang and he jogged downstairs to let Slade in.

He shoved a bag at Beau. "Bagels and cream cheese. I hope there's coffee."

"With that fancy single serving machine of Megan's, there's always coffee."

Slade followed him into the kitchen and leaned against the counter while Beau fixed their drinks.

"Don't mistake this for any kind of intimate girl chatter, but how are things going with Megan?"

Beau took a moment to think about it. Slade's question didn't bother him. The two of them had always had the closest relationship on the team. Plus, Slade knew that Beau was rootless. His mother had passed away, his father was pretty much a nomad and Beau had no intimate family to relate to. It was natural for him to want his friend to find the happiness he had. He weighed his words, choosing them carefully.

"I'd say things are good," he said in a slow voice. "You know me. I'm not one to jump into something in a hurry. But I will say this. She's the first woman I was happy to wake up with in the morning."

"A good sign." Slade clapped him on the shoulder. "I'm here if you ever want to talk. If not, I hope everything works out great."

"Yeah. Me, too."

"Hey, Slade." Megan hustled into the kitchen. "Did you bring goodies?"

He nodded. "Goodies and info."

"Well, let's get to them. I need to go into the office for a while."

Every muscle in Beau's body tensed. "Not by yourself."

"Excuse me?" She turned to him, indignation written on her face.

"You heard me. There's someone running around out there that wants to do you harm. If you want to go somewhere, I'm happy to take you."

Megan just glared at him. "Let's see. How about this. Megan, there are some very dangerous people out there who have painted a target on you. I would feel a whole lot better if I took you wherever you have to go. Not that you can't take care of yourself, but I don't want anything to happen to you. It would hurt me a whole lot."

Slade turned away to hide a smile.

Beau glared at her. "I—"

"Say, of course, Megan," Slade prompted.

Beau had already figured he'd be fighting a losing battle. He nodded his head at Slade. "Yeah. What he said."

It irritated him that the other two burst out laughing. Then he realized that if he wanted this relationship with Megan, he had to remember she was smart and savvy and had a definite mind of her own. He snaked out an arm and pulled her tight against his body, planting a hot kiss on her mouth. When they came up for air, he grinned at her.

"Okay. Now I can say, of course, Megan."

"I've got time enough for coffee," she told him. "And to hear what Slade has to say."

When they were all at the table with their coffee and bagels, Beau looked over at Slade and said, "Give."

Slade tapped his phone to bring up his Notes app. "My guy traced the license plate in that picture and nailed it to a 2005 silver Altima. It's registered to Sonia Menendez, but you can bet your ass she wasn't the one driving it."

Beau frowned. "So who is she, then, and why won't she be driving it?"

"She's a very respectable Hispanic woman who is pushing sixty and doesn't drive."

"But she has a car?"

"Uh-huh. Her grandson, Oscar, uses it." Slade took a swallow of coffee. "She bought it for him in her name, with money he gave her, because he didn't want it in his. I'll explain later. But his obligation for her doing that is to drive her to and from work every day."

"And she works where? Downtown? The northwest area? The east side?"

"At city hall, as a file clerk. It seems she's been there for years. But she doesn't drive and she said she was tired of taking the bus. She says she hates it worse when it rains. Thus the taxi service in exchange for putting the car in her name."

Beau frowned. "Why doesn't her grandson want it in his name?"

"He's the head of a small gang in South San Antonio. He doesn't want anything in his name that rival gangs can destroy." Slade shrugged. "I've never understood the mentality of gangs who think violence is the way to solve everything."

Every muscle in Beau's body tightened. "Are you telling me someone has sicced gang members onto Megan?" He curled his hands into fists and just managed to stop himself from banging them on the table. "Fuck. Just fuck."

"I don't think they give a rat's ass about Megan as a person, who she is or what she does," Slade told him. "They got paid to do a job. Period."

"I'll kill those fuckers."

Slade's laugh had a rough edge. "Fine, but can you wait until we get the name of whoever paid them?"

"Sure. Because I damn well want to know who that is. I've met Barry Maier a few times. I don't know him well, but even though I don't like him, I can't see him with Mexican gang bangers."

"You just never know about someone," Slade reminded him. "No matter. We'll get the name from them."

"Just how do you plan for us to do that?"

"Money. It's the one thing they understand."

"However much you have to give them," Beau said, "I'll split it with you."

"We can talk about that after we find out what we want."

Megan had said very little during this entire discussion. Beau cast a glance at her.

"What do you think, babe? Would that be Barry's style?"

She tapped her mug, a thoughtful look on her face. "Kneejerk reaction, I'd say no. But I've learned that you can never tell for sure what someone will do in any given situation. Or who they know, for that matter. The problem here is, I just can't see this as his style."

"In desperate times, people take desperate measures," Slade said.

"But is he that desperate yet? I mean, I don't think anyone but us is putting together all the pieces of this thing. No one else is interviewing the Golden Age players. No one else is looking into the strange coincidence of all these deaths. For the most part, they're just chalking it up to overexertion at an age when their bodies can't take it. No one except us has asked to see the autopsy reports, according to Megan."

"True." Beau nodded. "We may be ahead of the curve here. And if we are, it may be the best reason for them to shut you down before you can take it any further."

"We've all agreed someone has to be giving these athletes some kind of magic pill," Slade added. "Maybe they think they've perfected the formula at last and don't want anyone dredging stuff up that would kill the whole thing."

"All of this is possible," Beau agreed. "But maybe when we pay these gang members a call, we'll find out more. And by the way, when will that be?"

"Tonight. Oscar picks his mother up after work and takes her home, gets a quick bite to eat and waits for his gang to gather on the front steps of the house. Seven's the usual meeting time."

"How long will it take us to get there?"

"Maybe a half hour. I'll pick you up at six-thirty."

"Hold on, guys." Megan looked from one to the other. "You're going into South San, into gang territory, just the two of you?"

The men looked at each other and burst out laughing.

"Megan." Beau did his best to wipe the grin off his face. "I promise you these guys are like babies compared to the Afghan warlords and their followers. We'll be fine."

"I was thinking I'd bring Kari with me," Slade told her. "You two can chew each other's fingernails."

Now it was Megan's turn to grin, edged with a little embarrassment.

"Yeah, yeah, yeah. I keep forgetting you guys are Delta Force bad asses. Okay, have at it. And I'd love to have Kari visit with me. And if you guys don't mind eating late—after you've done your bad ass act—you can pick up Chinese on the way home." She looked at her watch. "Meanwhile, I have to get to the office. We're all of us in and out of the office on an irregular basis. So much of our work is done at home or on the fly. But Kendrick has us come in once a week for a staff meeting, so he can lick Linda Alfonso's butt and suck the guys' dicks."

Both men stared at her then burst into simultaneous laughter.

"I can't believe that came from your sweet little mouth," Beau said, grinning.

"Better watch out for this one, Beau." Slade winked. "She's a lot tougher than she looks."

Megan nodded. "And don't you forget it. Either of you." She carried her plate and mug to the sink. "I have to get going, so my chauffeur better be ready."

"In five, babe," Beau said.

When Megan had left the room Slade looked at Beau. "I meant it when I said you'd better watch out for this one. She's tough, she's sweet and she's a keeper."

Beau blew out a breath. "Don't I know it. I'm doing my best not to screw it up. She is for sure a keeper. It's just so different for me. I've never wanted a woman for more than five minutes before."

"It happens to all of us. And when it does, you hang on for dear life." Slade pushed back from the table. "Take care today. I'll see you tonight."

* * * *

Slade arrived with Kari a few minutes shy of six-thirty.

"Thanks for letting me hang with you," Kari told Megan.

"Oh. Are you kidding? I'm glad for the company. Maybe we can dissect those autopsy reports some more." She winked. "I've also got a bottle of Sauvignon blanc I've been saving."

"Works for me." Kari gave Slade a kiss and pushed him out of the door. "Okay. Go forth and do battle."

"Just where is this place we're going?" Beau asked as they pulled out into the street.

"South San Antonio," Slade told him. "Most people refer to it as South San."

He drove through the downtown area, the shops getting smaller and less glitzy. After two left hand turns, Beau saw they were now in an area of small houses. He noted as they drove down the streets the disparity in appearance. Some were maintained with immaculate care while others looked like a good strong wind would knock them over. The one Slade pulled to a stop in front of was one of the neater ones, a tiny bungalow with flowers in window boxes and young men lounging on the steps with hostile expressions on their faces. And the silver sedan with a damaged front bumper sitting at the curb.

He'd seen them before, in other parts of the world. It didn't matter what country it was, their attitude was always the same. *You've got it, I want it, I've got the power and I'll take it.* The power involved killing, torture, kidnapping and many other crimes. *Okay, been there, done that.* He could deal with these punks, because that was what they were. But he would follow Slade's lead.

The moment they got out of the car, the man sitting on the lowest step rose to confront them. His attitude was hostile, the look on his face a sneer, and his clothes, while sloppy, screamed expensive. Beau and Slade walked up to the steps, neither of them smiling, and by unspoken agreement were in their Delta Force mode.

"I think you guys must be in the wrong neighborhood," the man on the steps said. "You should get back in your car right now while it's still in one piece."

The men — Beau didn't think any of them were over thirty — all laughed and made obscene gestures. The thought of men like this being anywhere near Megan made his stomach roil. He and Slade stood there, both impassive, expressionless unless someone looked in their eyes. They didn't back up, they didn't argue, just stood there.

"You want something?" the man asked, not quite so sure of himself.

"Oscar Menendez," Slade told hm. "That you?"

"What you want with Oscar? You gotta tell me first."

Beau almost laughed. This was like something out of a B movie.

"If you're not Oscar," Slade said, "I have nothing to say to you."

Now the three on the steps behind whoever this was stood up, adopting what they clearly believed were threatening postures. Beau had to swallow a laugh. They had no idea what threatening was. But he had to give the guy credit. He made one more attempt.

"Nah. You tell me and I'll see if he can talk to you."

Slade sighed. "I'm sorry you feel that way, because I hate having to do this." With a flash of movement so quick none of them reacted, he reached out for the asshole's arm, twisted it behind his back and drove it up against his body until the man fell to his knees. Slade pressed harder, forcing the man to bend almost double so his face was close to the ground. When he tried to move, Slade just exerted more pressure. Rage mixed with pain on the guy's face, but there was fear in his eyes, too.

When the others on the steps rose, Beau moved forward, hands held loose at his sides, but his body in obvious ready-for-action mode. The gangbanger on the lower step didn't seem to get the message, because he rose, a challenging look on his face. Another second, another fast move and he had the man on his knees with Beau's arm around his neck at the critical pressure point. The others backed up so they were higher on the stairs, away from the action.

"Now," Slade told the jackass in front of him. "Oscar Menendez. Call him out."

"Hey, Oscar," he shouted. "Get your ass out here."

"I'm busy with my *abuela*," came a voice from inside.

"I know, but you better get out here. Now."

The screen door slammed open and a young man who could have been a duplicate of the one Slade was holding captive came out. "What the hell, Luis? You know —" He stopped and stared, clearly trying his best to keep the shock from his face. He looked at Slade. "What the fuck you doin', man?"

"I came to see you, but your right-hand man here was a little testy about that happening. I had to teach him some manners." He nodded at Beau. "It took a little more 'persuading' before everyone got the message."

Oscar looked from one to the other, unaccustomed fear in his eyes. "Okay. Here I am. You can let him go. We're cool. Just tell us what you want."

Slade released Luis, who stumbled backward, seemingly trying his best not to show the pain he was feeling. Beau did the same, and the two idiots all but threw themselves up the stairs.

"I have two questions for you." Slade's tone was cold and uninflected, what too many bad guys had come to realize was his killer's voice.

Beau wondered if the young punks had any idea who they were dealing with.

"Yeah?" Oscar threw back his shoulders and straightened in an obvious attempt to reassert his authority with the group. "What makes you think I'll answer them?"

Beau saw the muscles in Slade's face harden. *Not good, guys.*

"Are you looking for another lesson in discipline? I don't have time for that, so here's the first question. Are you interested in five hundred dollars cash?"

That stopped him, stopped all of them. They stared at Slade and Beau.

"You got that much? Let me see it?" A little of Oscar's bravado was creeping back. Beau knew Slade would let it happen. Oscar needed to re-establish his control over his group.

Slade put two fingers in his pockets and eased out the wad of cash. "I should also tell you that if you think you can just grab it, my friend here is a qualified marksman, as well as a sniper. He's carrying, and he can blow every one of your heads off before you figure out what's going on."

That made them all think. Beau could tell by the expressions on their faces that they were baffled by how this whole situation had come about. He had the feeling that these were not members of a very affluent gang. That if they ran drugs it was penny ante stuff, which he was sure was the reason they'd been picked for what they'd done. A chance to make extra money.

"What's the answer?" Slade asked.

Oscar scowled. "What do I got to do for it?"

"Answer the second question. A young lady received threatening texts, had her computer stolen and yesterday a car" — he pointed over his shoulder at the Altima — "that one, almost ran her down. In return for the answers, you get two things — the five hundred dollars and the ability to go to bed tonight without any broken bones."

Beau watched them all look at each other, trying to hide their sudden panic and the fear that had arisen when Slade had subdued Luis. Oscar looked at his 'gang' then back at Slade. He shrugged.

"Sure. Ain't no skin off my nose. A...guy we sometimes get" — he paused, swallowed — "medicine from said he needed a nosy reporter warned off. She was makin' trouble for him and his lawyer friend."

Beau had to stop himself from looking at Slade. *A drug supplier? What the hell?*

"Where does he get his drugs from?" Slade asked. *Is there someone else yet in this mix?*

"He says he makes them. That's why he can sell them cheaper than the other suppliers."

"I want his name, Oscar. There's another five hundred if you give it up."

Now Oscar looked worried. "Man, I can't give you no names. He'll —" He stopped.

"He'll what? Kill you? I have a feeling he's not the killing type."

"No, not just that. He —" Oscar swallowed. Hard.

Beau had to wonder what the whole difficulty was in giving up the name. *If the guy isn't not the usual type of drug dealer, what does he have over Oscar that makes him reluctant to reveal the guy's identity?*

The air was thick for a moment with the battle of wills. Then Oscar caved.

"Felix. His name is Felix. That's all I know."

"And how does Felix know when you want your *medicine*?"

"We always lookin' for it. He comes by about once a month and sells us a bunch of different stuff."

There was a little more back and forth before Slade gave him the other five hundred.

"One more thing," he added, as he handed Oscar the money. "Felix comes by again, I want to know. You call me." He pulled a cell phone from his other pocket and handed it over. "There's one number in here. Mine. And don't use this for anything else or I'll know. And one more thing. If any of you go anywhere near that reporter again, threaten her in any way, or even just think of her, we'll know it and come back and kill all of you."

Oscar took the money and the phone and backed up the stairs. The others just sat there, Luis still cradling his arm. Slade and Beau eased away and got into the car. When they were a block away, Beau burst out laughing.

"You are so damn good," he told his friend. "If you ever get tired of Delta, you could get a job as an actor."

"Some of us are just naturals," Slade joked. Then he sobered. "Now, we need to find out who Felix is. I got the feeling they knew his last name, but I could be wrong."

"Maybe." Beau gave a dry, humorless chuckle. "We could always go back and beat it out of them."

"If we can't find Felix, we may do just that. But how many pharmacologists named Felix can there be in San Antonio? I've got the impression he isn't part of the regular drug trade. I'll bet he works at his profession in one of the pharmacology companies. We can start there."

"Right. Whoever is running this game wouldn't hook up with someone off the streets. He'd have to be able to trust the product."

"Megan's great with research," Beau reminded him. "She's the one who found the list of athletes who had died of an apparent heart attack, even though they're spread all over the globe. I'll bet she can run every possibility through all her search engines and see if anyone has a friend or relative named Felix."

"Good. Let's pick up the Chinese food, go back to Megan's place and put your girl to work."

Chapter Sixteen

Felix navigated the streets of South San Antonio with a familiarity borne of the number of trips he'd made to this destination. He also felt comfortable there, having grown up in a similar neighborhood for the early years of his life. Then his mother had married a man with money and, before he could sneeze, he'd been living in a big house, with a large bedroom and a world of opportunities open to him. He'd also acquired a stepbrother who he'd discovered looked at the world much like he did. The fruits of their relationship were ripening now with this new project. The good thing about it was they didn't publicize their connection, for a number of reasons, so there was no thread connecting them if it all went south. They had plausible deniability.

Less than a month had passed since his last visit, but he needed the money he got from selling his products to the street gangs. The experiments with his new pharmaceutical were becoming more and more expensive. He had gone through most of the money from previous 'projects' in his determined effort to create what he was calling to himself a wonder drug. If this worked, he and his stepbrother would be rich beyond their wildest dreams. One more test run would do it. He was positive.

Thus the trip to the South San neighborhood to peddle what he now called his side product. He pulled up in front of Oscar's house, glad to see the man and his 'boys' hanging out on the steps. It was close to seven, the time of night when they began to hatch whatever mischief they could create. *Good.* That meant they'd be eager for the product.

"Hola!" He climbed out of his car and walked toward them, holding the small backpack he used to carry the goods.

Oscar rose to his feet, eyeing the backpack. *"Que pasa?"*

"I have a new supply for you. Can you use it?" He snickered. "Dumb question, right?"

"Uh, yeah. But first we gotta talk about something."

"Talk?" Felix frowned. "About what? I'm not changing my price. You know that, so what's to talk about?"

"About the two *mercenarios* who paid us a visit." The look in his eyes was cold and hard. "That's what. Not cool, *mi primo,* for guys like this to come after your *familia.*"

A tiny prickle of unease stabbed at Felix. "Mercenaries? What mercenaries? Who were they? What did they want?"

Oscar looked at his gang then back at Felix. "They weren't the type you asked questions to. They talk, you listen."

Didn't ask questions? The trickle of unease was fast becoming a river. All the muscles in his stomach cramped into a gigantic knot. If Oscar had been intimidated by them, Felix knew bad trouble was coming. "What did they want?"

"They wanted to tell us if we didn't stay away from your *chica* reporter, we were dead meat." He took a step forward. "They meant it, Felix. They looked like they could kill us with their bare hands, hide us where no one would find us and not miss a beat."

Bile rose in his throat. "How did they find you?"

Oscar waved at the silver sedan. "Through that. And don't ask me how, because I don't know and they didn't say. And trust me, I wasn't about to ask them. But if you want anything else with that reporter, find someone else to do it."

Felix struggled to hang onto his temper. "Did it occur to you he found you because of the stupid way you handled things? That you drew attention to yourself with such a stupid stunt? You might as well have posted a sign that said 'Oscar Menendez and his gang did this'."

"You said you wanted her taken care of," he objected. "We took care of her. She ain't bothered you today. Right?"

Felix curled his hands into fists, tamping down a surge of rage. *Is everything going to fall apart because I involved my dumb-as-rocks cousin?* "I wanted her scared enough to drop the story she's working on, not the victim of something that will just make her dig harder. I didn't think *mi familia* was made up of fools and idiots."

"Watch it, Felix." Oscar's eyes flashed with a hint of anger. "You asked for a favor. You didn't even pay us for it. We did what we always do. You don' like our work? Fine by me. Don't ask us to do nothing again."

He could call them fools and idiots, but hadn't he known that from the beginning? He was most angry because his stepbrother had been right. He'd handled this all wrong. Bungled it. And he had no idea how to make it right, except to accelerate the tests to achieve success before she could find the answer she was digging for. He was so close. Almost there. He was sure this last batch would do it. They just had to get it distributed and monitor the results.

And now his stepbrother was breathing down his neck to do just that. Of course, smart as the other man was, he hadn't yet brought up what would happen when they went public and people began tying the deaths of all those other athletes to the trials of this drug. He was aware that there was a certain amount of mortality in high-risk drug tests, but he'd never been able to find one where the numbers were this high.

Fuck, fuck, fuck.

"Got it. No more things outside our little business deal. *Esta bien.*" And he hoped that didn't fall apart. He held up the backpack. "Are we doing business tonight or do I take this someplace else?"

Oscar looked at the others, then nodded. "We doin' business. Come in the house."

Felix followed him inside, wondering if that tiny chill racing along his spine was a signal he'd pushed his luck here one too many times.

* * * *

Megan demanded to know every detail of their little errand, so, over dinner, Beau gave her chapter and verse.

"I'm too familiar with the South San gangs," Kari told them. "Not much scares them." She grinned. "Except two Delta Force soldiers, right?"

"You got it." Slade lifted one of her hands and placed a light kiss on her knuckles.

A tightness seized Megan as she looked at the two of them. They had such an incredible, intimate relationship. *Will I ever have that with Beau? Do I want it?* The answer, no matter how she tried to avoid it, was yes. But a man who had made a career out of being footloose and unattached might not be too comfortable settling into something like that. The last few days he'd said and done some things that made her think it might be possible, but she was going to be very careful. A lot would depend on how things stood when he left next time.

"Do you think Oscar will use that phone and call you if Felix does show up?" Kari asked Slade.

"I'd say he'd be more afraid Slade would come after him," Beau chuckled, "and dismember him if we found out Felix had showed up and Oscar didn't call."

"We'll just have to wait and see," Slade added.

The words were hardly out of his mouth when the other burner phone he'd purchased buzzed. He took it out and looked at it.

Beau lifted an eyebrow. "You think Felix made contact again with Oscar so soon?"

"Anything is possible. I'm hoping we scared him enough that he won't pull any kind of shit with us."

He pressed Talk to answer the call. Megan watched him, looking for some indication of what was being said on the other end, because Slade sure gave nothing away.

"Yeah. Uh-huh. Uh-huh. Okay. Good. Now throw the phone away and forget we ever met."

"What did he have to say?" Kari wanted to know, the minute Slade disconnected.

"It seems our friend Felix happened to show up tonight with some of his usual merchandise to sell. Oscar says it's sooner than usual so he figured the guy needed money."

"If he's the one making whatever it is the athletes are taking, and I'm pretty damn sure he is, he manufactures the synthetic dope to peddle to get money for his work. It seems he needs a sudden influx of cash."

Megan shifted in her seat on the couch. "Did he get any information for you?"

The grin on Slade's face, she thought, was pure evil satisfaction.

"He did better than that. He got a picture of him and one of his car." He pulled them up and passed the phone around. "I'm going to shoot this to my guy who found Oscar for us."

"And we need to search for a Felix in San Antonio who is a pharmacologist," Beau pointed out. "Someone who makes and tests drugs."

"And who has a relative who is an attorney," Slade added.

"He has to have a lab somewhere," Megan mused. "He must be a highly skilled pharmacologist if he can create something like whatever they are giving the athletes, so I'm sure he works for a top-level company. He can't use their lab for what he's doing, though, because it would be too open to question. So where would he set it up? This isn't like a home-grown meth lab in a house or a garage. Not an apartment. Too chancy. He'd need privacy."

"And I'll bet the attorney he's working with is Barry Maier," Kari added. She looked at Megan. "You said yourself he represents a lot of the athletes who have died. What better conduit to test these drugs than such prime material?"

"I wonder if those athletes know what they're taking," Beau mused. "I mean, they'd have to be aware it's some kind of experimental drug. That you can't get it from a doctor or a pharmacy. Aren't they taking a big chance?"

Megan held up one hand and ticked things off on her fingers. "Consider this. You're an athlete aging out of your sport. Your best years are behind you and maybe you aren't ready to retire yet. A man you trust, your attorney, comes to you and tells you he has a magic pill that can make that all go away. That can give you one or two more years at the top of your sport. You'll perform better than you ever have before and endorsement money will increase exponentially. Who would say no?"

"Are they so stupid," Slade asked, "that when they see other athletes in what we'll call the test group dropping dead, they don't worry the same thing will happen to them?"

Megan shook her head. "I know these people. They all want to think they're invincible."

Beau shook his head. "I guess I just don't get it. I mean, risking your life? For glory?"

"And a lot of bucks," Megan added.

Slade looked at Megan. "Beau said you're the search engine expert."

She laughed. "Well, sort of an expert."

"Remember," Kari reminded her, "you sniffed out that something was going on and dug up all those athletes to connect the dots. I have faith you can find Felix."

Megan brought her laptop to the table, booted it up and began her search. She knew the others were filled with curiosity and was grateful they didn't pepper her with questions while she was working. It turned out to be easier than she expected.

"Got something," she said, smiling.

"So soon?" Beau smiled. "I'm impressed."

"It was much easier than I expected. I started with the most probable sources, and…"

At that moment Slade's phone rang. "Yeah?"

"I'll wait until he's finished with the call," Megan whispered to Beau.

They waited, expectant, when Slade disconnected, but he shook his head. "Not what we hoped. He traced the car but it's owned by a shell corporation. He used every trick he's got and couldn't break through all the walls. He did say he'd keep trying, though."

"Someone with a lot of brains set this whole thing up," Kari told them. "If Felix's 'lawyer buddy' is Barry the Bear, you can bet he tied up that shell corporation with a nice tight bow. I'm sure he set this up to be able to make purchases for whatever lab work is being done—maybe to set the lab up to begin with. He's also smart enough and devious enough not to leave any strings hanging for someone to pull. Slade, just tell your friend thanks, but not to waste any more of his time. He can let it go. If this turns out to be what we all think, I can bring it to our office, we'll open a case file and get subpoenas for all their records. Megan, what have you got?"

"I stated with the easiest databases, pharmacologists in San Antonio, Texas. It's one of several profession-specific databases online. And voilà! There's a Felix Sandoval who works for LQS Pharmaceuticals. They're located in Castle Hills, not too far from the airport. It seems he's one of their top pharmacologists, according to their website."

"No shit?" Slade shook his head. "He's taking a big chance working on an illegal product."

"More so because he's also concocting those synthetic drugs he sells to Oscar's gang," Beau added. "And who knows who else."

"Do we have a home address for him?"

Megan nodded. "He lives in Olmos Park."

Slade whistled. "Big bucks there. He must be pulling down a hefty salary from LQS."

"Or he's supplementing it with income from his little sideline," Beau added. "Did you check where Barry lives?"

She tapped the keys on her computer. "He lives at the Dominion, on the city's northwest side. Not surprising. A lot of athletes own homes there—many of them Barry's clients. Also a very wealthy community."

"You wonder just how much money is enough," Slade mused.

Megan gave an unladylike snort. "For some people, there's no limit."

"What about a connection linking Barry and Felix?" Kari asked.

"Let me see what I can do."

She was peripherally aware of Beau getting up and making coffee for everyone, and setting a full mug next to her. She smiled her thanks and went back to her search. She knew the others were conversing in whispers so they wouldn't disturb her, as her fingers flew over the keyboard, but she blocked everything out.

Half an hour later, she looked up from her laptop.

"I'm not finding what we want," she told them. "They attend some of the same events, contribute to some of the same causes." She rubbed her forehead. "I feel it, guys. It's right there below the surface just waiting for us to find it."

"Maybe we can pull the strings from different places," Kari suggested. "Megan, can you work your magic and pull up a list of Barry's client athletes who are lucky to still be alive?"

Megan looked at Beau then back at Kari.

"If it's a little on the dark side," Kari assured her, "I'll take care of it. But can you do it?"

She nodded. "A friend of mine installed a program on my laptop that allows me to do a lot of things. He did it when I was having so much trouble getting background on Barry. When I first thought he was the one behind all of this, I was trying to find some connection with somebody — anybody — that he could be doing this with. But don't ask me about my friend." She grinned. "I'd have to kill you."

"Hell, I'll beat the shit out of anyone who even tries to insinuate anything," Slade said. "Have at it."

Working the program, it took her less than half an hour before she had Barry's entire client list up.

"I'm not seeing this," Kari said, covering her eyes. "And don't tell me how you got it."

They all laughed a little, even though anyone who knew her would know she wasn't kidding.

"Here it is." Megan compiled the list into a single document. "Now I'm going to filter out their athletic clients who are past thirty-five, then further by looking for those having years where the success is unusual."

She sent the filtered list to everyone's cell phone and they each sat and studied it.

"Should we be warning these people?" Megan asked.

"I'd like to," Kari said, "but since I didn't get the information in any legal manner, I'm kind of hamstrung."

"I'm not," Slade pointed out.

"Neither am I," Beau added.

"But that's going to take time. First contacting them, then getting them to believe us. We need to find that damn lab."

"Well, they're damn sure not making it in a garage."

"It would have to have specific requirements," Kari told them, "such as ventilation for toxic fumes, running water, stuff like that. And duh." She smacked her forehead. "How incredibly stupid am I? Let's search under the name of that shell corporation."

"Let's try all the names," Slade told them. "My guy said they have shell on top of shell on top of shell. I'll send the list to everyone."

They had been at it again for more than half an hour, Megan growing more and more frustrated because she knew it was all there just out of reach, when she hit the jackpot. She stared at the screen for a moment, as if unable to believe she'd found it.

"Guys." She looked over at them. "I've got it. At least I've got the facility."

Beau stood up and came to look over her shoulder. "They sure lucked out."

"Uh-huh. A dental lab went belly up—I checked the previous owner—and they didn't have to do much conversion."

"I'll bet Felix visits the lab at night," Beau suggested. "He works all day so that's his only time there."

Slade looked at him. "Are you thinking what I'm thinking?"

"I know what you're thinking." Kari got up from the table to refill her coffee mug. "Just be very careful."

Slade winked at her. "Darlin', careful is our middle name."

"Are you going now?" Megan looked at Beau as he got up from the table.

Slade answered for them. "Just as soon as it's full dark. Gives us a chance to print out a map of the area and memorize, and get our gear together."

"Gear?" Megan frowned. "What kind of gear do you take to follow some guy?"

Beau laughed. "I'd tell you, but then I'd have to kill you." Then he sobered. "For one thing, I'd like to have some night vision goggles, since we won't want to use flashlights and give ourselves away. Also, since we have both Felix's home address and the location—we think—of the lab, we don't need to follow him."

"It's dark already," Slade pointed out. "We don't know what hours Felix works at the lab. Remember, he still has to go to his day job. I'd like to go check out the lab. Maybe we'll get lucky and his lawyer friend will pay him a visit tonight."

"That's almost too much to hope for," Kari told him. "When I get to the office tomorrow I'm going to condense all the autopsy reports into one so the thread is visible. Megan, if you send me the list of athletes who had a stellar year for their age then died of a so-called heart attack, I'll put it with everything else. I'll get a copy of the report on your attack yesterday, even though it just says reckless driving. It still rounds out the picture. Then I'll take it all to my boss and see if we can move forward with something."

"What will he do?" Megan asked. "Doesn't any investigation have to be generated in the police department?"

"Yes." Kari nodded. "But Kip can go to the chief of detectives, lay it out for him and get something going. Pearce Gentry, the chief of Ds, is a good friend of his and very sharp. He knows Kip wouldn't come to him without something hot." She looked over at Slade. "And if you can bring us anything from tonight, so much the better."

"I live to please," he teased, and bent down to give her a gentle kiss. When he straightened he turned to Beau. "Let's get our shit together and see what we can find out."

* * * *

I've just got a bad case of nerves.

Felix repeated it to himself over and over as he worked in the lab. The whole episode with Oscar had unnerved him and made him jittery. He never should have called the man in the first place. Strike that. He never should have gotten mixed up with him to begin with.

Life has a funny way of linking circumstances together, he thought. If his mother hadn't married a gringo, he never would have acquired a stepbrother who'd grown up to be a hotshot lawyer. If one of his mother's side-shoe relatives hadn't contacted him with a way to make a lot of money creating drugs to sell on the streets, he might not have looked at opportunities outside his regular position. If he hadn't been almost caught making a delivery one night, because Oscar was under surveillance, he might not have called on his stepbrother, now a well-known attorney, for help.

So mix one attorney representing high profile athletes with one chemist, add a bottle of bourbon to stimulate the brain, and voilà! This little side business, which could make them all wealthy beyond any expectations, had been created.

And now there was the possibility it would all turn to shit.

He had never expected the athletes to die. He'd been prepared for a bad reaction to the pills, but nothing like this. Nor had he expected Megan Welles with her reporter's nose twitching to start putting the pieces of the puzzle together. And now they were hovering on a dangerous ledge. Even if the pills worked this time, would someone besides Megan start digging and put the pieces together? And what would they be able to do about Welles herself?

He couldn't decide if he wanted a bottle of antacid medicine or a bottle of bourbon.

Take a deep breath. You have work to do.

A sound outside caught his attention. He paused to listen, straining to hear anything else. The way the building was designed, there was a large interior room that he'd set up as the lab. No windows, no trace of light ever escaped. He always turned on a light in the one office that held his desk. If anyone wondered about his car in the parking lot, they would think he was doing office work.

Why would someone come snooping around, anyway? No one, not even Oscar and his thugs, knew about this place. And his legal brain of a stepbrother had buried the ownership of everything, including his vehicle, under so many layers of shell corporations it would take years to unravel everything.

He hoped.

He went back to work on his testing, focusing on the combination of ingredients but still half-listening for another sound. At last, unable to concentrate, he turned off the lights in the lab and eased his way to what had been the small lobby of the building. He crouched down and duckwalked over to the front window, peering over the windowsill at the parking lot.

Nada.

Not a damn thing. Just his car. Not even a light. His paranoid stepbrother had insisted on disconnecting the lights in the parking lot. He stayed there, crouched in an uncomfortable position, for a good ten minutes before making his way back to the lab. Flicking the lights on, he collapsed onto the high stool he used at the work counter and drew in a slow breath. He sat there until his racing pulse had returned to a somewhat normal rate.

Hell!

This was all getting to be too much for him. So what if he'd been the one to suggest this one night when the two of them had been splitting a bottle of bourbon? To bring up the idea of creating a drug that extended an athlete's playing life at the top of his or her game. To get excited as they discussed all the possibilities and, most important, the fortune they could reap. But somehow, somewhere, things had gotten out of hand.

It was that fucking sports writer. She was going to ruin everything. His cousin had made a mess of the job of taking her out of the picture. Now too many eyes were on everything. He'd told his stepbrother he needed to use all the resources at his disposal to make sure this thing didn't turn to shit. But now where were they? In the biggest pile of it imaginable.

"We can always move the entire operation overseas," his stepbrother had reminded him.

Assuming we get out of this with our skin intact.

Swallowing his fear and misgivings and mentally crossing his fingers, he went back to work on the formula.

Please let this be the time it works with no drastic side effects.

Chapter Seventeen

Megan and Beau were having breakfast the next morning, drinking coffee and trying to stay calm as they waited for a call from Kari. The two men had returned to Megan's last night to report on their recon of the supposed drug lab. They'd arrived and left with the same level of stealth, gathering their info without alerting Felix. Then they had turned everything over to Kari before she and Slade had left.

Beau had just taken a sip of coffee when his cell rang and he looked at the screen.

"It's Slade. Maybe Kari has some news."

Megan lifted her eyebrows. "So fast?"

"Let's find out. Hey, Slade. What's up?" He listened, punctuating the silence every so often with an *uh-huh*.

Megan did her best to curb her impatience until he hung up at last.

"Well?"

"Whatever she took to her boss must have struck a chord. He met with Pearce Gentry right after Kari briefed him and gave him what she'd put together. He's already opened an investigation and assigned a team to it."

Megan widened her eyes. "For sure? That's fast. Thank you, Kari."

"One of the things they're doing is digging up everything they can find about Felix to see who the attorney is he's connected to."

"It's Barry," she insisted. "I know it is. He's in the best position for it."

"Kari agrees and so does her boss. And here's the kicker." He paused for effect.

"Well, come on," she pressed. "Don't tease me."

"Kip Reyes, Kari's boss, is related to one of the athletes who died."

"What?" Megan's jaw dropped. "Are you kidding me?"

"Not even a little." He grinned. "You sure pulled the tiger's tail this time, babe."

"Oh, My. God." Her brain was racing a mile a minute. "So what are they doing first? What's happening? Tell me, tell me." She felt like a kid at her own birthday party.

"For one thing, Kip himself is going to talk to Barry. He thought about having him brought down to the station, but he's waiting for whatever final link they find to tie him to Felix."

"They can do a search," she pointed out. "They have access to things I don't."

"Plus," he added, "they can question people who might have seen the two of them together or heard Barry mention Felix."

"Would he be so stupid?" She tucked a strand of hair behind her ear. "I mean, if he and Felix are involved in this illegal operation, he's not dumb enough to mention his name and let anyone connect them. Just in case."

Beau shrugged. "If they had a relationship before all this happened, it might have come up in conversation."

"Maybe Barry represented him in something and that's how they got together."

"Pearce did say they'd get a warrant at once for the lab, telling the judge they received information that they have probable cause to believe illegal drugs are being manufactured there. That knocks down one domino. He expects to move on it this morning." Beau looked at his watch. "I hope within the hour."

"And Felix himself?"

"A little trickier. They're looking to see if he's ever been fingerprinted. If he has, they can match it against any prints they collect at the lab."

"What about the pictures Oscar took when Felix delivered he drugs?"

Beau took a swallow of his coffee before answering. "Slade sent everything to Kari's phone and she gave it to Kip. But Oscar is no more coming in to answer questions than I'm going to parade along the Riverwalk in a pink dress."

Megan burst out laughing. "The image defies description."

"Yeah, well, don't hold your breath. But Kari did say they are going to bring Felix in as a person of interest."

"Will someone keep us up to date?"

"As much as possible." He smiled at her. "I know you're anxious to get this done, but they have to do it right. Okay?"

"Yeah. Okay." She nibbled on her bottom lip. "I need to go to the office. I can't access LexisNexis from my laptop, or a couple of the other mega search engines they have there. I want to see what else I can dig up, now that I have more search parameters."

"Okay. I'll take you. Let me call Slade back and see if he's hanging around town this morning and wants to get coffee."

"Good, I'll run and shower and dress." She was so excited it almost bubbled over. All she could think was *Big story, big story, big story.*

The athletes who were part of this program were foolish for believing in a pipe dream, but she still wanted justice for them. Maybe if others read it, they'd think three times before getting suckered into a program like this in the future.

By the time she was showered, dressed in jeans and with her hair pulled back into a ponytail, Beau had cleaned up the kitchen from their breakfast and was waiting for her.

"Slade called as soon as you headed upstairs. They got the warrant and are getting a squad together to move on it as we speak."

"Yes!" She pumped her fist in the air.

"Kip Reyes is on his way over to Barry's office. As soon as they call him that the building has been breached and what they've found, he'll go in and have them get Barry for him."

"God, Beau." She wanted to dance. "I can't believe it's happening."

"It's all because of you," he reminded her. "If you hadn't smelled something suspicious, they'd still be making the poison and more athletes would die."

"Okay, let's get going. Is Slade going to meet you for coffee?"

"Uh-huh. And Kari will be keeping us up to date on what's happening."

"Let's go, then."

"Wait just a sec. Your car is ready. The body shop called. Do you want to go pick it up first?"

Megan shook her head. "I want to get to *Sportsweek*. I'll call the garage and give them my info over the phone. I've done it before, plus they know me. Then, if I ask very nice, could you pick it up after you leave Slade?"

He cupped her chin and tilted her face up to his. Heat blazed in his eyes. "How nice?"

"Very, very, very nice."

"Then I think it can be arranged."

He kissed her then, sliding his tongue into her mouth and tangling it with hers, licking every inner surface until her toes curled and her sex throbbed with the beat of a jungle drum. She forgot time and place, even who she was as she fell into the erotic cloud that enveloped her. By the time he lifted his mouth, she wasn't even sure where she was any more.

"Um," was all she could say.

He grinned. "I agree. Okay, let's get you to work."

* * * *

"Why are you calling me at my office?"

Felix gripped his cell phone so hard he was afraid it would break. If his stepbrother had been in front of him, he might have done the same thing to his neck. He'd had to go outside to make this call, telling the security guard he had to get something he'd forgotten in his car.

"I'm calling you," he ground out, "because everything has gone to shit."

"What? What the hell do you mean?" The voice on the other end was both irritated and belligerent.

"The security system at the lab sent a warning to my other cell phone. Remember how we set it up? If there was a problem it dings me and I can pull up the cameras?"

"Yeah. So? Who the hell would bother with that little building."

"The cops, you asshole. That's who. The cops are all over the place."

There was dead silence.

"Hello? Are you there? You better not have hung up on me."

"I'm here." The voice was flat and hard. "You'd better get your ass out of town this second."

"What?" Felix almost shouted the word. "No. You have to help me. This is what you do. Put on your lawyer suit and get me out of this jam."

"Felix. If they've found the lab, there is no getting you out of this. Go to the bank. Get the cash from the safe deposit box and get the fuck on the next plane to nowhere."

"But—"

"Hold on." There was an interminable silence. Then, "The fucking district attorney is in this office. Right now. You'd better disappear, because that's what I'm going to do."

The connection went dead. Felix stared at the phone as if willing the voice of his stepbrother to still be there. His hand was shaking so much he struggled to put the phone back into his pocket. He'd have to get out of there. *Shit.* His keys and everything were in his jacket in the lab. He nodded to the security guard, entered the building again and hurried to the lab as fast as he could without calling more attention to himself.

"I have to go out for a little bit," he told his two assistants who were working at the counter. "But I'll be back soon. Just keep on with this process."

He shrugged into his jacket and headed for the door to the corridor. But the moment he opened it, nausea surged up into his throat and his hands began to shake. Standing in front of him were one of the vice presidents and two men in suits with badges clipped to their lapels. And a uniformed policeman.

The man in front held up a hand to prevent him from walking out.

"Felix Sandoval? Detective Dunning. We'd like you to come with us, please. We have a few questions we'd like to ask you."

Felix was shaking so much he struggled to speak. "A-About what?"

"Just a project you've been working on."

"Am I under arrest?" *Sweet Jesus. How has this happened?*

Dunning shook his head. "Not at this time. But we do have some questions for you."

"Felix?" The vice president frowned. "Can you tell me what this is all about?"

No. No, I can't.

"I don't know," he bluffed. "I'm sure it's a misunderstanding of some sort." He looked at Dunning. "I'd like to call my attorney."

The detective nodded. "As soon as we get down to the station house."

But then he realized he had no attorney to call. His attorney was in the same predicament and maybe had a head start. By now he could be on the run, headed out of the city to…wherever.

Now what do I do?

* * * *

Megan disconnected the call and set her cell back down on her desk. Beau had called to say Slade was going back to Kari's office and he was heading to the garage to get her car.

"Are we all set on the bill?"

"Yes. Good to go," she assured him.

"Fine. I'll come by the office when I have it. Do *not* leave that place without me. Do *not* go anywhere. With anyone."

She stopped smiling as irritation crept through her. "I appreciate your concern, but I'm not one of your teammates. You don't get to give me orders. I was taking care of myself before you came on the scene and I'll keep doing it when you're gone."

As soon as the words were out of her mouth, she wished them back.

"I'm sorry, Beau. I didn't mean it to come out that way."

"I understand." His tone of voice was flat, uninflected. "But you're right, you're not part of my team. When they receive an order, they don't argue. They follow it, because they know that's the way to the best outcome."

Oh, God.

"I said I was sorry. Listen, can we talk about this later?"

"Of course."

It was the total lack of emotion in his voice that got to her. *What did I do?* He was just thinking of her. It was that damn chip on her shoulder that got in her way every time.

"I'm not just throwing my weight around," he told her. "I'm serious, Megan. They've arrested Felix and Kip Reyes is at Barry's office, as we speak. But we don't know who else is involved in this with them, or who might come after you for revenge, or to somehow protect themselves. Promise me you won't leave that office."

And there's that old kneejerk reaction again.

"All right, already. I hear you." She blew out a breath of exasperation. "Jeez. Come up to the offices when you get here."

"See you soon."

She tapped the icon in her tablet for the local ABC affiliate to see if there was any breaking news, but nothing came up except the regular programming. *Too soon*, she thought. If they'd just arrested Felix, there hadn't even been enough time yet for word to get out. But when they brought Barry in, all hell was sure to break loose. She hoped she could be there for that. Maybe Kari could pull some strings for her.

She turned back to her computer and the most recent search. She'd tried everything to find a connection between Felix and Barry but so far she had come up short. This was taking longer than she expected.

What she should do was call Jason Aponte and ask him if anything unusual was happening in his office. Maybe he could give her a heads-up on the situation at his office. She had just picked up her cell to dial when the ringtone signaled an incoming call. She checked the screen. *Jason Aponte, Good.* Maybe he had information for her.

"Hey, Jason. What's up?"

"What's up is the story of the century, if you want it."

Excitement sizzled in her veins. *Does he know what's happening? Is he going to give me inside information?*

"Of course, I want it. Come on up to the office. I can even give you a cup of our miserable coffee."

"No." His voice dropped. "I can't risk anyone hearing this but you. I know you've been asking about the athletes who died, most of whom were our clients. I can tell you everything you want to know. Including a big surprise."

She tapped her pen against her teeth. Beau had said not to leave the office, but going downstairs to meet Jason wasn't dangerous. *Right?*

"Okay. There's a little boutique coffee shop right off the lobby. How about if I meet you there? I'm heading down now."

She was already out of her cubicle and heading for the hallway and the elevator by the time she disconnected the call.

"I'm on my way to get a hot story," she told Kendrick as she stuck her head in his office.

"What story? Where are you going?" He half rose from his desk chair. "Wait a minute, Welles. I might want someone to go with you."

Yeah, that's not happening.

"I'll fill you in when I get back upstairs."

"Wait!" he shouted after her, but she was already in the hall.

Luckily for her, the elevator came at once. She fidgeted all the way down, grinding her teeth when the car made three stops. At last they reached the lobby and she hurried out toward the coffee shop, then stopped when she saw Jason waiting for her not far from the building entrance.

"I thought you were going to wait for me in the coffee shop? We can talk in there at a corner table. No one will hear us or bother us."

He shook his head. "No. We need complete privacy. Come on." He grabbed her arm and tugged her toward the entrance.

Megan looked at him, noticing a wild light in his eyes and the twitch of a muscle in his jaw. She planted her feet as firmly on the floor as she could and tried to yank her arm away from him.

"Jason, what's going on? What's the deal here?"

He dragged her over to a wall of the lobby, out of the way of traffic. "You just couldn't keep your fucking nose out of our business, could you?"

She stared at him. "What? What are you talking about?"

"If you had just waited until I set up interviews for you, let me guide you, we could have put the right spin on this. But no, you had to keep digging and talking to people."

Megan took a deep breath and let it out on a slow exhale.

Calm. Keep calm. Find out what the hell this is about.

"Jason, I think we should sit down over a cup of coffee, and —"

"We're not getting any goddamn coffee. We're getting out of here."

She tried to jerk her arm away from him. "I'm not going anywhere with you until you tell me what the hell this is all about."

"All about? All about? It's about you being so goddamn nosy you fucked everything up."

"Everything what?" She tried to tug her arm away again. "What the hell are you talking about?"

"You know what I'm talking about." He tightened his grip on her.

There was an edge to his voice and his breathing was erratic.

"Jason, tell me right this minute what's going on."

"I already told you. I said I'd get you interviews. I could have managed the whole process with you. Then, when the pills worked — when the water boosted them — you'd have the biggest story of all. But you had to keep pushing and pushing. Stupid cunt."

Shock almost immobilized her. "Are you talking about the athletes and Barry?"

"*Barry?* What the fuck does he have to do with this? He wouldn't know an opportunity if it was tattooed on his forehead. I was the one who came up with the idea. We were going to be rich." He gripped her arm even harder. "I heard the district attorney was at the office. He got a call while he was talking to Barry and asked where I was. I just managed to get out of there. Damn you, Megan. You just had to stick your nose in where it didn't belong."

Ohmigod! It's him! He's the one!

Megan forced herself to take a deep breath. "Jason, I still think a cup of coffee would do you some good — "

"I don't want any fucking coffee." He spat the words. "They've already arrested my cousin and they came to the office looking for me."

"Uh, they weren't looking for you. They wanted Barry."

"Barry again. What a laugh!" His fingers dug harder into her arm, painful in their pressure. "At least while they danced around him, it bought me enough time to get out of there and get to the bank to clear out the money I stashed."

"Money?" She frowned.

"From selling the goddamn pills and water to the athletes. Are you stupid?"

"Athletes? The ones who died?"

"Jesus." He drew her so close she was almost plastered to his body. "Will you shut the fuck up? Now we're going to walk out of here nice and easy."

She called on every bit of self-restraint to stay calm. "Where are we going?"

"To get my other car so I can get the hell out of here."

"You don't need me for that," she pointed out. "Just let me go back to my office. I'll never tell anyone you were here."

"Right," he sneered. "You think I'm stupid? As long as you're with me, they can't get me. You're my insurance. Even those macho assholes of yours won't bother me if they think you'll be hurt. I know they're right on my trail. That fucking Felix will throw me to the wolves. You're my ticket out of here. Now come on. Move your ass."

"But—"

"And just in case you're planning to yell for help, don't. I'd hate to shoot you or anyone else, but I will if I have to." Something pressed hard against her side. "This ought to tell you I mean business."

She slid her hand down and her fingers touched cold steel. *Gun!*

Holy mother!

All she could think of was if she got out of this she'd never argue with Beau again. If he told her to stay put, they'd need a tank to move her. Assuming, of course, that he ever talked to her again.

Chapter Eighteen

Beau was fighting the traffic on the Interstate to get to Megan's office, doing his best to control his irritation with the one woman who had ever gotten under his skin like this. He was trying to figure out how to deal with this situation when his cell rang. The readout had Slade's name.

"Did you miss me already?" he joked.

"Where the hell is Megan?" Slade's voice sounded just like it did when they were in the middle of a mission.

"What do you mean?" Beau frowned as he whipped around a slow-moving car. "At her office. Why?"

"No, she's not. And she's not picking up on her cell phone."

A cold knot twisted in Beau's stomach. "Did you talk to her editor? What's his name? Kendrick?"

"Yeah. He said she poked her head in his office and told him she was on a hot story and she'd be back."

"Well, she doesn't have wheels so she can't have gone far. Are you going to tell me what's going on?"

"Everything's gone to shit." There was a slight pause. "Barry's not the one. Not the attorney. Not Felix's cousin. It's Jason Aponte. Felix cracked under questioning, once they confronted him with all the evidence. He said Jason's the one behind this whole thing. The two of them came up with the idea one night as a way to make a lot of money."

"Where's Jason now?" Beau was almost afraid to hear the answer.

"They think he's with Megan. Kip Reyes went to talk to Barry Maier. While he was there, he got a call saying Felix had given up Jason in hopes of working a deal for himself. Jason must have overheard him after that and known it was all over."

"What makes you think he's got Megan?" Beau was doing his best to stay calm, even as he honked at traffic and began swerving in and out. *God damn it.* He wanted to throttle the woman, even as fear swamped him.

"He needs a hostage to get out of town. Felix said he blames her for the whole thing falling apart. And she's nowhere to be found. Wait. Hold on a second. I've got another call coming in."

Beau did his best to keep from screaming while he waited for Slade to come back on the line. He needed to be cool. He could yell afterward, but right now he needed that icy mission calm.

"Yeah, Beau? Still there?"

Where else would I be? "I'm here."

"Okay, that was Kari. The cops just called her boss. Jason's at Megan's building. It seems he's got her in the lobby and he has a gun. Reyes is on his way and he's bringing Kari with him."

Don't panic. You haven't panicked all these years. Think of this as a mission, a hostage rescue. You've done a hundred of these.

Megan, why the fuck didn't you stay in your office the way I told you to? How can I protect you if you don't listen to me?

"That's no place for them." Beau snapped the words out. "This isn't a party, for fuck's sake."

"Reyes is no novice, Beau. He'll make sure they're both out of the way. But they're the ones who set this all in motion. No one was going to tell them to stay home."

"What about the people in the lobby? I mean, there have to be some getting on and off elevators, moving around."

"The police have a squad on site with a hostage negotiator. He talked Jason into letting the others go."

"But not Megan." Each word was like a knife in his heart.

"No." Slade's voice was both somber and sympathetic. "Not Megan."

"God damn it," he exploded. "I told her to stay in the goddamn fucking office. Just that one thing. Stay put. Don't leave. What was so hard about that?"

"You can ask her later. Right now, we have a situation. Listen, I'm already at the building. How far away are you?"

"About ten minutes if I can get around all the fucking traffic."

"The cops are at the front of the building, with the sidewalk blocked off. You'll see where command is set up. Kip Reyes said the rescue team has plans for the building and he's cleared the way for them to share with us."

"I'll meet you there in less than five."

He didn't fucking care if he got a speeding ticket. Ten tickets. He just had to get to Megan. *Why the hell didn't she just stay put like I told her to? Why couldn't she just understand I have her safety at heart? That I'm not trying to cramp her style?*

Beau pulled off the Interstate onto the frontage road and turned into the parking lot for Megan's building. It wasn't hard to see where the action was. Barriers had been set up to block off an area just back from the entrance to the building — double glass doors with floor to ceiling windows on both sides — and it was obvious cars had been moved to clear as much of the area as possible. An oversized black van was parked next to a table set up beneath a temporary awning and men in black gear and helmets stood waiting for orders.

SWAT.

The sight made Beau's stomach knot.

At the perimeter of the parking lot sat vans with the call letters of three television stations on them and pressing as close as they could get to the barriers were reporters with microphones and videographers with their cameras hoisted on their shoulders.

You won't do Megan any good if you fall apart.

Deltas did not fall apart. He kept repeating it to himself, and in moments he was in mission mode, everything else cleared from his brain. He left his car in a No Parking zone and jogged over to where Slade was arguing with a man who looked like he was in charge.

"I don't care if the president of the United States himself sent you on a mission," the cop was saying. "We have our protocol and regulations here. No civilians. Period. We've got it under control."

"Doesn't look that way to me." Slade's tone of voice was that lethal one he used when he was about to vary from mission protocol. "The perp is still inside and he still has the hostage."

"And you think you can do better than a trained hostage negotiator and a trained squad."

A telltale muscle twitched in Slade's jaw. In another minute, he might cold-cock the lieutenant.

"I'm telling you that hostage rescue is one of the things my team and I are trained for. And we do it in situations much more dangerous than this. What's the object here? Saving the hostage or following protocol?"

Beau edged closer to where they were standing, just as a tall man in an expensive suit stepped up to them. He would have bet money this was Kip Reyes. In another minute, it was confirmed.

"You want to put your two cents in here, Kip?" the policeman asked. "Go ahead. Everyone else is."

"Charlie, no one's trying to jump all over procedure," Reyes said in a voice calmer than Beau's would have been. "But he's been in there with her for close to an hour and he's not coming out. You need to try something else."

Charlie stared at Kip then threw up his hands. "Okay, okay." He looked at Slade. "What's your plan?"

At that moment, Beau stepped up next to Slade and his friend's lips curved in an icy smile.

"He's right here. Beau, this is Lieutenant McIlwaine. Lieutenant, meet Beau Williams, the best damn sniper in the world."

The cop loosened a fraction, rolled out the plans for the building and bent over them with Slade and Beau. Ten minutes later, they had it together.

"I'm going to station my sniper across the street on the roof of the office building directly across from here," McIlwaine told him. He slid another sheet over, a diagram of the area, and pointed to a structure. "Right there. Just in case he gets out of there with the woman. My guy never misses."

Beau wanted to tell him that if anyone was acting as a sniper, it would be him. But then he realized if he did that, he couldn't go inside with Slade. Fuck it all. He and Slade would just get this done, the way they'd completed hundreds of other missions.

He and Slade both had their handguns, which had been locked in Slade's car. Now they checked them to make sure both were loaded and ready.

McIlwaine dialed a number that Beau assumed was Jason's cell phone. If the man would answer, it was the lieutenant's job to keep him talking. Beau and Slade moved through the parking lot around to the side of the building where two other cops were guarding that entrance.

"Just to let him know he couldn't get out this way," one of them said. "We did not want him leaving with Miss Welles."

"Good thought," Beau told them.

The door was out of sight of the lobby, the corridor perpendicular to it. That gave Beau and Slade the chance to slip in unnoticed. From that point on, they would use the hand signals that were so much a part of them. Jason was still looking out of the front door, with Megan standing in front of him perfectly still, a gun pointed at her head. With his free hand, he held a cell phone that he was shouting into.

Good, Beau thought. *McIlwaine's doing his part. He's got him connected with the hostage negotiator.*

"No, no, no," he shouted. "Don't give me your shit. I want safe passage for myself and Megan Welles out of here or no deal. Don't push me. I've got an itchy trigger finger and I might just scratch it."

"He's on the edge," Slade whispered to Beau, who nodded.

The two men moved with practiced stealth until they were in their agreed upon positions. MacIlwaine hadn't been too happy with their plan, but he had to concur that, if there was no other choice, a dead criminal was better than a dead hostage. His own sniper had been told to shoot to kill, if it came down to that.

The two men moved as stealthy as cats, with not even a whisper of a sound. Jason had not shifted his position except now they could see the hand holding the gun was shaking. *Not a good sign.*

Slade signaled to Beau, who nodded.

Soundless, they moved up until they were close enough to reach Jason. The man was so unhinged and focused on the phone he didn't hear them.

"Jason." Slade called out his name.

Jason whirled, pointing the gun at the sound, but it did him no good. Slade was right behind him and pounced, grabbing the hand with the gun and removing the weapon in one smooth, quick move. Then he closed his fingers over the man's wrist and bent his arm behind his back.

"Don't even think of making a move," he warned in what his men called his voice of death.

Beau shoved his gun into the small of his back, grabbed Megan and pulled her against him, holding her as tight as he could. He just stood there with her while the police surged through the front door. One of the uniformed officers took charge of Jason, handcuffing him, then two of them marched him out the front door. Beau was somewhat aware of insanity outside — people shouting, reporters trying to get statements, onlookers buzzing with speculation. But his main focus was on Megan and the fact that she was safe in his arms.

"Give me your keys," Slade said. "I'll bring your car around to the other side."

"I need to chat with you, Donovan," McIlwaine said.

Slade nodded. "Hold on a minute."

Beau stood there with Megan, wordless, for long moments. Then he took her hand and led her out of the side door, where Slade had her car idling.

"Get her home," he told Beau.

"Doing it right now." He paused. "Thanks."

"No thanks necessary. Ever."

Before the media could hunt them down, Beau pulled out of the rear exit of the parking lot and headed for the condo. He wouldn't forget this day — or the unfamiliar fear he'd felt — for a long time.

* * * *

For Megan, the next two days went by in a blur. Everyone wanted to know about the two Delta Force soldiers who had taken down the criminal, but Beau and Slade were making themselves invisible. Kip Reyes gave Kari a day off to hunker down at the ranch with Slade, but he kept her in the loop. She, in turn, passed everything along to Beau and Megan. When she called, Megan put her phone on speaker so both she and Beau could hear.

"Jason Aponte and his step-brother Felix are facing multiple murder charges," she told them. "One for each athlete who died."

"Good." Megan spat out the word. "Too bad they can't kill him, revive him and do it all over again."

"Did you ever find out what was in those pills?" Beau asked.

"Mega caffeine," she said, "just as we thought, along with some other ingredients to boost it. It overstimulated them to perform at a higher level. In addition, they had a special water Felix had created that boosted the effects of the pills. They drank excessive amounts of it because the caffeine affected the kidneys and their bodies craved the liquid. They were making money on both the pills and the water, while destroying the bodies of the athletes."

Megan let out a sigh. "Evil, greedy people."

"Amen to that," Kari agreed. "Our office is busy sorting out the paperwork, getting indictments, all the things that will go into bringing this to court."

"How's Barry the Bear taking this?" Megan wanted to know.

"He's been somewhat silent through all of this, busy distancing himself and the law firm from Jason Aponte."

"So he had nothing to do with this?"

"No." She snorted a laugh. "Too bad. I'd like to see his ugly face in front of the judge, but he wasn't involved at all. Anyway, he'll be busy dealing with any blowback and trying to figure out how this all happened without him getting a sniff of it."

Megan just wanted everyone to leave them alone so she and Beau could be together, shut out the world and do their own thing to wipe away the vestiges of the nightmare. She had received so many calls that she'd stopped answering and let it all go to voicemail. The one thing she did do was write the story about two people so greedy they didn't mind killing athletes to make themselves rich.

Kendrick, knowing he'd be in trouble if he gave the story to someone else, had asked her to put it together, but he needed it at once. She wrote it from home and emailed it to him. *Sportsweek* put out a special edition and it seemed many of the news outlets picked up the story. She now had more offers from other media than she knew what to do with, including a very lucrative offer from a major daily newspaper. Television networks wanted to interview her, local stations wanted her on their morning shows. She had become the new golden girl of sports reporting.

But all she wanted was to hide away with Beau, who had for some strange reason withdrawn into himself. They'd made love the night of the big crisis, erotic and unrestrained, but since then, even though they slept in the same bed at night, he hadn't touched her. Not even a soft kiss. In bed he made sure to lie as far away from her as possible. She kept expecting him to move his things into the guest room. He was there, but he wasn't. They were like two silent shadows occupying the same space. She wasn't even sure why he was still there.

She kept herself busy writing up her notes and considering the offers that had come pouring in. She begged off any media appearances until the following week, pleading for time to recover from the situation. If they didn't want her then, so be it. Kari called a few times but, realizing Megan's head was somewhere else, just wished her good luck, said she and Slade were so relieved she was safe and told her to call when she wanted to talk. Meanwhile she waited, more tense than she'd ever been for Beau to tell her what was wrong.

The morning of the fourth day after the crisis, Slade called. She didn't have to hear more than Beau's side of the conversation to know what it was.

"You're leaving," she guessed.

He nodded. "Downtime is up."

He rinsed his coffee mug and headed upstairs to pack his duffel.

Her mind had been so focused on other things she hadn't realized their departure date had just crept up on them.

She tried to smile. "Off to save the world again?"

"Just doing our job." He didn't even look at her as he zipped up his duffel. "Teo's on the way to pick me up."

She drew in a deep breath for courage. She couldn't let him leave with things like this between them.

"I've been trying to give you space," she told him, "waiting for you to tell me what's wrong. I can't wait any more. I can't let you leave with things like this between us."

For a tense moment, she was afraid he wouldn't answer her. When he did, she almost wished she hadn't asked him.

"I can't do this anymore, Megan."

Her heart felt as if a knife had been stabbed through it.

"Do what?"

"This." He pointed to himself then her. "Us."

She dug her nails into her palms, determined not to fall apart.

"So, we're done? Just like that? I thought we were building something here." How could she have been so wrong? She knew she'd come into this with low expectations, just as she knew Beau had started out just looking for a good time during his leave. But things had changed. She hadn't imagined it. What the hell had happened?

He studied her for a long moment. "I never expected to have feelings for someone the way I do for you. I always thought relationships could destroy you. I guess I was right. I should have paid attention."

"I don't understand." And she didn't. "What went wrong?"

He rubbed his jaw. "Listen. I know I don't bring a hell of a lot to a relationship, but what I can do is protect the woman I love from danger." He paused. "But not if she's too fucking stupid to listen to me."

She stared at him.

"*That's* what this is about? Because I didn't stay in my office?"

"You put yourself in harm's way because you didn't do what I asked. You thought you knew so much better. I'm sure you figured Jason was harmless, but I'm in a line of work where we don't think *anyone* is harmless. I did my best to keep you safe, but you fucked it up."

She wanted to pound on his chest or scream at him or hit him over the head.

"So you're going to throw everything we've been building away because I, what, disobeyed an order?"

"You're independent. I get that. But you also need to be smart. And if you loved me and trusted me, you would have paid attention to what I said. You almost got yourself killed because you thought you knew better."

As angry as she was, she had to admit he was right. She had sensed something a little off when Jason had called her, but she'd been too hungry for the story, too sure she knew better what she could do.

"Okay." She wet her lips. "But we can work that out. I've been independent and fighting in a man's world for too long. I need some adjusting, too. Can't we at least talk about this?"

"Not now." He looked at his watch just as the doorbell rang. "That's Slade. Time to go."

"Please don't leave like this." She followed him down the stairs. "Please, Beau."

They were in the foyer now. With his free hand, Beau opened the door to Slade, standing on the little stoop.

"Beau?" She twisted her hands together.

"Take care of yourself, Megs. Maybe you'll do it better with someone else."

He shouldered Slade out of the way as he stepped out.

Slade frowned at her, but she just shook her head and closed the door. Then she sank to the floor, dropped her head into her hands and did something she hadn't done in a long time. She cried until her throat was raw and her eyes burned. Then she cried some more. It seemed she just wasn't meant for forever.

Chapter Nineteen

The story was more than a nine days' wonder. It filled not just the sports news but general news for weeks. Megan agreed to the interviews on the local channels, which led to invitations to appear on some national shows. She'd barely been back in her townhouse before both her cell phone and her landline were ringing like crazy with offers. The story was the biggest scandal to rock sports in years and the media was playing it for all it was worth. She was busy keeping up with her schedule and writing a series of articles on what had turned out to be a huge scandal in athletics.

Gus Kendrick was shocked when, the day after Jason Aponte and Felix were captured, she told him she was leaving. Obviously realizing he might have screwed up a good thing, offered her a big raise plus a bonus. When she told him she was taking the story elsewhere he threw a fit, insisting the story belonged to the magazine. Megan told him he could either let her leave without a problem or she'd send a letter to the publisher listing all the times Gus had taken her work and given it to someone else.

The publisher had called her himself and, when he couldn't change her mind, offered her such a hefty sum to write articles for that magazine that she'd accepted. *Sportsweek* was, after all, still the premier online sports publication. But she'd refused to work with Kendrick so the publisher had hooked her up with a different editor. She'd also refused to stay on staff, not with all the calls she had received. Among those was a publisher who wanted her to write a book about the situation, an opportunity that interested her a lot. She got an agent, negotiated a deal with a hefty advance and had a deadline of one year to finish it.

She was thankful for all the work, able to immerse herself in it so she was exhausted by the time she went to bed at night. Of course, that didn't mean she slept. Most of her nights were filled with tossing and turning and a longing for Beau that was painful in its intensity. One minute, she cursed him for being so bullheaded about everything, the next, she beat herself up for not listening to him. But they were such opposites. He was used to orders being followed and she was used to fighting for everything.

If he just hadn't waited until the last day to tell her what was wrong, she was sure they could have talked it out, learned to deal with each other.

This is why I swore never to fall in love.

But she had. She'd fallen and hard for the man who looked like a carefree surfer but underneath it all was a hardened soldier and an incredible lover. And a man with a heart he'd kept locked away for so long.

Team Charlie left in early September, just at the start of the football season. In addition to her book deal, the series on Golden Oldies and the race for perfection in athletics, she was doing a companion series on current athletes nearing retirement age and why they felt retirement was a good thing. She attended several football games, her new superstar status bringing her invites to celebrity suites. But after a while, it felt like she was just plodding through each day, like wading through water. She'd give it all up if she could just see Beau walk through her front door. She had her independence, but at what cost? And had he wanted to take it away from her, or was he just protecting a woman he—loved. *Loved?*

Kari had called several times, but Megan just couldn't make herself spend time with the woman. As hungry as she was for information about Team Charlie, she knew she could heal if she cut it all out of her life. Besides, much as she hated to admit it, she was jealous of what Slade and Kari had and destroyed that she and Beau in the end didn't have the same thing.

In late October, she broke down and agreed to have lunch with her. They met at a favorite café on the Riverwalk on a perfect fall day. The sun was shining, the temperature was in the seventies, and mariachi music was playing in the background. Megan should have been in a great mood, but instead she couldn't shake the depression.

She had made up her mind not to bring Beau into the conversation, but her need got the better of her.

"I hate myself for asking," she said as soon as they'd taken the first sip of their margaritas, "but how is he?"

"Not good," Kari told her.

Megan frowned. "What do you mean?"

"Slade says he's closed himself off from almost everything. When they aren't on a mission or training, he cleans his weapons and spends time either at the gym or the target range, or sometimes on long hikes in the wilderness. He wears himself out so he can fall into bed at night and sleep."

Megan raked her fingers through her hair. "I hate that he's doing this. At least before he'd go out and have a good time, even if it was all temporary."

"He hasn't been with any women. That should tell you something."

"Yeah? Tell me what? That our situation ended so badly he'll never have another relationship?"

"No." Kari shook her head. "That there's just one woman for him."

"He has a funny way of showing it."

Kari sipped her drink. "I hope you don't mind, but Slade managed to pry it out of him. Pried being a mild operative word."

Megan shrugged. "Beau can say what he wants."

"That's not the point. It's very unusual for him to confide this kind of stuff in anyone. He's really hurting, Megan."

She shrugged, tamping down her own pain. "So am I. He knows where I am any time he wants to see me."

"But would you see him?"

"What's the difference?" Megan tossed back the rest of her drink. "He'll never bend and I don't want to break. Besides, either he's off on a mission or stationed hours away. I swear I don't know how you handle it."

Kari's lips curved into a tiny smile. "As a matter of fact, they've been reassigned to a new home base."

"They have?" Megan was almost afraid to ask. Before, their home base had been Fort Bragg in North Carolina.

"Slade pulled some strings and got them reassigned to Fort Sam."

Fort Sam Houston was now Joint Base Sam Houston, a combined military operation with extensive training facilities.

"I guess that means you'll see a lot more of him."

"You bet." Kari got a faraway look in her eyes. "A whole lot more. Their new posting would give you more time for you and Beau to learn about each other."

Megan shrugged. "I'd say that ship has sailed. You're so lucky you found your forever." Megan hoped she didn't sound like a jealous cat, even though she was.

Kari rested a hand on Megan's arm. "You'll find yours, too, Megan. I promise you it's there. You have to reach out for it."

"Yeah, well..."

When they parted after lunch, she did promise to keep in touch more with Kari and Kari promised not to nag her about her situation.

"Just give some thought to reaching out to him, though, will you?" Kari asked.

"I think he has to reach out to me. He's the one who shut it down."

Kari shook her head. "Lord save me from stubborn people."

October slid into November. Kari invited her for Thanksgiving dinner, but she just knew the whole team would be there, so she begged off. She thought about a quick trip to California for dinner with her parents, but they told her they'd decided to take a cruise. So she spent the holiday at the convention center, helping to serve the mammoth dinner put on every year by restaurant owner Raul Jimenez for those who had no other place to go.

Then it was December. Megan spent a lot of time working on her book, hoping to block out the sights and sounds of Christmas, but they seemed to follow her wherever she went. While everyone was celebrating, she became more depressed than ever. After yet another sleepless night, she made up her mind that she'd take the first step. If it was over for real, then she'd deal with it. But she had to take one more chance.

She left a message on Kari's voicemail, asking if she'd call her and help her with something.

* * * *

Slade looked at his sniper, sitting at a table cleaning his rifle for what had to be the hundredth time.

"If you don't get your head out of your ass, I'm going to chop it off."

Beau shook his head. "Yeah? You and what army?"

"The United States Army," Slade snapped. "Everyone's sick and tired of you acting like there's nothing to life but missions." He held up his hand. "Don't say it. That's the quickest way to lose your humanity."

"Thanks for the tip."

"I have orders from my wife. Christmas is in three days and if you don't get your act together, you're uninvited for dinner."

Beau smiled a tiny bit at that. He could just see Kari saying that.

Slade sat down in a chair cornerwise from Beau. "I'm going to say this one more time. Go see the woman. Beau, it's obvious to anyone with eyes you're in love with her. Hell, you haven't even gotten laid since you left her place. For Beau Williams, that's a rarity."

Beau put down the cleaning rag and looked at Slade, hoping the misery he felt didn't show in his eyes. He hadn't thought walking away from Megan would hurt so much. Or that he'd miss her the way he did. He just knew if he had it to do all over, he'd handle everything in a different way. But he figured he'd screwed up that opportunity.

"Even if I wanted to fix it, I couldn't. I don't know how."

"Well, then, aren't you lucky that you know someone who can help you?"

Beau lifted an eyebrow. "Because you're such an expert?"

"No, my wife is. We went through our own tough times. I think everyone in Special Forces does, because of the life we lead and the way we have to discipline ourselves. Beau, try to understand that you and Megan are alike in so many ways, not the least of which is fierce independence. You're used to giving orders to take care of people and she's used to making her own decisions. You need to cut each other a little slack."

Beau turned his attention back to his rifle. "You don't even know if she'll see me."

Slade grinned. "It just so happens this very day she asked Kari if there was a way to get in touch with you."

For the first time in weeks — make that months — he felt a flicker of hope.

"And what did Kari tell her?"

"Nothing, yet. She passed it along to me, hoping I could kick some sense into you. My advice is to go to her, tell her you love her and the two of you work out how to handle things."

"Look at you, the big relationship guru."

"Damn right. You can thank my wife for that, so I'd listen to what she says."

Beau's heart gave an unfamiliar leap. *Can I do this? What if she says it was too late? No, it can't be, not if she was asking Kari for my contact info.*

"I don't have a car."

Slade reached into a pocket and pulled out a set of keys. "Take mine. Kari's picking me up in an hour. Get to it, buddy."

Beau shoved the pieces of his rifle back into the case and handed it to Slade. "Can you put this in my spot for me?"

"Yeah, but don't you think you should at least shower and change first?"

Beau shook his head. "I might change my mind. Wish me luck."

* * * *

Megan was working on a chapter of her book, trying to concentrate and not having much luck. She'd decided not to venture out of the house until after Christmas. She was so sick of the holiday and the depressing good cheer. She had little to be cheerful about.

You have a great career.

She gave a mental swat to the devil on her shoulder. Careers were wonderful but they didn't keep a girl warm at night and they didn't give her great sex.

The holiday was everywhere, for crying out loud. Carols played in stores and over loudspeakers. Intelligent people ran around in Santa hats and sweaters with snowmen and reindeer. People she didn't even know kept wishing her a Merry Christmas. The displays were enough to break her heart, projecting holiday cheer while she was so engulfed in sadness she could hardly think. She wanted to go to a deserted island until the holiday was over.

Just then her doorbell sounded. Groaning in exasperation, she saved the document and trudged downstairs.

If this is another person trying to sell me Christmas cheer, I won't be responsible for my actions.

She yanked the door open and her jaw dropped. Beau Williams stood on the little stoop in his cammies, looking rough around the edges and nervous as a tick.

"Beau?" She just stared at him.

"Can I, uh, come in?"

All her breath was trapped in her lungs and she was sure her heart had stopped beating.

"Megan?"

She just kept staring at him. Was he real or had her imagination conjured him up?

"If you want me to leave, just say so."

She snapped out of her shock, reached for his wrist and yanked him inside. She dragged in his duffel and slammed the door. They stood there, just looking at each other, as if each of them was afraid to move. Then, taking a physical leap of faith, she jumped up to wrap her arms around his neck and her legs around his waist.

"Kiss me, soldier boy," she demanded.

He did, his hard lips pressing against hers until she opened for him so he could sweep his tongue inside. He licked the inside of her mouth, sucking on her tongue and even biting down on it with a gentle touch. He had one arm beneath her ass, holding her against him while his other hand cupped her head to keep it in place. He tasted so good and so familiar. She had missed this so much. They broke the kiss only when they needed to breathe.

Then they looked at each other, gazes locked.

"I'm sorry—"

"Forgive me—"

They both burst into thready laughter.

"Let's try that again," he told her in an even voice. "Me first. I'm sorry."

"Me, too." She nuzzled her face against his neck. "Can you forgive me for being such an independent bitch?"

"If you can forgive me for being a controlling asshole."

The stared at each other and burst into laughter again.

He carried her into the living room and sat on the couch, settling her on his lap.

"I hear you're pretty famous now."

She flicked a hand in the air. "A tiny bit. But I'm having fun with it."

"At least something good came out of that fucking disaster."

"That's how I keep looking at it."

"I just want you to know how proud of you I am."

She felt herself blush. "Thank you. I'm pretty jazzed myself."

There was a long pause.

"Megan." He sighed. "I'm not sure I know any other way to be except what I am. I've never loved anyone before and my training and instinct tells me to protect you one hundred percent. That shows how much I love you. That's who I am. All I can promise is if you give us another chance I'll try not to strangle you with it."

"I've had to fight for every success my entire life," she told him. "Most of the time in a man's world, so I strike back when a man gives me orders."

"But I—"

She held up a hand. "Let me finish. But I can go overboard, too. I should have realized that with everything going on that day you just wanted me to stay safe. If I had insisted Jason come up to the office and he refused, I could have figured out how to stall him until you got there. So we both made mistakes, and I nearly lost my life because of mine. I promise you I won't do that again."

"And I'll try to be less…possessive."

She laughed. "If that's even possible."

He turned her face to look at him and the emotion in his eyes nearly slayed her.

"Can we try to make it work? I've never wanted to be with anyone the way I do with you. Never thought about—" He paused and swallowed. "About building a life together."

A funny little flutter set up in her stomach. "Me, neither."

"So Christmas can be a new beginning for us? I'm not promising anything except my best effort."

She studied his face, seeing so much there. "Only if you can tell me how you feel."

"I've never said this to anyone before." He buried his face in her hair. "I—love you, Megan. Please help me to love you the way I want." He kissed her ear and whispered, "Now it's your turn."

She'd never said it, either, but somehow, the words came easily to her. "I love you, Beau. I'll love you the best way possible."

"That's all I ask."

She eased herself off his lap. "I see you came right from work."

"When Slade told me I had a chance with you, I didn't want to waste a second. I was afraid I'd lose my nerve."

"Why don't you come upstairs and I'll wash away all that grime?"

The heated look he gave her almost scorched her skin.

"You know what happens when we take showers together."

"I'm counting on it."

Her hands were shaking so much when she stripped off her clothes she could hardly turn on the shower. But then he was there with her, tall and naked and hard everywhere. They stepped beneath the spray of water and washed each other at the same time, hands skimming over curves and muscles, feeling hard ridges and soft flesh. His cock was so swollen she had trouble getting her fingers around it, and the thought of it filling her made her pussy contract with want.

They were both shaking with need when they turned the water off and dried each other with big towels. But there was no uncertainty when he lifted her and carried her to the bed, stripping back the covers. No foreplay this time. They were both so hungry that they were beyond ready.

"I hope there are still condoms in that nightstand drawer," he said in a voice rough with need.

"There hasn't been anyone else to use them."

"Good. And there never will be."

He sheathed himself and slid into her in one swift motion, his cock filling every inch of her. He began to move in the motion they'd become used to, both so ready foreplay was unnecessary. It seemed just seconds before they both exploded in an earth-shattering orgasm, shuddering and crying out.

"I love you," he murmured in her ear.

"I love you, too."

"Megan?" He had his lips close to her ear.

"Mmm?" What did he want? She could hardly think.

"Merry Christmas."

She hugged him close to her. "Merry Christmas."

And one thought echoed in her mind.

This is what forever is like.

Want to see more from this author?
Here's a taster for you to enjoy!

Night Heat
Desiree Holt

Excerpt

Dumb, dumb, dumb.

Of all the dumb things she'd ever done in her life, this one ranked right at the top of the list. *How did I ever let myself be talked into it?*

Okay, so this was a great article she'd been selected to write. Maybe there'd be something that would help her make the leap from writing to reporting. Not that she didn't love her job, but she continued to look for ways to switch from magazines to news.

But career choices aside, the closer Jill Danvers got to Bluebonnet Falls, the harder butterflies tap-danced in her stomach. She hadn't seen Gabriel Carter in ten years. Not since the summer she'd given him her virginity and her heart and he'd trampled on both by marrying someone else. After that, she'd made a conscious effort to ignore the town and any news about it. She sure didn't want to read about how well Mr. and Mrs. Gabriel Carter were doing.

Still, no matter how hard she tried, she hadn't found a way to get him out of her system. Her secret guilty pleasure, the hot lover who invaded her dreams and left her breathless, sweaty and tangled in her sheets when she woke. Gabe Carter was the yardstick by which she measured every other man she met.

Now, in just a few minutes, she'd be face-to-face with him again. Just the memory of his hot, firm body made her nipples harden and a pulse throb between her thighs like a jungle drumbeat. The singing of the tires on the pavement was a counterpoint to the thudding of her heart.

"Get a grip," she scolded herself. "He's probably flabby, bald and missing half his teeth."

She only wished. Seeing him again would be a lot easier if he were, him being someone else's husband and all.

Yes, let's not forget the husband part.

She wheeled her Chevy Blazer up the Interstate 10 off-ramp and turned right onto the two-lane road into Bluebonnet Falls. Five more miles and she'd be facing her personal Armageddon.

"You can do this," she said, her words disappearing in the wind. "Smile, shake his hand, make your arrangements and get on with it." If she was lucky, maybe her homecoming wouldn't be a big deal to anyone. She could do her story and get away pretty much unscathed.

The notes for her *Life in America* assignment were tucked away in her Coach portfolio. She'd worked very hard to get where she was, scrabbling her way up the publications ladder to finally get the position at one of the country's top magazines. *Life* had been running her *Slice of Life* series of articles on small towns and large cities and she'd seen a lot of the country.

This time, she'd be focusing on Bluebonnet Falls and its upcoming bicentennial celebration. Normally, she'd be looking forward to this type of assignment.

'It's a good story,' her editor had pointed out. *'Besides, it's your hometown, so you ought to give it a special slant.'*

Then she'd learned Gabe was chairing the bicentennial steering committee. *How on earth can I handle seeing him again? Working closely with him?*

"Damn it!" she shouted into the breeze. "I don't want to do this."

Driving down Main Street, she thought how little the place had changed. Ten years later and every stone and storefront seemed exactly the same. Time had stood still.

She pulled into a space in front of the Hoechler Building where Gabe's office was, got out and fed coins into the parking meter.

"Jill? Jill Danvers? Is that you?"

At the sound of her name, Jill turned and squinted at the tall, willowy blonde who walked up to her. Her stomach knotted. *Jennie Foster, the biggest gossip in high school.*

Jennie pulled off her sunglasses and stared at Jill. "Well, this is quite a surprise. Long time, no see."

And with good reason. "How are you? You look great."

Jennie's stick figure had filled out so she now had curves. Her hair, now a lustrous shade of champagne instead of dishwater dull, framed her oval face and her outfit complemented her lightly tan skin. The whole ensemble screamed *money.*

"Oh, thanks, but you know, it's a constant struggle." She laughed. "Although three kids will keep you from sitting around too much."

"Three children?"

"Yes, indeed." She waved her left hand at Jill, the diamond wedding band and engagement rings flashing in the sunlight. "Married Jim Schroyer when we graduated A&M and the kids just started popping out." She laughed again, an easy, unselfconscious sound.

"It's good to see you," Jill said, surprising herself.

"Same here. I'll tell you, I wasn't sure we'd ever see you around here again. You know, the way your aunt and uncle swept you off after your folks died."

Jill wondered if anyone in Bluebonnet Falls had guessed the real reason she'd left and never come back. She and Gabe had kept pretty much to themselves so their big romance—or whatever it was—hadn't been front-page news. By September, things had changed. The death of her parents had provided her with a plausible excuse to leave.

"Well," Jennie went on, "are you planning to stay for the big celebration? It's not for a couple of weeks yet."

"Yes, I am. I'm doing an article about it for *Life in America*. I came early to do some research about the town's history and interview some of the people involved with the event."

"Wow! That's just too great." Jennie eyed her shrewdly. "I guess you'll be meeting with Gabe Carter about it, since he's the chairman."

"Yes." With an effort, Jill kept her voice calm. "As a matter of fact, I'm on my way to see him right now."

"Great. Good luck."

Good luck?

Jennie hugged Jill briefly. "Lordy, wait 'til I tell everyone. Jill Danvers back in Bluebonnet Falls. Wow."

Jill watched Jennie clip-clop down the street in her sandals, fishing a cell phone from her purse. The woman was busy punching in numbers and seconds later had the phone pressed to her ear.

So much for trying to keep a low profile. By tonight everyone in the Falls would know Jill Danvers was back in town. Smoothing imaginary wrinkles from her skirt with nervous fingers, she walked into the building. As she rode the elevator to the third floor, she counted to ten then twenty. Anything to calm herself.

In a minute, she would be facing the sexiest man she'd ever met. The one who still held her heart even if he didn't know it. She had to keep reminding herself he was married to someone else and out of reach. She swallowed a sigh.

Get serious. Gabe Carter is just another man.

Yeah, right. And the Grand Canyon is just another ditch.

Then the elevator whooshed open. She walked the few steps to his suite of offices and pushed open the door. And caught her breath.

Gabe stood at the reception desk, talking to the woman seated there. At Jill's approach, he looked up and smiled. "Hi. Can I help you?"

That deep voice rumbled from his chest and long-forgotten waves of desire washed over her.

Just her luck that after all this time he was more mouthwatering than ever. His tall, muscular body was still trim, his hair a deeper golden brown, the laugh lines on his face more prominent. The sleeves of his soft cotton dress shirt, ocean blue like the color of his eyes, were rolled back at the cuffs, exposing tan forearms with a light dusting of golden hair. Jill needed every ounce of willpower not to throw herself at him.

She swallowed against an instant panic attack and took a calming breath. "Hello, Gabe. Nice to see you again."

His eyes widened and he stared at her with an expression close to shock. He reached out and took her hand. "Jill? My God, is that really you?"

"In person."

His gaze raked her from head to toe. She knew what he saw. She was still slim but she had filled out so now she had curves, rounder breasts and hips that flared just enough. Her makeup was more sophisticated and she knew the green of her simple tailored outfit complemented her eyes and brought out the auburn highlights of her thick chestnut hair. She had taken great pains to create the image she wanted to project to him, to let him know what could have been his.

She felt naked under his penetrating look. Ten years hadn't put out the blaze that roared through her the minute he touched her. Maintaining her professional poise took superhuman effort. *This might turn out to be a lot more difficult than I thought.*

His hand was warm against hers, reminding her of the last time he'd touched her in intimate places. The last time they'd made love. She'd never forgotten the feel of those slightly roughened hands gliding over her skin, touching her in intimate places, teaching her what love was about.

"Well." He released her hand with obvious reluctance. "You certainly have grown up, haven't you?" He grinned, a dimple flashing at one corner of his mouth.

"Haven't we all." She tried to match his nonchalance.

"Christy." He turned to the woman at the desk. "You may not remember Jill Danvers. She was a year or so ahead of you in school, I think. Jill, this is Christy Malone. The heart and soul of the office."

Christy blushed at the compliment.

Jill smiled. "Nice to meet you."

"Same here. Gabe's been looking forward to seeing you again." Her eyes flashed. "We're all so excited you're writing about the big event. Won't that just put us on the map?"

"Well, that's my intention." *So Gabe's been looking forward to seeing me, has he?* If only it were for the right reasons.

"Hold my calls until we're done," he told Christy. "Come on, Jill. Let's go into my office and talk."

His hand rested just at the small of her back as he guided her out of the reception area. Her skin burned where he touched her and images of his naked skin next to hers and his hands stroking her flashed through her mind. As memories aroused her body, her panties dampened and her nipples tightened.

Not good.

With an effort she blanked her mind.

The office reflected the man well, solid and with a strong sense of masculinity. Lots of leather and wood, with rich brown carpeting to soften footsteps. Western-themed art hung on the wall and appeared to have been selected to reflect the geography of the area. But the absence of any personal photos struck her as odd. Not of Robin, or their child or the three of them as a family.

Interesting. What does that mean?

She moved toward one of the chairs in front of the desk but Gabe motioned to the couch against one wall.

"We don't need to be so formal, do we? After all, we're not exactly strangers."

That's the problem. I wish we were.

"You're right," she said instead. "But it has been a long time since we've seen each other."

"Too long." He flashed his gorgeous white teeth at her again. "Lord, Jill, it's so good just to look at you."

"You look pretty sharp yourself." There. She had just the right tone of nonchalance. "I gather from these digs your law practice is flourishing."

He leaned back against the couch, one leg crossed over the other, one arm thrown along the back. "I have to admit I'm happy with the way things are going."

"And Robin? How is she these days?"

Gabe's jaw tightened and his eyes darkened. "Robin? She's fine, I guess. I'm sure she'll be interested to know you asked about her."

"Well, give her my best." *Along with a pint of hemlock.*

Robin Fletcher and Gabe had been a long-standing couple through high school and college. Before That Summer. Following her graduation from the University of Texas, Robin had taken off to spend three months in Maine with relatives.

'I think she's in a snit,' he'd told Jill when she'd asked.

'About?'

'We're examining our priorities. I told her some days I feel swept along on an uncontrollable tide.' He'd grinned. *'A tide named Robin. She didn't take it too well.'*

So Gabe, with one semester of law school left, had been at a loose end. Without Robin in the picture, the summer had belonged to them. They'd hardly mixed with anyone at all, unwilling to share even a minute with anyone else. In those three short months Jill's life had turned upside down. She'd fallen in love with Gabe and her parents had been killed in a highway crash.

Even after ten years, the day of the funeral was still burned into her mind — and not just because of the grief.

* * * *

Ten years earlier

It seemed the whole town turned out for the Danverses' funeral. Afterward, they filled the house to express condolences and sympathy. Jill had stood graveside between her aunt Karen and Uncle Joe, numb with despair and craving the feel of Gabe's arms around her. When he walked into the house he gave her a brief hug, murmured soothing words and said he'd be there when everyone left.

She was in the kitchen pouring coffee for herself when she heard Robin's mother and another woman on the other side of the door.

"I see Robin's home."

"Yes, just last week. We wanted her to have this summer after graduation before she starts working."

"I guess she and Gabe will be announcing their engagement?"

"Oh, of course. I'm hoping for a December wedding. The holidays are a great time for a celebration, don't you think? Although for some reason Robin wants a quiet one right away."

The words ripped Jill's heart open. *How can this be true?* Forgetting the coffee, she went in search of the man who'd whispered exquisite words of love and the future to her, only to find him on the patio with his arms around Robin in a lover's embrace.

Sick at what she saw, she ran from the house, away from everyone, trying to swallow the flood of tears.

Even when he spotted her and called after her, she kept on running. *So much for all Gabe's wonderful promises.* Maybe to him it had been nothing more than a way to pass the summer until Robin got back. Maybe everything was a lie, couched to get her into bed.

Gabe found her sitting on a bench in the park.

"Get away from me," she snapped. "I hate you — you are such a liar."

"Jill, please." He crouched down in front of her. "There are things going on I can't tell you."

"Things that made you lie to me?" She spat the words out.

"They weren't a lie." His voice was low. "I promise you that."

"Then why are you marrying Robin?" She managed to hold back the tears.

"You'll find out soon enough, but I can't tell you now. Please believe me."

"Not any more. I believed you once. Look where it got me." She jerked away from him and ran into the deepest part of the park. She hoped he'd follow her then hoped he wouldn't. When she discovered she was still alone she stopped running and allowed herself the luxury of a good cry.

By the time she returned to the house, everyone was gone. Uncle Joe and Aunt Karen were waiting with worried looks and a note from Gabe that said only *We have to talk. I'll try to explain.*

Explain what? He'd said he couldn't tell her the reason.

"He's called several times," Aunt Karen said. "He waited for you as long as he could, but then he had to leave. He said he'd keep trying until he got you. Honey, I don't know what's wrong but shouldn't you at least talk to him?"

"I did." She stared at her hands in misery. "We have nothing left to say to each other."

"Jill." Aunt Karen put her arms around her. "This has been a tough week for you. Today you buried your parents. Maybe you're blowing things out of proportion. Whatever is wrong between you and Gabe, at least give the man a hearing?"

Maybe. And maybe not. She was still crying tears of anguish for her parents, but then to see Gabe with Robin that way, to overhear the conversation…

Jill crumpled the paper and threw it into the trash. "All right. If he calls, I'll talk to him."

She ran upstairs and curled up on her bed, tears welling again in her eyes and choking her raw throat. Somehow exhaustion claimed her and she dozed off. When she woke, her room was filled with darkness broken only by the shaft of light from the street lamp shining through her window. She splashed cold water on her face in her bathroom, blew her nose and pulled her hair into a ponytail before going in search of her aunt and uncle. She'd made a decision and she needed to act on it before she changed her mind.

"I'm going back to San Antonio with you," she told them when she had herself somewhat composed. "Can I stay with you until I find a place of my own?"

"Of course, honey," Uncle Joe told her. "As long as you like. But Gabe…"

"I'll talk to him. I said I would. But that's all. I want to leave here." The phone was ominously silent. *So much for his need to talk to me.*

She spent most of the night packing everything she could fit into her car, anxious for them all to get an early start. The faster she left Bluebonnet Falls, the faster she could get away from the pain of her parents' death and Gabe's betrayal.

When the doorbell rang, she figured it was her neighbor coming for the extra key. But when she pulled the door open, Gabe stood on the porch looking as if his night hadn't been much better than hers. His clothes were rumpled and his eyes were red-rimmed and shadowed. Deep lines were carved into his face and he badly needed a shave.

"Go away." She started to shut the door.

"Robin's pregnant," he blurted out. "Four months."

Jill stared at him, the pain in her chest like a sharp sword. "Get the hell away from me." She slammed the door and ran up the stairs, holding her hands over her ears as the doorbell rang again. "Don't answer it," she yelled. "Do not open that door."

Karen stared up the stairs as the doorbell rang again and a fist pounded on the heavy wood. "What shall I tell Gabe?"

"Tell him…oh, tell him to go to hell."

A week later, with a perverse need to enhance the pain squeezing her heart, she did an Internet search and in seconds a picture of the new Mr. and Mrs. Gabriel Carter stared up at her. When a magazine offered her a job as a travel writer if she'd spend a year in Europe, she took it. The only way to keep her fragile heart from shattering altogether was to stay as far away from Gabriel Carter as she could, and never see him again.

About the Author

A multi-published, award winning, Amazon and USA Today best-selling author, Desiree Holt has produced more than 200 titles and won many awards. She has received an EPIC E-Book Award, the Holt Medallion and many others including Author After Dark's Author of the Year. She has been featured on CBS Sunday Morning and in The Village Voice, The Daily Beast, USA Today, The Wall Street Journal, The London Daily Mail. She lives in Florida with her cats who insist they help her write her books, and is addicted to football.

Desiree loves to hear from readers. You can find her contact information, website details and author profile page at http://www.totallybound.com.

29167094R00178